WHO WE WERE

LINDSAY DETWILER

Who We Were © 2017 by Lindsay Detwiler

Who We Were is a work of fiction. All names, characters, events and places found therein are either from the author's imagination or used fictitiously. Any similarity to persons alive or dead, actual events, locations, or organizations is entirely coincidental and not intended by the author.

For information, contact the publisher, Hot Tree Publishing.
www.hottreepublishing.com
Editing & Formatting: Hot Tree Editing
Cover Designer: Claire Smith
Interior Designr: RMGraphX
ISBN-10: 1-925448-63-0
ISBN-13: 978-1-925448-63-4

10 9 8 7 6 5 4 3 2 1

To my mom

CHAPTER ONE

"Last time," I mutter, taking a deep breath so I don't shatter into a fit of rage. This has to work, or everything is going to fall apart.

I steady my hand, pull on my eyelid, and try not to jab my eye out as I pop the lens in.

Blinking a few times, I ignore the burning sensation. Once my eye stops watering, I look at myself in the mirror.

"Yes! Finally!" I scream, jumping up and down for theatrical effect.

The contact burns like fire, but I don't care. No nerd glasses for me tonight. Now it's on to the smoky eye shadow before I get dressed. My fingers fly to my palette as I glance at the clock on my phone. I have twenty-two minutes before we have to leave.

Correction: I have twenty-one minutes before the always punctual Mitch starts freaking out about how we're going to be late and I have to get my ass in the car.

Working carefully on my eyelid, I try to remember all the

steps from the YouTube video I watched this morning. Ten minutes later, I've blended until I'm bored, and I move on to the other eye. Seven minutes after that—hey, I've sort of mastered it—I've finished my second eye. I inch back from the mirror to appraise my face. Other than the eyeliner being a tad wonky on my left eye, they look pretty even.

Despite my eyes being so bloodshot they make me look like a drug addict, I've done okay. Although I have fiery eyes I want to pluck from my head, ditching the glasses was a smart move. I'm not the nerdy Maylee my classmates probably remember… at least not completely. I've even twisted my mousey brown hair into a fancy updo—also thanks to YouTube.

Yep, I'm going to give her at least somewhat of a run for her money. I won't be totally fading into the background with my ho-hum looks. Isn't that everyone's fear on a night like tonight?

"Hey, what the hell are you doing in there? Aren't you ready yet?" Mitch calls from the hallway. He's probably already dressed, shoes tied, keys in hand.

"You know what they say. Better to be late and look good…."

"Actually, I don't know anyone who says that," he retorts. Always has to get the last word.

I sigh, parading out of the bathroom. Mitch stands down the hallway. I was right. He's wearing his expertly pressed dress shirt, his tie is creepily perfect, and his shoes are tied. His hair, always picture-worthy, stands up every which way, an illustrious example of messy with a touch of perfection.

I hate to admit it, I really do, but he could be a model.

Life's so not fair. He gets the perfectly shiny, unfrizzy locks, smooth skin, shimmering eyes.

I get the dull hair fit for a librarian, skin that's either dry as hell or shiny in a not-so-sexy way. I get the boring brown eyes. You'd think the Big Guy could've at least sort of evened the score a little, huh?

"I'm almost ready."

"Whoa. Heavy-handed on the makeup, huh?"

"Shut up."

"No, no. Looks good," he says, hands up defensively.

"Really?"

"Honestly. I just think you're going through too much trouble for people we don't even care about anymore."

"That's the point."

"What is?"

"I'm doing this *because* I don't care about them. I want them to see how little I care about how they treated me. This is my chance, Mitch, to be like 'hey, remember the mousey girl you made fun of? Well, she's doing all right for herself now.'"

"So you're doing your eye shadow as a form of 'screw you'?"

"Sort of."

He rolls his eyes. "Women."

"Well sorry, Mr. Hotshot. Not all of us were super popular. You're probably excited to go back so your loyal fans can flock to you."

"It was never like that."

I sigh. He's sort of right. I'm being a bit dramatic. Not that

I'd admit it.

"I just have to get dressed and I'll be back."

"You have five minutes."

"We're going to Michaelangelo's, not the White House. What, we'll miss a few appetizers if we're late?"

"Hey, you're the one who is all about this. If it were up to me, I'd be spending my Saturday elsewhere."

"Yeah, at work."

"Still better than this."

"Just stop. It'll be fine. It'll be good for us to reconnect."

"You are not going there to reconnect, and we both know it."

"Okay, so I may or may not be going to snoop a little on certain people."

"Or one."

"It's not all about her."

"Well, I'm pretty sure last week you said, 'Oh good, the wench wrote on Facebook she's going.' I'm thinking it's a little about you wanting to see her."

"Okay, well whatever. I'm going to get changed."

I stomp back to the hallway, feeling cranky. My stomach rumbles, reminding me of how few calories I've eaten today. In my room, I yank the royal blue skintight dress from the hanger. This is *my* color; the saleslady even said so last week.

Before slinking into the dress, a perfect mix between formal and casual, I reach for my secret weapon—the super plumped-up push-up bra Shauni recommended. It's made with some hydro technology to give natural curves. I can definitely use it. I don't want whispers about me to be about how my boobs never did come in.

I strap the contraption—which promises to add two full cup sizes—to my chest, thankful to see that it delivered as promised. I step into the dress and pull it up my body, huffing a little as I get to the top. I'm watching in my full-length mirror as I do it, which is never a good idea. When I've finally wiggled it up enough, I pause to appraise the situation.

Okay, so when I bought the supertight dress in hopes of losing weight, I may have overestimated my dedication to the diet. What was I supposed to do, though? Turn down all those chocolates Shauni brought to work?

If I just sort of suck it in a little, it will be okay. I assure myself I can pull this off. Just a few hours, and I'll be golden. I'll have them convinced I haven't gained a single ounce since high school.

As I struggle with the zipper, though, I realize I have a second problem, a problem I've never, ever encountered in my twenty-eight years.

The bust area is too snug.

I guess I forgot about the superbra when I tried on the dress. I now have a new appreciation for what my bustier friends go through. I have another choice today. I can ditch the bra and opt for the flat look. Or I can try to stuff it all into the dress.

Never one for rational when it comes to my looks, I, of course, opt for the second choice. I've dealt with too many years of merciless no-boob comments to succumb to them again. Dammit, I'm a grown woman—I'm going to have boobs for this, one way or another.

I do a little dance that probably looks way too intimate

from another view. I've quit watching in the mirror, too afraid to see. I shove down on the fake boobs in the bra, yanking the blue fabric up around them to get them locked and loaded, and contort my arms in a way that certainly is going to pull a neck muscle. I guess all of my exercise classes these past few weeks have paid off, though, because I'm able to pull the zipper up.

I breathe, but not too deeply. I can't afford it.

I'm in. I'm afraid if I move too much I might snap right out. My ribs are crunching a little. If I wear this dress too long, I may have permanent damage.

What the hell are you doing, Maylee? I ask myself. Maybe Mitch is right. Maybe this isn't worth it.

The real Maylee wouldn't give a shit what people thought of her. The real Maylee wouldn't stuff herself into a ridiculous dress. Any other Saturday night, I'd be in my favorite Edgar Allan Poe T-shirt and a pair of sketchy jeans.

I guess that's the thing about high school reunions, though. They make you snap a little. At least I can admit to it. This has to be the first step to admitting psychosis, right?

Mitch thinks I've taken it too far. Shauni, of course, thinks I'm doing the right thing.

"Show those snotty jerks just what you've become," she told me yesterday. "Especially the blonde. Show her you've won."

I'd smiled, munching on my lunch of celery and carrot sticks in my attempt to shed a few more ounces of water weight. Nevertheless, the whole time I was asking myself a very hard question: Have I really won? If I'm going to so much trouble to fool my classmates into thinking I've done so well for myself, aren't there deeper problems than booblessness and a flabby waistline?

Maybe the problem isn't my body type, my hair, or any of it. Maybe it's because at twenty-eight, I thought life would be a little different, a little bit more… grown-up.

Looking in the mirror, however, I know I can't pretend to be all introspective and mature about it. Even though I know it's ridiculous, there's a part of me deep down that does want to show her I've done okay for myself, no matter what. I want the girl who tortured me in high school, who convinced me I was a mousey nerd, to realize I blossomed.

Even if it is a bit of a lie. Or a lot of a lie.

"Let's go," Mitch yells from the living room. I sigh.

No more introspection. It's go time.

It's time to face my past.

HIGH SCHOOL
FRESHMAN YEAR

Feet flat on the floor and hands crossed, I sit at my desk—front row, of course. I'm wearing my hot-pink Nikes, brand-new for the first day of high school, and an Aéropostale T-shirt—also pink. My classmates file in, high-fiving each other, jumping around the room, not worrying about whether their pencils are sharpened or if they have a notebook. A ball of paper pelts me in the back of the head, and I groan.

Gina, Ariel, and Jillian are all in lunch right now. Figures I'd get split up from them in the schedule. At least English is my favorite class. I sit silently awaiting the mercy of the bell, the beginning of class, and the end of the reminders I have no friends here.

"Hey, sorry to bother you, but do you have a pen?" I turn to the girl who claims the seat beside me. While some of the boys jump off the seats and two of them pretend to strangle each other in the back corner, I'm happy to see someone else just calmly sitting.

"Sure, here let me find one," I say, digging for my pencil pouch in my JanSport. I find a pen—pink of course—and hand it to her.

"Thanks so much. I can't find my pencil case. I'm

Josephine, by the way."

"Hi. I'm Maylee. Are you new?"

"Yeah. Family just moved in from New York City." Josephine flashes a killer white grin. She's dressed in a superstylish blouse, skinny jeans, and sparkly ballet flats. She looks like she's twenty-six instead of fourteen, her platinum blonde locks curled perfectly around her face.

"Get to your seats, now!" Mr. Jones bellows, his military-like voice ricocheting off the walls. The boys in the back corner instantly stop, panic on their faces as they dash to their desks. There won't be any crazy stuff happening in this class, not under Mr. Jones's watch.

Mr. Jones paces in front of our desks. I turn to Josephine to give her a look. She gives me an "Oh no" look back, and we giggle.

"Ms.... what is it... Ms. Keagan... what's so funny?"

I feel my cheeks warm.

"Oh, Mr. Jones, she was just smiling because Hamlet *is her favorite play. We were talking before class about the whole 'To be or not to be' quote and how most laymen interpret it incorrectly. It's really not as inspirational as people take it. It's really just about Hamlet questioning whether life is even worth it." Josephine stares at Mr. Jones pointedly, her killer smile flashing.*

Mr. Jones eyes us suspiciously as I hold my breath. He seems satisfied with her explanation, though, gives us a grin— at least by his standards—and continues.

I mouth "thank you" to Josephine for saving me.

Maybe I do have friends in English after all.

CHAPTER TWO

At eighteen, when asked in the yearbook what my life ambition was, I'd said to travel the world. I'd said it with the confidence every eighteen-year-old speaks with, the confidence life is going to work out exactly how you choose. I had this idea that if I worked hard and lived life right, I'd get to dictate my path.

Now, I sort of laugh when I think of that girl. Who the hell did she think she was, telling life what she wanted?

The eighteen-year-old would've probably been sad to meet this twenty-eight-year-old version. The most traveling I do is the three-mile drive to work every weekday. Once a year I go to Atlantic City with Shauni for a weekend, and once a year Mitch and I head to the beach in Maryland.

Whoa, world traveler, slow down, huh?

Even if my youthful version could forgive my lack of traveling, she probably wouldn't forgive all the other things going on in my life. Or more accurately, not going on.

In fact, if my eighteen-year-old self could see me now, she'd probably burst into tears and beg to stay in school a few more years just to put off the sad, inevitable future a little longer.

Okay, so I'm being a bit dramatic again. My life's not so bad, I know. I live in a nice apartment, even if I do share it. I've got a steady job I love, good friends, a bit of disposable income, and thirty-two pairs of shoes. I go for a manicure a few times a year, and I can even afford to nurse a daily coffee habit. Living the American Dream, huh?

But there are plenty of other things missing from the dream, things I thought would be worked out by now.

I mean, the love life thing would be nice. I don't even mean a husband and kids, the whole stereotypical, semisexist view of what women want. I just mean a man in my bed every once in a while would be nice. Maybe even, I don't know, a movie or dinner out with a member of the opposite sex. I don't want to get crazy or anything, though.

I'm not a nun. Although I'm a bit mousey, I'm not totally repulsive, at least from what I've been told. However, for some reason, whether it's my somewhat rampant sarcasm, my thick brown glasses, or maybe just karma, I seem to repel men.

The good ones at least.

There've been a few notable stops in my romance train, but some are more accurately described as notorious.

Stop 1: Jonathan

This stop occurred junior year. He was a sophomore— go ahead, say it. Cougar. Okay, I'll admit I don't mind the title. I was the nerd girl in the airplane-window thick glasses, bowl cut, and conservative clothes. He was the sexy tennis player with some nice forearms and some gorgeous green eyes. When he started talking to me in Trigonometry class, I couldn't believe it. He took me out for milkshakes, and then he took me to his backseat for a little… well… shall we say shaking? Two days later, I found out someone dared him he couldn't sleep with the flat-chested book nerd. So yeah, loss of virginity not going down in the books as romantic. First train wreck of many.

Stop 2: Josiah

Senior year. I loved him. He was probably my first real love.

I broke up with him. Sometimes, I still wish I hadn't.

Stop 3: Ricardo

All you need to know about this is he was a foreign exchange student from Mexico. He introduced me to tequila one night. I fell hard… for him, and literally, I fell over in his dorm. We actually lasted a year until he had to go back to Mexico. He proposed; I said no. I was focused on my teaching career and didn't want to be distracted with, you know, a wedding. That was that.

Stop 4: The man who shall remain nameless

Year two of college. Shauni set me up with a cousin of her brother's girlfriend's mom's aunt's neighbor. He showed up, sweaty, bald, and a bit "snorty." As in, he snorted every thirteen seconds due to severe allergies. I could've looked past it. After all, I suffer seasonally as well. When he slurped his spaghetti noodles with gusto, I refused to ever see him again and also sent Shauni a strongly worded text. I refused to ever speak about him, swearing Shauni to secrecy about our date. Thus, he will forever be the nameless man.

Stops 5-8:

At twenty-three, I hit a very low point in my life. When tragedy struck, I spun out a little. My bio clock was ticking and I needed to find someone. Stops five through eight on the train were a succession of relationships lasting a month or two each. Two of them I met at the local bar. One I met on the job. One I met through Mitch's friends. Regardless, the pattern repeated. We went on some dates, I grew clingy, and I started talking marriage. Want to scare away a twentysomething man who has never had a serious girlfriend? Say the M-word. Lesson learned.

Stop 9: Jeremy

I'll call him the heartbreaker. Twenty-seven. Lasted nine months. I thought he was the one. He was not. We'll leave it at that for now.

So yes, the romance train did pull out of the station. There were quite a few broken tracks, detours, and engine failures along the way. Pretty sure it's now stranded somewhere in the middle of nowhere.

I can't say I'm completely faultless in this. I can't say I'm just a bad-luck lover who can't catch a break. I mean, you already know I'm a bit sarcastic. I speak my mind. I'm not one of those girls who tries too hard—the exception being today. Nothing ever seems to work in my favor when it comes to romance, though.

Shauni says I try too hard, go for the wrong guys, and am too picky. She's one to talk. She basically has sworn off all men unless their name is Ed Sheeran. Yep, she's a cougar as well, I suppose.

Ten years after high school, things obviously aren't exactly going as I had planned. I'm not traveling, and I don't have a steamy love life to speak of.

At least I'm not going to my ten-year high school reunion alone, though. Right? That has to count for something. The only thing worse than going to a high school reunion with a terrible significant other is going alone, right? So there's that.

Looking to my left as Mitch silently drives, focusing on the road, I realize how sad my eighteen-year-old self would be with this fact, too.

Mitch is certainly, as I said already, not a bad-looking companion to a high school reunion. He'll turn some heads. But at eighteen, I don't think I ever pictured myself at our high school reunion on the arm of my brother.

Yeah, not quite every girl's dream. Not quite the way to get people talking in a good way.

"You're quiet," Mitch says as we near the restaurant. Our classmates really went far out. Our big one-oh is at a tiny hometown restaurant. Mitch is right. This is a bit lame already. I'm having pangs of regrets, and we haven't even arrived.

"Just thinking about how much my life didn't work out."

"Stop being dramatic. You're just feeling like that because we're going here. That's why I didn't want to come. It's just a big 'look at how awesome I am' show when really, most everyone here probably thinks their life sucks."

"Not you. You've done well."

He shrugs. "So I have the job I wanted. It doesn't mean my

life's perfect."

"True," I admit, looking out the window. "You've got some loser sister living in your apartment."

"Stop digging for compliments. You know I didn't mean it."

I turn to look at my brother now, a rare moment of seriousness between us. "I know. But I don't think having your sister live with you at twenty-eight was really what you had in mind after you graduated from law school."

"I have three bedrooms. What the hell would I do with them anyway? Plus, you pay rent. It's helping me pay off my loans."

I smile at his words. They're partially true. I also know he could probably pay off his loans without my meager rent contribution. Mitch always looks out for my feelings, though, at least with the big stuff.

"Well, you could be filling them with sexy hookers," I say, grinning. He gives me a look. Right. Not his style. "Cats?"

He looks even more exasperated. "Nelson is enough cat for me. Trust me. I've sworn off them. You're ridiculous. Just stop."

I laugh, but then it hurts a little. "Ouch," I say, grabbing my rib cage.

"Okay, that thing is clearly a health hazard. Are you sure you're going to make it?"

"Just have to make it through a few hours."

"Oh, sounds fun. It's not too late. Let's ditch this crap for some actual fun."

"No, we're here now. I just want to see her. I'm curious.

Facebook doesn't do her justice. She has a lot of head shots."

"What are you hoping? She got fat?"

"Maybe a little."

"You're such a jerk."

Mitch gets out of the car. I take a small breath. Here we go. Ten years. *Let's go show them where life got me.* I push away the feelings of being old and the nerves of facing people from my past, good and bad.

Mitch is right. This is silly. My life is fine.

I chant this mantra to myself as I gingerly step out of the car, trying not to make any sudden movements that might tear my dress. As I wobble, though, and Mitch takes my arm, I can't help but think maybe life isn't fine.

Everyone else, except Mitch and a few others, have moved on from this dinky town, have chased after their dreams. How many of them achieved their life ambitions? I haven't even started living out any of mine.

I'm twenty-eight, I can't find love, and I share an apartment with my twin brother.

What the hell do I have to show off anyway?

The sign "Welcome Class of 2006" taunts me as we near the restaurant door. I'm a little dizzy, maybe just from nerves.

"Are you okay?" Mitch asks as I stumble a bit.

"I'm fine. These shoes are just hard to walk in."

He looks down at my feet. I'm wearing ballet flats.

"Did you eat today?"

"Yep." An apple and a few carrot sticks. Oh, and some celery.

"You sure?"

"Yes, I'm sure. What am I, five?"

"You look a little gray. Maybe tomorrow you'll do something really crazy like, I don't know, start eating again."

I shrug, smacking my lips together one last time to make sure the lipstick is evenly applied. The prospect of a ginormous burger paired with about eighty-nine french fries does seem to be calling my name. Just a few more hours, then it's back to normal.

Maybe Mitch is right. Women are a bit crazy, I suppose.

CHAPTER THREE

"Oh, it's so good to see you! Look at you two! You haven't changed a bit."

Rory Eliot's voice is as screechy as I remember, and the incessant smile still hasn't left her face. Apparently her optimism hasn't evaded her either; I'm pretty sure the eye wrinkles I have as well as the extra ten pounds of weight are, in fact, changes.

"Now, here are your name tags. Make sure you're wearing them. At the end of the night, we'll have a door prize drawing. You have to be wearing your name tag to win. Isn't that lovely?" She hands me a huge square. I notice my name is spelled wrong but do not want to hear her apologize ninety-eight times. I just smile, saying thank you. Then I awkwardly try to figure out where the heck to stick the name tag reading "Mylee." Do I stick it on my bare skin since I'm wearing a strapless? Over my boob? I certainly am not placing it near my stomach. No need to draw attention.

Mitch watches my odd dance of moving the sticker around.

I finally settle on half on my bare skin, half on the top of my dress.

"You ready for our shining moment?" he asks, grinning, ushering us toward the bar in the middle of the restaurant where all of our former friends, foes, and acquaintances appear to be gathered.

"Not sure it's going to be shining."

"You look great, Mays."

I try to let go of the fact he is using the nickname I hate. After all, he's paid me a compliment.

"You too. Let's go."

As we enter the room, I scan the people. Some of the faces jump out at me from the past. There's Ron, the gamer boy who asked me to prom. It was after the whole Jonathan scandal, so I'd said no. I hadn't gone at all. He's aged well, looks good. Maybe I should've said yes.

I see faces from all the familiar high school cliques— jocks, band nerds, and my people, the bookworms. Despite the passing of ten years, they still congregate with the familiar.

I pull Mitch toward a small group I'm actually glad to see.

"Maylee, oh my goodness! Has it really been ten years?" Ariel says, pulling me into the circle. She holds a mojito in her long, slender hand. If it weren't for the frizzy curls, I wouldn't have recognized her. She's lost at least fifty pounds and looks like a diva. Gone are the wire-rimmed glasses and the freckles. She's gorgeous.

I hug her, trying not to spill her mojito. By the smell of her breath, this isn't her first. "Good to see you," I say, meaning it.

Jill, Susan, and Gina are all there too. It's a mini reunion of nerdigans. We've all overcome our geekiness, at least at the surface. Maybe everyone's ditched their glasses for tonight.

We catch up, talking about jobs and husbands—Jill and Gina have theirs with them. We talk about the past decade, how much we can't believe time has passed, and how sad we are we've lost touch. We go through the motions. I am glad to be here. It's comforting to reconnect with a piece of who I was. When I planned on coming tonight, I hadn't really thought about this part of it, which is a shame.

Mitch wanders back from the bar, carrying a beer for himself and a Long Island for me. I guess I'll give in and have a drink.

As Jill talks about her two-year-old at home and whips out the pictures typifying motherhood—sleeping baby, baby smiling with birthday cake, etcetera—I only half listen. I'm scanning hard now, looking for the real reason I'm here.

Twenty feet across the room, I see a familiar shade of blonde hair. Her back is to us, but recognition sinks in. I'd know her anywhere. The girl who tortured me, who haunts my memories of high school. She was the bane of my existence. Anger bubbling, I realize maybe she still is, even if I don't want her to be.

I sip on my Long Island, spying as she chats with Wayne, one of the football players. She's giggling, twirling her hair in the signature man-killer move. Things haven't changed.

As if on cue, she says goodbye to Wayne, rubbing his shoulder and turning to come our way. A few feet from us, she stops. We lock eyes. This is the moment.

She's wearing an olive-green dress cut to fingertip length, asymmetrical on the top with only one strap. On anyone else, it would be reminiscent of vomit. On Josephine, though, it perfectly warms her alabaster skin tone and emerald eyes. Her skin is smooth, perfect, not a wrinkle or crease in sight. She's wearing killer heels but walks with grace befitting a runway model. Her makeup is flawless, her contouring and eye shadow on point.

She's the picture of perfection every guy from our graduating class probably remembers.

I slam down my Long Island, the room quieting. Confidently, I stomp toward her, eyes burning a hole in her face.

"Josephine. Hi. Remember me? The girl you tortured? The girl you said would never be good enough? Here I am. I'm damn happy. You didn't win."

Then I bitch slap her as my former classmates gasp in unison.

***

Okay, let's start over, so I can give you the real story.

Josephine *did* rub Wayne's arm and lock eyes with me. But that's where the truth stops.

I didn't bitch slap her. I didn't confront her. For years, this was how I pictured our encounter.

I know what you're thinking. I'm crazy. I'm the one with issues, not her. I should let it go, it was so long ago. Who cares what she thought of me?

Maybe you're right. Maybe it has been a long time. But a woman never forgets being belittled. Words hurt. Attitudes hurt. Sometimes the past doesn't want to relinquish its grip, especially when the grip almost ruined your life.

I should clarify. I don't sit around wallowing in pity or making voodoo dolls of Josephine. In fact, up until five months ago when I received the invitation for tonight, I'd barely thought of her. Sure, when I saw the evil antagonist in a movie, I'd think *Oh, there's Josephine*. At exercise class, when our instructor tells us to think of something motivating, I picture her face, her perfectly trim body she flaunted around, and I kick it into high gear. When we're told to visualize a target during kickboxing, I alternate between her face and the face of my boss at the diner I worked at during college.

Other than that, she'd pretty much left my thoughts—until tonight.

When I snap out of my pretend moment and back to reality, I realize we're still staring. Mitch, standing right beside me, takes another swig of his beer. Perhaps he had a flash of the bitch slap scene, too.

I wait for her to make the first move. Will she slap me? Ignore me? Apologize? Does she even remember me?

My questions are soon answered.

"Maylee and Mitch, I can't believe you're here! It's so good to see you," she says, beelining for me. My stomach tightens. She approaches… and then she does something gag-worthy.

She hugs me. As in a tight, swaying a little, friendship hug.

Jill, Gina, and Ariel look uncomfortable. They're not really sure what to do. I get no backup from them. Mitch makes a little choking sound, still downing his beer.

I pull back as soon as it is socially acceptable.

"How are you?" I offer coolly. I'm not letting her know she's getting the best of me.

"I'm great. You know, just trucking along. How about you two?" I notice she isn't really looking at me anymore. She's eying my brother.

"Good. Same. Trucking along."

"Yeah, can't believe it's been ten, huh? You two look amazing though."

"Thanks," Mitch responds.

I stand, my lips pursed, my toe tapping.

Perhaps I'd have rather had the slapping scene. She continues talking social niceties as if I'm not her biggest enemy from high school. In fact, she acts as if there was nothing between us, which just infuriates me. Does she not remember? Or is this part of her manipulation?

She was always golden at manipulation, at being the overtly sweet girl with the internally nasty demeanor. Right now, though, she just seems the picture of perfect maturity, of a life put together.

I'm annoyed. I don't know if it's because she is acting oblivious to the way she treated me, or if it's because maybe I am, in fact, just being an immature weirdo hanging on to the past.

Josephine turns back to me. "Honey, do you need some Claritin or something? Your eyes look really, really red. Allergies? Your nose is a touch red too."

The sweetness drips from her voice. Oh no. She hasn't risen above. She's still the same Josephine. The same undermining Josephine.

"No, I'm fine, thank you. Just some contact issues."

"Oh, that's right. I do remember you were a glasses wearer, right?" She winks at me. "Breaking out the contacts for tonight, huh? Never a great idea. Takes some time to get used to them. Do you have your glasses in the car? I can get them for you." She smiles sweetly. I just sigh.

I decide I need a break from all of this. "You know, I think I'll just swing by the restroom. Maybe I can fiddle with them a bit. Or just throw them out. My eyesight isn't that bad anyway," I say. Mitch doesn't even notice. His gaze is glued to her, and I hear them continuing the conversation as I waddle off, still barely able to breathe from the dress situation.

As I rush off to the bathroom, the light-headedness surges again. I suddenly don't feel well. Maybe it's the Long Island—I am quite a lightweight. Or maybe it's because I am starving. I feel a bit woozy, but tell myself I'll be fine. I'm almost to the bathroom door, though, when it happens.

I tip over. I try to put my hands out to stop my fall, to grab the wall, a table, anything, but I can't seem to manage. It happens too fast. I stumble over my own feet, trying to catch myself, to steady my feet. I just end up getting tangled up on… well, nothing really. I do an odd roll onto the floor, trying to stop my fall but failing miserably, a flailing tangle of limbs hitting the ground.

The next thing I know, I'm lying on my back on the floor, gasps audible around me despite the music playing and loud conversations.

My head hurts. The room's a little spinny. I'm a whole lot of disaster, just like my high school days.

You can put the girl in a nice dress and do her makeup, but you can't take away her tendencies for disaster or clumsiness, I suppose. Guess I'm not fooling anyone.

***

"Are you okay?" a husky voice asks as a blond, spiky-haired guy leans over me. He must be an inch from kissing me. My heart flutters a bit. I look up at him, his almost royal blue eyes peering into mine, framed by brown glasses matching mine—when I'm not torturing myself with contacts. The smell of his aftershave wafts toward me. I like it.

Then I remember what happened. The fall. I grab my head. Shit, this is embarrassing.

"I'm fine, I'm fine," I say, struggling to get up to my elbows at least.

"That was quite a fall," he says, true concern in his eyes. Looking at him again, more closely, I recognize him. Okay, so I'm at my high school reunion. Not a surprise I know him. The name comes back, fighting through the fog of time in my hazy mind.

Benson. Benson Drake. The only male in the school who could rival me for the ultimate nerd title. He was quiet, though, a true loner. A guitar player, a back row sitter, an intense bookworm, he didn't really say much to anyone, not even his fellow nerds. We had a few conversations, but he was a bit shy even for my type.

I'm surprised he's here at all.

Of course, I can't really judge. I came with my freaking twin brother. Oh, plus I'm currently lying on the floor with people whispering about whether or not I'm trashed.

Benson reaches for my hand, but the independent woman in me kicks in. "I'm fine, really. Thank you," I announce. Getting up, though, is a bit harder than I imagined. The dress is still too damn tight, so getting myself up is a bit of a challenge. I struggle, and shove, trying to still suck it in so it doesn't all fly out. I imagine I look like an octopus trying to maneuver on dry land. Not a pretty sight, obviously.

That's when the final, reunion-shattering disaster of the night happens.

As I'm leaning up, struggling and stretching to gracefully bring myself to my feet, Benson still crouched down, I hear a distinct rip. I squeeze my eyes tight, not wanting to recognize the truth, although the free feeling near my chest area tells me all I need to know.

I still don't open my eyes as I ask Benson, "Was that my dress?"

"Uh, yes." I hear pity in his voice.

"How bad?"

"I mean, I don't think it's bad." I open one eye to look at him. He's grinning and blushing.

I glance down.

Oh yeah. It's bad.

Think Jennifer Lopez's plunging neckline at the Grammys revealing.

Except I don't have Jennifer Lopez's… um… assets. The fake Wonderbra is now showing, all of its glorious padding dazzlingly on display.

"Oh my God, just great," I practically whimper. Benson takes off his jacket and hands it to me.

"Here, take this."

"Thanks," I say, truly meaning it, shoving myself into it, squeezing it shut over my dress, which is now much looser. On the plus side, I can almost breathe now. On the downside, my boobs are hanging out, I've made a fool of myself, and my dress is slowly wiggling down my hips, just to mention a few points.

He offers his hand. This time I take it. I've learned my lesson about independence, at least for tonight.

I glance around for my brother. I'm ready to ditch this reunion. This was, in fact, a terrible idea. Screw the door prize. I'm ready for some Netflix, my pajamas, and ten more years of ignorant bliss. Next reunion—if I ever come again—I'm wearing yoga pants while swearing a vow of sobriety and red meat.

The jacket is helping, but it's not completely covering me. My dress is still on a downward descent. I'm pretty sure half the reunion is buzzing about my fall—the other half not talking about it only because they're too drunk to care. I don't really want to wander back in and have condescending eyes stare at me. I've had enough attention for tonight, none of it really positive. I scan the room, finally spotting my brother.

He's still with her.

Where the hell is the loyalty? I fall and almost split my head open, and he's still chatting it up with Josephine.

What's even worse? I see it. The hair twirl. The smile.

Oh Lord, I will be talking to Mitch tomorrow.

"Can I take you home?" Benson asks, breaking into my thoughts, seeing exactly what I'm seeing.

"Would you mind?"

"Not at all. I think Mitch is occupied."

"Suppose I don't want to interrupt." I pull out my phone and send Mitch a text with a few expletives in it. "Are you sure you don't want to stay, though?"

Benson grins. "As much fun as it is realizing I'm still the geek in a sea of popular, I think I'm good."

I nod. We head toward the door, passing Rory. "You aren't

leaving already, are you? We haven't even started the games. Plus, there's the door prize."

"Not feeling well," I say. Benson ushers me toward the door.

"Oh, I get it." Rory winks.

I pause. "No, we're not…."

Rory throws her hands in the air. "Hey, no judgment here. I always thought you two would be adorable together."

I tilt my head, and Benson just shakes his.

"That was sort of weird," I say, peeling the name tag from my chest and tossing it to the ground. Littering is the least of my worries today.

Benson smiles. "She always was quite the gossip, huh?"

We saunter to the parking lot, and I wait for Benson to lead me to his car. We stop in front of a '69 Dodge Challenger. It's a sweet ride, even for a self-proclaimed car nonenthusiast.

"This is your car?"

"I've got a thing for classics. At least one of my life goals came true."

"So, I'm sorry, we've barely had a chance to talk," I say as I climb into the front seat, still trying to hold the jacket in place. I buckle myself in, pulling the belt tight around my chest like a bandage. He climbs into the driver seat, starts the car, and we sit for a minute. He turns down the radio so it's just our voices filling the interior.

"You still live in town?" I ask once we're settled in. I exhale, finally able to stop worrying about my dress falling completely down.

"Yep. I actually just moved back a few months ago. I have a small cottage on the outskirts. Pretty secluded, just like I like it. Gives me plenty of writing inspiration. You?" He puts on his seat belt before pulling out of the parking lot, his headlights casting a glow on the road in front of us.

"Uh-huh. We have an apartment on Maple Avenue. Wait, did you say you're a writer?"

"I am. At least trying to be."

"What do you write?"

"Novels. Fiction."

"Sweet. Any books published?"

"I have one submitted to an agent right now. I'm working at Jack's Place, too, to earn income until I get my writing going. I bartend there a few nights a week."

I smile. "That's awesome, Benson. I know how much you loved books. So cool you're going after your dreams."

"How about you? Everything working out how you wanted?"

"Not quite. I mean, I'm working at a preschool as a teacher's assistant. I love my job, I do. But, well, things haven't gone quite as planned."

"They never do. There's still time."

"I guess. Well, hey, thanks again for offering to take me home."

"No problem. Where to?"

"Left at the light."

Emboldened, I turn on the radio to the pop station. The newest Justin Bieber song blares loudly. I sing along, the Long Island wearing off a bit, but still hanging in my system enough to give me a sense of bravado. Benson smiles. "You're different."

I look over at him. "Is that a good thing?"

"Yes. I mean, you're still Maylee, but you're more confident. I like it."

"I think you're different, too."

"I'll take it. I think getting away from high school is good for some of us, huh? The outliers? I definitely think life on the outside of high school has been better."

"In some departments, I guess."

We drive, the Bieber song still playing. "So, you have anyone in your life, you know, romantically?" I blurt. There's no point in trying to talk about the weather. I mean, he's already sort of seen my boobs.

"No. Nasty breakup. Sort of why I'm back."

"Oh. Sorry."

"It's okay. Heartbreak is good for writing."

I nod. When we get to our place, I tell him thank you again.

"You're welcome. You know, the reunion sucked. But it was good seeing you. Really good seeing you."

"A little too much of me, huh?" I laugh. He shakes his head, grinning.

I start to squirm to take off the jacket. "Just keep it. I'm sure I'll see you at some point to get it back."

I pause, looking at him. "Maybe. Good luck with your writing."

"Thanks."

I stumble out of the car, tripping on the curb. I turn around to wave at him casually. He waves back. I smile. It's nice to see one of my kind doing well for himself. No one in their right mind would call Benson Drake a nerd now.

Okay, the writing thing is a bit nerdy.

But he's definitely a hot nerd. I stumble up the stairs to our apartment to rip off the rest of my dress and pluck the contacts from my eyes.

HIGH SCHOOL
FRESHMAN YEAR

It's December of my ninth-grade year. Just like at junior high, I've carried on my reputation. The bookworm, the front row sitter, the teacher's pet.

I can't help it. I love school. Genuinely love it. I've even decided to pursue teaching once I'm done here. My dad jokes with me about how I'm such a nerd that I'm choosing a job in education so I never have to leave. He's sort of right.

My parents don't understand where my nerdiness comes from. Both Mom and Dad were basically hippies in their day, preferring illicit smoking activities to studying Shakespeare. In fact, when I tell Mom I earned an A on my Hamlet *test, she asks who the hell that is.*

Not that my parents don't support me. They think it's cool to have what they call a brainiac in the family.

"We have the smarts and the sports. A perfect balance. Looks like you're both setting yourselves up to support me in old age," Dad jokes.

The sports, of course, refers to Mitch, the superstar hockey player. Everyone thinks he's already slated for a scholarship. He does well in school, too, but he does well in a way acceptable to the popular kids. As in, he doesn't go around quoting Emerson. Plus, he has perfect vision. I just have these wide-rimmed glasses.

Mom says they make me look sophisticated. I think she's just trying to make me feel better.

Winter formal is around the corner, and everyone is in a tizzy about who is going with whom. Gina is ecstatic because Will, lead chess club player and mathlete, just asked her to go with him. She's been chatting all day about what color dress she's going to wear.

I'm happy for her, but I'm also a little jealous. I've got my eye on my winter formal date.

Adam.

He's top trumpet player in the band. His perfectly smooth brown eyes make me melt. He sits in front of me in science class. Last week, I even worked on a lab with him.

And I made him laugh—really, truly laugh. Not at me, but with me. It's sad, but I picture myself on his arm, ditching the glasses for once and looking good. I know, though, that it's a pipe dream. He'll probably never ask.

"You don't know that," Josephine says over the pasta surprise we're eating in the school cafeteria as I confess to her what I've been thinking.

"Come on, Jo. I'm a nobody."

"You did make him laugh." Josephine holds up a fork accusingly. "Why don't you just ask him?"

"I can't do that."

She sighs, winking at me. "You know, maybe I could talk to him for you."

"You'd do that?"

"Yes. You know how I am. Men can't resist my charms."
She laughs. She says it teasingly, but I know a part of her is serious.

Jo and I have grown as friends over the past few months. Ever since she saved me from Mr. Jones's wrath the first day, we've been spending more time together.

Ariel, Gina, and Jill have been a little cold toward her. They don't like new additions to our junior high friends group.

I admit, she can be a little off-putting. She's very confident. I don't think it's a bad thing. It's good to have self-esteem.

Jo winks at me. "Stay here. I'll mosey over to his lunch table, see what I can do."

I smile, so happy to have her as a friend. How awesome. I love Ariel, Jill, and Gina, but none of them would have the bravery to do this.

I try to act natural, but I can't. I feel nauseous. Plus, I don't want to be jamming a meatball into my mouth when he looks over. I watch with nervous anxiety.

Josephine saunters over, her hips swaying a bit. I can't help but notice all the guys pause to glance. She shoots them all a come-hither look. If I did it, they'd probably just think I was having a seizure. She's a natural.

She approaches Adam, who is sitting with a group of friends. She leans over the table, and I see her smile. I can't see Adam's face. Maybe that's okay.

She twirls her hair around her finger, and I can read her coy expression from here. She tilts her head back in laughter, the conversation seeming to last forever. My stomach clenches, and I'm tapping my foot like I'm at the dentist instead of the cafeteria. The anguish over waiting to hear what happens is worse than the root canal I had last month, seriously.

Eventually, she shrugs, gives a little wink, and slinks back to the table.

"Well, what happened?" I ask as she sits down. She takes a bite of her frozen yogurt, a neutral expression on her face.

"Well, I talked to him about you."

"And?"

"It's sort of bad news, May. I'm sorry." She grimaces.

My heart sinks. I knew it.

"Yeah, he says he wanted to ask someone else."

"Oh. Well, yeah, I figured as much." I try not to let the disappointment come through my voice.

Josephine averts her eyes, twirling her hair. I pause, wondering why she's acting so subversive. It can't be.

"I hope you don't mind. I didn't expect this, not at all. But you're right. He's so cute."

I don't know what to say, didn't expect it. I just shrug, sinking my fork into my pasta before twirling it around. I try to pretend I'm not hurt, that it doesn't matter, but the pain of rejection burns. I should've known better. I'd never get the guy.

"Oh, don't be silly. You two are way better together anyway," I finally say, plastering a smile on my face as I nod.

She reaches for my hand, consoling me. I'm probably imagining the condescending look in her eye. "Help me pick a dress this weekend, huh? We can find you one too. You know, you don't have to have a date to go."

I just nod.

I want to tell Gina about it next period in Trig, but I can't find the words. It's too embarrassing. I try to convince myself it doesn't matter. I convince myself Jo didn't mean for this to happen.

Something burns inside, a painful consideration.

Maybe Jo isn't the friend I thought she was after all.

I brush it aside, though. When you're the front row sitter, you can't be too choosy about your friends. Plus, it wasn't her fault.

It couldn't be Josephine's fault.

CHAPTER FOUR

In my leggings and a T-shirt with a cat on it, with a pint of Ben & Jerry's, I park myself on the sofa. I've tossed the superbra into the back of my closet, not wanting to keep it on but not quite ready to let go of it. You never know when you'll need some extra cleavage, right? I flip through the menu on Netflix, taking forever to decide on what to watch. Nothing calls to me. I'm caught up on my favorites, in a show hole. Plus, I'm still feeling kind of crappy from the night's events.

I check my phone. The only text is from Mitch. Wow, is it informative.

Mitch: K

I'm telling myself he's staying for the illustrious door prize and not for the reason I think he is. I will not have that woman slash she-devil get her hooks in my brother. He's too good for her. I mean, yes, he drives me crazy sometimes, and I frequently think he's an ass. But he's my brother. And she's… well, she's Josephine.

It's times like tonight I wish Mom were still here. She was never one to shy away from the truth. She called it like it was. She'd probably be trying to leap in the car right now to go vandalize Josephine's car or something. Hey, I never said she was perfect. Pretty sure she's the reason my nerdy self inherited a pretty un-nerdy trait: my bluntness. It's an odd mix… an introvert who verges on sarcastically frank from time to time.

If nothing else, Mom would make me feel less shitty about myself. She always told me there was more to life than work and impressing people. If she were here, she'd probably be loading me in the car to go out for some ice cream or dancing or even a beer—after we finished the vandalism, of course. Priorities.

But she's not here. I swipe away the thoughts. No use tossing myself down the rabbit hole of complete self-pity, self-loathing, and melancholy.

I turn on *Jane the Virgin,* deciding to rewatch an episode to take me out of my funk.

As often happens when one is overcome by a wash of sadness, two things occur:

1. One episode turns into three. I unlock an "achievement" on Mitch's Xbox for watching three episodes nonstop. Not so sure this is truly an achievement I'll be bragging about.

2. I don't stop at the halfway mark I promised on the ice cream. I demolish it. Then I go to the kitchen for some

cookies. In my defense, I *have* only had vegetables and fruits for the past eleven days.

I start to doze off, giving up on Mitch's return home. Maybe the door prize was a night out with Rory herself. There's a thought. My brother and Rory.

At two in the morning, Mitch sneaks through the door, but I instantly wake up. I'm a light sleeper. I blame my extreme paranoia coupled with my childhood fear of cat burglars.

"So," I say, stretching, wiping some cookie crumbs off my shirt, "fancy seeing you here. What, did you get lost? Reignite a lost flame? I thought reunions were for losers?"

He has a huge, goofy grin on his face. The grin I've only seen a few times before.

"Well, it turns out you were right. It wasn't so bad," he says, running a hand through his hair.

In my heart of hearts, I know as soon as I look at him. I know what has him smiling, or more accurately, who. I just don't want to admit it.

"So who were you with?"

He shrugs, hesitating enough to confirm my suspicions, busying his hands with a bag of cheese-flavored popcorn on the counter, even tossing a few pieces into his mouth for good measure.

"Please, for the love of God's green Earth, tell me it isn't who I think it is." I stand, showing just how serious I am.

"Maylee, she's not so bad, really," he says, a mouthful of popcorn causing him to mumble.

I close in on him, grabbing his shoulder. "You've got to be

kidding me. Not so bad? After all the crap she pulled?"

"It was ten years ago, for Christ's sake. It's not like she murdered puppies in her spare time."

My jaw clenches. "She made my life hell."

"I know. But people change," he says, softening. "Maylee, I don't know, something just clicked."

"Unclick it." My arms are crossed. Anger from high school bubbles back up.

I shouldn't be surprised. Of course Josephine would warp him under her spell. She did that with every guy in high school. I don't know why I'd think anything would change now. A bitch slap at the reunion would be too forward for Josephine's style. She's much craftier than that. Of course she would go the underhanded route.

But this is my brother, for God's sake. Rational, rule-following, head on straight Mitch. He parties a little sometimes, but keeps his eye on work. Climb the work ladder, make good decisions Mitch.

This is not the type of man to fall for Josephine's tricks.

Then again, Dina did do a number on him. I don't think he's gone on a date in nine months.

So of course, Josephine picked the perfect time to swoop in.

"Maylee, seriously. Just stop. You don't even know her anymore. She's different. She's a yoga instructor now as well as a nutritionist. She's living in State College, all alone."

"She *would* be a yoga instructor. She's certainly into herself enough."

"Do you realize what a jerk you sound like right now?"

"Do you realize you're telling me you have the hots for my biggest enemy right now?" I huff, still frustrated.

Dammit, though. Mitch is making me feel guilty. Maybe I *am* being ridiculous.

Besides, they're not getting married or anything. It was one night. She'll saunter back to State College, Mitch will get drowned in appeals, and all will be well. She can go back into oblivion, only existing in my horrific memories from high school that I can shut off at any time and banish to the land of irrelevance. He'll meet a perfect girl, one I introduce him to. They'll get married and make perfect little nieces for me to spoil. I'll be best friends with my sister-in-law, not in a weird, stalker-like way. In a monthly manicure, girl's night out for margaritas kind of way. It's going to be fine.

"You know, if you weren't so busy eying up Miss Namaste, I could've used your help."

"Oh, I heard all about the help you needed."

"No thanks to you, I found my way home quickly."

"I heard you *busted* out of there." He snickers at his lame joke, and I cringe.

"Creep," I retort. "I'm going to bed."

"Hey," Mitch says, stopping me. I turn in the hallway to look at him. "Thumbs-up on the high school reunion idea."

I grimace. "Turned out real well."

"I don't want to say karma," he says, shrugging with a stupid smirk on his face.

I roll my eyes as I head to bed, trying to put this god-awful night in the books.

Tomorrow, it's back to Maylee, the seminormal, glasses-wearing girl who's been out of high school for a decade and still doesn't know what the hell she's doing in life.

CHAPTER FIVE

"No, Johnny, don't put that in your mouth!" I dash across the room, grabbing the tub of paste from the four-year-old's hands.

Why didn't we just use edible paste at this point? Kids were drawn to it like… well, like kids to paste. After redirecting Johnny with a coloring book, I wipe my brow. It's only ten in the morning, and I'm already anxiously awaiting nap time, which is still two hours away.

Shauni sips her coffee, and I head over to finally fill her in on the reunion situation. Just as I'm opening my mouth to begin the story again, Shauni dashes over to the other corner of the room to redirect a girl who is slapping another for taking her Barbie.

The job is truly exhausting. Brain warping, eyelids held open with toothpicks exhausting.

"I'll just wait until after work to tell you," I shout as I head to take a girl to the bathroom.

"That good, huh?" Shauni laughs, another kid hanging on

her leg.

You'd think working with your best friend would be awesome, would give you plenty of time to talk. But when your workplace is swarming with fifteen children under the age of five, including a few with attention issues, talking is not really an option.

Ever.

I'm not complaining. I love the kids, paste eating, Barbie slapping and all. This is the part of my life that makes me feel alive, makes me feel as if I'm doing *something* with myself.

I just wouldn't mind two or three minutes of calm every once in a while.

I help Cora wash her hands and take her back to the playroom, ready to contain any more disasters. My job is never boring. I've seen pretty much everything you can see, from a Pop-Tart meltdown to a caterpillar poison control emergency.

Don't ask.

"Johnny, no!" Shauni yells, and I dash over for backup when I see the situation at hand. I help her pull him off the bookshelf before disaster strikes. Johnny is our acrobat slash gymnast slash Evel Knievel.

"Okay, time for a story," Shauni announces, fluffing her layered, shoulder-length hair, a trickle of sweat running down her cheek. "Who wants to read *Clifford*?" She says *Clifford* in her Mary Margaret voice, the one the kids love. They scramble to their mats, thankfully.

"Go take a break," Shauni whispers. I gladly oblige. We work well like this, knowing when we can give each other a break, constantly running to each other's aid. We keep each other sane in this sometimes insane environment. I glance at the kids and then at the clock. If past trends dictate anything, I have a good three minutes until the room again erupts into chaotic crying. I use my time wisely, going for a coffee refill for the both of us as the sound of children's laughter fills the room.

Those giggles make it all worth it.

Before I can even get to the pot of coffee to get some liquid energy, the equivalent of liquid gold in the preschool center, I hear it.

Tears. Shouting. Three minutes was apparently asking way too much.

***

"God, those devils were wild today," Shauni says.

"Shauni," I whisper. "You can't say that."

"Why? You think their parents don't agree?" she says nonchalantly. A few parents in the lobby eye her suspiciously, shrug, and then leave with their kids.

While I can certainly be accused of being blunt from time to time, Shauni is often accused of being downright abrasive. She grew up in Texas, and she's a Texan to the core. She's not afraid to say what's on her mind. She's not afraid to stand up for her rights.

And she's not afraid to tell parents their children are devils, even if she is head preschool teacher.

Shauni blasted into my life at the University of Pitt. I was the bookworm—surprise, surprise—trying to blend in with the curtains when my roommate dragged me to my first party. Shauni was the girl on the table singing the "Shots" song after guzzling them.

We were quite an unlikely pair.

I quickly learned the girl in fishnets and a halter top had spunk and heart. When I found out that behind the party-animal girl on campus was a girl who volunteered her time on Saturdays at the same soup kitchen I did, I realized maybe we weren't very different in the fundamental ways.

Which was true. We shared a fundamental love of several things.

1. Charity

2. Books

3. Shoes

What more did a girl need?

Honestly, Shauni is my absolute best friend. She's there to support me when I need someone to cry to. She's there to give me a swift kick when I'm being dumb or pitying myself too much. She's crazy loud and crazy outgoing. She's also kind and tenderhearted.

Plus, she's so good with the kids.

"Coffee Barn?" she asks, referring to our usual after work haunt. I nod, anxious to finally get the opportunity to tell her about the reunion.

"I can't wait to hear about the boob buster incident," she says.

I almost ask how she knows already but then remember we live in Smallsville, USA. My boob buster incident was probably front page news.

"Oh, it was lovely."

"At least you were memorable," she says, winking. Of

course Shauni would see my boob busting as a good thing.

"Well, that's not the only gossip I have for you."

Shauni literally rubs her hands together before leaning down to put some loose Lego away. "Oh, sounds good."

"Hardly."

"Well, let's get this stuff cleaned up so we can go talk about all the juicy tidbits."

"Let's."

We work quickly, shoving toys back in their color-coordinated bins and wiping down the tables with disinfectant, and head out the door to our favorite coffee shop.

***

"The usual," Shauni says with a wink when Matt asks her what we want. He's wearing the signature red Coffee Barn T-shirt and some killer, tattooed biceps. Shauni is entranced.

I might be a little, too.

After we both get our fix of eye candy and I secretly admire his hands working the espresso machine—perhaps wondering what kind of damage they could do in bed—we head to our usual table by the window, both offering a coy "thanks." Yeah, we're crazy flirtatious.

"Okay, spill," she demands as soon as we sit down. Her red lipstick, which she reapplied on the way over—perhaps something to do with tattooed Matt—is rubbing off on the cup already, but she doesn't notice. She's staring at me, impatiently motioning for me to get to the story.

I sigh, shaking my head. "It was a disaster."

"Yeah, I gather that. I want all the sordid details."

I walk her through the entire scene. The Rory encounter,

the fantasy slap moment, the real Josephine moment. The boobscapade, as I'm calling it.

"Wait, back up, tell me more about this Benson guy. Why haven't I heard about him?"

"Because I barely know him."

"Well, sounds as if he knows you now."

"I knew him a little in high school. Really nerdy and quiet."

"Oh, you were much better by the sounds of it," she says pointedly. I can't argue. "What's he like?"

"Well, he's a writer. He says he moved back to town—"

Shauni interrupts with a huff. "Not what's he like personality wise. I mean what's he look like? Good, bad, tell me."

"You're shallow."

"I'm in my twenties. These are the years to be shallow."

"If you want to be alone."

"I'm fine with that. Now stop stalling. Tell me."

Shauni's heard all sorts of embarrassing details. She's heard the details about my vomit situation at Barnes & Noble in front of a group of sexy men. She's heard about some of my love-life disasters. For some reason I can't explain, however, this question makes me clam up. The thought of describing Benson is… nerve-racking. I start to stammer. Shauni smiles.

"He's sexy."

"I didn't say that."

"You don't have to. Did you two bang?"

"Shauni, seriously?"

Shauni shrugs. "Don't be so prissy. It's a fair question. Isn't that what you go to these awful reunion things for?"

"No."

"Right. You go to stick it to your old frenemy. So now we've established you found some possibility in the man department, tell me more about the wench. Did you get any good digs in? Did she get plump? Tell me."

Now it's my turn to sigh. "Not even close."

"What do you mean?"

"I told you this whole thing was a disaster."

"You mean worse than splitting your dress disaster?"

"Like my brother has the hots for Josephine disaster. Like he ditched me to hang out with her. All evening."

Shauni's jaw drops. She is, for once, speechless. "You're not serious."

"Very."

"Do you think this was her plan all along? Do you think she's just been waiting for the reunion to strike, to take a shot at you when you weren't expecting it?"

I crack a smile. "Really? Calm down, Sherlock. I think we should give the blonde more credit. She's a plotter by nature. If she wanted this, I think she'd have accomplished it sooner."

"Well, it's just so weird."

"Tell me about it."

"Listen, let's not freak out. It's probably just a one-night thing. How far do you think it went?"

I almost spew out my coffee. "Ew, stop. This is my brother. I don't want to even think about...."

Shauni throws her hands up. "I'm just gauging the situation."

"For me or for yourself?"

"Hey, I've told you I think Mitch is hot. But lawyer… so not my type. Too pretty boy."

"Well, apparently not for a yoga instructor."

"Wait, she's a yoga instructor?"

"Plus a nutritionist. Oh, plus she owns her own yoga place."

Shauni shrivels up her nose as I stir my latte. "So no plumping up, I take it?"

"No. She looks perfect. As always. Arms sickeningly toned. Perfect skin and hair. The whole package."

"Well, like I said. It was a one-time thing. Mitch is too smart to fall for her. It's fine. Throw the whole thing in the past."

"Done. I'm ready to move on. No more reunions."

"Okay, but about this Benson…."

"*Shauni.*" I give her the warning look. She smirks.

"Fine. Subject change. Friday night plans. Go."

"Pajamas and Netflix?"

"Stop being old. Let's go out."

"I don't want to."

"You can't sulk forever. Forget about him."

"It's not about him. It's about me being tired."

"Well stop it. This is the prime of your life. It's my duty as your bestie to make sure you enjoy it."

"Please don't use the word bestie. Now who is the nerdy one?"

"Whatever. I'm going to get a refill."

"On your latte, or on Matt?"

"I wish."

I smile as she sways her hips to the counter.

I sip the last drop of coffee in my cup and think about what Shauni said. She's probably right. This whole Josephine thing is over. It was a mistake going to the reunion, but not a huge one. It's over now. We can all go back to being our twenty-eight-year-old nobodies, which sounds perfectly fine to me.

***

My hair is in a greasy ponytail and my shoelaces aren't even tied. Heck, I didn't even have time for dry shampoo on my roots or for a swipe of powder.

You know the song about bad days? Well, if it were on the radio right now, I'd punch it. Because this is certainly one of the days it was talking about.

I fly through the door of the center. I have one minute to spare. Parents are already heading to the classroom. I whir by, my purse almost taking out a woman on the way.

"Excuse me," I shout, running like an incompetent bimbo down the hallway to the classroom. I practically skid past the doorway, grabbing the doorframe to fling myself inside.

"I'm here," I yell as Shauni turns. When her gaze lands on me, she practically jumps.

"What happened?"

"Well, where should I start? My alarm didn't go off this morning for some unknown reason. Nelson accidentally escaped out the front door when I was trying to leave, so I then had to chase him down the hallway. His meowing woke up Mrs. Churchfield, who proceeded to give me a ten-minute lecture about how Nelson cannot be meowing so early in the morning. I couldn't find my car keys, I got every red light on the way here, not to mention the fact I haven't had time for coffee or to pee or to even brush my teeth."

At this point, Shauni looks glazed over, and I'm about to burst into tears.

"Okay, breathe. Go pee. I'll get some coffee for you. We have about a minute. We can pull it off."

I nod. "Thank you." I head to pee, passing the woman I almost took out with my purse. She glowers. I'm sure she's thinking twice about leaving her child with me. Hell, I would too.

After I get myself somewhat situated and try to fluff my hair in the mirror, I head back to help Shauni get the kids settled down. She hands me a coffee. I toss it back as if it were a shot.

I'm feeling an ounce better. Just an ounce. The coffee has helped.

But this whole day still blows.

We get through the workday with only ten tearful outbursts, one Band-Aid, five screaming tantrums, and six paste-eating attempts.

"Want to go get coffee?" I ask, my eyes practically drooping out of my head after the kids have gone home.

"Would love to, but I have a dentist appointment," Shauni replies practically.

"How adult of you."

"Gotta try in some areas, huh?"

"I guess. See you tomorrow." I trudge out of the center after helping to clean up. On my drive home, a sappy love song comes on. Not just any sappy song. *The* song.

I flip the radio off. Today seriously can't get much worse.

I pull into the apartment parking lot, prance through the front door, and find Nelson sleeping by the fridge. I pat him on the head before beginning my get-home ritual—sweatpants, a coffee or glass of wine depending on the day, and a chocolate bar.

Today is definitely a wine day, in case you haven't guessed.

I turn on the television, Nelson cuddling with me. An hour later, Mitch moseys through the door, flinging his keys on the counter. I notice he doesn't have a stack of papers with him as usual. His tie is loosened.

He's whistling. I think it's some song about sunshine.

"What are you so happy about?" I scowl. He looks at me on the sofa.

"What are you so mad about?"

"I'm not. Just tired. Seriously, what gives?"

"Nothing. Just a good day."

"Thursday is never a good day."

He just keeps on whistling, heading to the fridge for a beer and some leftover pizza.

I toss Nelson off my lap, stomping over to him. Arms crossed, I demand, "Tell me what's up."

He looks at me sheepishly. "You don't want to know."

I squint at him. It can't be. There's no way. But I have to know.

"Tell me."

"I have a date," he admits before sipping on his beer.

"With who?"

He pauses, looking me in the eyes. He shrugs. "Jo."

"As in Josephine, my blonde-haired enemy from years ago?"

"As in Jo."

If this were a cartoon, steam would be rolling out of my ears right now while the teakettle sound effects played. Red, puffy clouds of steam. Instead, I calmly breathe a few deep breaths and paint a smile on my face. "Why are you going on a date, dearest Mitch, with this woman?"

"Maylee, I like her. It's fine. Get over it."

I just stare, his goofy grin making me want to gag. He's totally taken by her. He's fallen for her.

And there's not a damn thing I can do about it.

***

"Of course we can do something about this," Shauni says the next day when I tell her the horrific news.

"What? Forbid him from seeing her?"

"No. But we can do something. First, we need to figure out how serious this is."

"They're dating. It's too serious."

"I mean, is it just an infatuation? Is it love? We need to know."

"How do we do that?"

"Do you know where they're going?"

"Yep, I heard him on the phone last night." I roll my eyes. I almost upchucked listening to his little flirtatious conversation. "He said something about Jack's Place around seven."

"I'll pick you up at seven fifteen."

"For what?"

"Just be ready. Wear something sneaky, like black pants

and a black shirt. We need to blend in."

"Shauni, what are you planning?"

"Don't worry. It'll be fine."

"I've heard that before."

"And, we've been fine, right?"

"Other than almost being arrested?"

"It was one time. And we weren't. We were fine."

I sigh. Once the woman got an idea in her head, there was no point in stopping her.

CHAPTER SIX

"I am *not* wearing this."

"Of course you are. You have to. We can't get caught."

"Don't you think this is going to look weird? We're going to be in a bar."

Shauni had burst through my apartment door at exactly 7:14 p.m. *She must be serious if she's on time,* I'd thought.

Now, she's shoving me into a tan trench coat, a black flapper-style wig, and a pair of shades.

She's sporting a red bobbed wig, aviators, and a black leather jacket. She clearly gave herself the better choice.

"Come on. We'll just go, get a look at the couple, and leave. I just want to get a feel for what we're dealing with."

"Don't you think this is extreme?"

"Okay, you're right. We should probably just sit back while Mitch and Josephine get close. If you're really lucky, there'll be a wedding soon. And some little nieces jumping around calling you auntie." She starts to take off her wig, testing me.

"Okay. Okay. We'll go. Just for a few minutes."

Shauni claps her hands, jumping a little bit. "This is so exciting."

"Okay, James Bond. Let's get moving."

I have to admit, the wig, the secret mission—it is rather exciting. I scratch Nelson's chin before following Shauni, ready to take on the world.

Or spy on my brother. Same thing.

***

I cough a little when the overpowering scent of alcohol and cologne hits my face but try to quiet it. We both stand in the doorway of Jack's Place, appraising the scene. The music, country and western, blares through the dingy, dark setting. A rowdy group of bikers chant across the bar. Sprinkled at random tables, couples ogle each other seductively, laughing loudly, sipping way too many drinks.

Shauni elbows me. "Over there," she whispers.

I see him sitting across the way with the familiar flash of blonde hair. Josephine's back is to us, so Shauni leads us around the bar. We're far enough away to not draw attention. With the better angle, we can keep an eye on them.

We climb onto our stools, me not very gracefully in my trench coat. I can't peel my eyes off them.

"Watch the body language," Shauni instructs.

The thing is, I already am.

They say twins have this twin speak thing, this twin telepathy thing, that lets us know what we're feeling. Right now, I'm getting a tingle because I think I'm getting it. I'm not reading his mind in a supernatural way, or weirdly connected to him. I'm not Sookie Stackhouse, after all—although I would be totally fine with the whole sexy, mysterious vampire bonus that goes with the mind reading.

Still, I see the way he's smiling. I see the way he's scrunching his nose, the way he's flinging his hand through his hair. I know without a doubt what he's thinking or feeling.

In all honesty, it doesn't take twin telepathy to know this is more than just a one-night thing. He's totally into her. I've only seen him this way one other time—the time he was really in love.

"Shit," I murmur, smacking a hand on the bar top.

"Agreed," Shauni says, seeing the same thing I'm seeing. "He's crazy about her."

"This is bad."

"Get ready to hear auntie."

I jab her with my elbow. "Let's not get crazy."

"Maylee, I don't think it's one-sided. Look at how she's looking at him."

"She's faking it."

I turn to look at Shauni. Even through the glasses—yes, we're still wearing them—I can see her squinting. "Come on," she says.

"So now what?"

"Now we move to phase two."

"Which is?"

"Drink our faces off and pretend your brother isn't dying to bang your worst enemy."

"God, I'm drinking right now. Bartender?" I raise my hand to flag him down as if I'm hailing a cab. I don't do this scene very gracefully. Shauni bursts out laughing.

I turn toward the cash register at the far right of the bar. The bartender's back is to us. He's wearing a tight shirt and some pretty tight jeans.

"Nice ass," Shauni says a little too loudly, and the bartender turns. My stomach flips with embarrassment.

When I get a good look—although dark from the glasses—my stomach plummets to the floor.

"Oh my God," I say through gritted teeth, trying to be a ventriloquist so he can't read my lips.

"I know, right?"

"No. Oh my God. It's Benson."

"Damn, he *is* hot. Nice." Shauni reaches to give me a high five. I bat her hand away.

"I can't talk to him. Not like this."

"Relax. It can't be worse than last time. Plus, you're in disguise. He won't recognize you."

"What about my voice?"

"Make it higher pitch. Or fake an accent." She snorts, knowing this won't work. Some help she is.

Benson strides over until he's right in front of us. "Can I help you two?" He acts very casual, not batting an eye behind those thick brown frames. Maybe Shauni's right. He doesn't recognize us. These disguises are good.

I sort of try to deepen my voice, make it sound husky, sexy. It comes out more like a screechy record player. I go with it.

"Two mojitos."

Benson nods, staring at me. I worry I've blown my cover.

"You two want me to turn down the lights?" he asks. My cheeks heat.

"It's fine. We just have sensitive eyes," I say. Benson smirks, shakes his head, and walks to the bar to make our drinks.

I turn my attention back to Mitch. He's still flirting with Jo. I actually feel a little weird now, spying on my brother. This probably wasn't a great idea.

A few minutes later, Benson returns with two of the best looking mojitos I've ever seen. I dig right in. Benson sort of lingers nearby, pretending to check on the bottles of a nearby patron. My heart beats a little harder than usual. My palms are sweaty, but maybe it's the booze already setting in. I readjust on my barstool. Shauni leans in.

"It's working. Mitch doesn't recognize us. He just looked over and didn't bat an eye. Plus your little high school lover is none the wiser."

"He's not my lover."

"He should be."

"Stop it."

Benson glances over, hearing us arguing in hushed whispers. He smiles, cleaning a glass.

"Can I get you a Long Island?" he asks. I turn to Shauni in confusion. He's looking at me, but he can't be talking to me.

"I have a mojito," I say, husky voice again.

"I thought at the reunion you were a fan of Long Islands?"

Shauni chokes on her drink. I feel my face warm.

We haven't fooled anyone.

Benson chuckles. I get flustered, shoving my glass down while trying to slink away. I'm ready to make a run for it, mortified about the wig, about the glasses, about the fake husky voice. About the fact Benson Drake probably thinks I was secretly trying to spy on him in this crazy outfit.

I spin on my stool, deciding to make a fast getaway. My trench coat belt gets hooked awkwardly on the bar somehow. Before I can catch myself, it's happening again.

I'm heading toward the ground, ready to kiss the floor.

****

This time, I land on my side. My glasses and wig have sailed through the air. Several patrons are standing around, some laughing, some pointing, some probably scared. No doubt someone's probably uploading a video of my klutzy move to YouTube as I lie on the floor.

Benson crouches down in a move becoming all too familiar.

"You okay?" He reaches for my hand. A part of me just wants to stay on the floor, crawl under a barstool, and pretend this isn't happening.

Again.

I sort of peer down to make sure there isn't a replay of the whole dress-splitting incident. Mercifully, there are no rips.

"I'm okay."

I reach for his hand, and he helps me up. A second time.

"This is becoming a habit, huh?" he asks. The other patrons, realizing no one has been mortally wounded, go back to their drinking and talking. I think they're a little sad I didn't do something really interesting like crack my head open.

"I'm mortified. I'm sorry. It's not what it looks like. I can explain all of…."

"This?" Benson hands me my wig and glasses. I blow my real bangs out of my eyes. He shakes his head. "You know, if you want to ask me out, you could just ask for my number. You don't have to keep throwing yourself at my feet."

"Honestly, that's not what was happening."

"Yes, it is," Shauni says, peering over my shoulder now. She still has the wig and glasses on. She reaches across me to offer her hand.

"Shauni. Nice to meet you. I've heard so much about you."

Benson shakes her hand. Now he's blushing. "Really?"

"No. She's lying," I say, trying to cover.

Before I can think too much about my fake accent or how mortified I truly am, I hear footsteps behind me. Shit. I forgot about the whole purpose of the disguise.

"Here. You two can cover this, right? Does your undercover pay allow you to get meal reimbursements?"

I close my eyes, exhaling. I turn to face my brother, who is shoving a bill in my face.

Yep. Just as I expected. He's pissed. Although I can't quite blame him.

"Mitch, I'm sorry. We were just...." Okay, so what could I say?

Nothing.

"Save it. Let's go, Jo. Let's go somewhere where there's a less unsavory crowd."

I see Jo give Mitch a playful wink. I almost felt bad for this whole scene. Almost.

"Dammit, why did you have to fall? We'd have been fine if you hadn't fallen."

Mitch stops in his tracks. "Actually, your disguises are atrocious. I knew it was you two as soon as you walked in.

Seriously, if you're going to be sneaky, tip one: Don't wear sunglasses in a bar."

Shauni looks thoroughly disappointed.

"Tip two? Don't bring the purse your brother bought you for your birthday last year."

At this, I glance at the handbag I'd tossed on the bar.

Shit. What an idiotic move. I glance at the navy Louis Vuitton with the huge fake diamond ring key chain I love plastered right on the front.

Busted.

Mitch and Josephine slink out of the bar. Shauni and I clutch our wigs and sunglasses in a cacophony of cheesy country music and yelling drunks.

"Still have a Long Island?" I ask as I turn to Benson.

"Do you two always get in this much trouble?"

I shout "No," as Shauni shouts, "Yes."

I spend the rest of the evening sipping on a Long Island, putting off going home in case our apartment was the backup date plan, and trying to avoid eye contact with the man who has now picked me up from the floor twice.

CHAPTER SEVEN

"Did you look in the fridge?" I ask the next morning when I finally drag myself out of bed.

He wordlessly shuffles through some papers on the counter.

"Hello?"

He continues flipping through the papers. I stomp toward him.

"Okay, I said I was sorry. If you look in the fridge, there's an 'I'm sorry' case of beer."

He looks up from his papers. "So you spy on me with your friend in a freaky disguise, you try to ruin my date over some stupid high school grudge, and you think a case of beer is going to make up for it?"

I shrug, scooching my right bunny slipper in a circle.

He exhales and yanks open the fridge. He verifies I'm telling the truth and turns back to me. "It's a start."

"I'll take it. Seriously. I know it was dumb. I just… I hate the thought of her with you. I don't trust her, Mitch."

"I appreciate your over-the-top but somewhat noble worry.

But I'm fine. Jo's fine. Maylee, it's been ten damn years. Can we just let this whole high school thing go?"

I sit despondently on the stool at the kitchen island. "I know. I know. I'm sorry. I can't just forget all the crap she did. She's not a nice person."

"People change."

"Not that much."

"You've changed."

"Not that much."

"Okay. So you still wear your bunny slippers from junior high. But you *have* changed. So has she. Can you please just give her a chance? I'm not saying get best friends bracelets or anything."

"Then what are you saying?"

"I'm saying don't creep on us at the bar when we're on a date."

"I guess that's somewhat reasonable."

"Can you manage?"

"I'll try. Just answer this. How serious is this thing?"

"I don't know yet." Cue the goofy grin.

"That's what I was afraid of."

"What?"

"You've got the grin."

"What grin?"

"The grin. You like her."

"There aren't wedding bells in the air, so chill. Besides, I think if you gave her a chance, you'd like her."

I make a pretend throwing up noise. Mitch rolls his eyes.

"You're so immature."

"Screw you."

He raises an eyebrow. "That's the best you've got?"

"Okay, lawyer boy. I'm out."

"Where you going?"

"To get coffee with Shauni and then shopping. Of course."

"No shoes, right?"

"No promises."

Mitch was already on my case about my random shoes around the apartment.

"No high heels. That Benson guy is probably tired of you throwing yourself at his feet."

"I do not throw myself at his feet."

"Um, okay. It's just happened twice now."

"It's not like that."

"Whatever you say."

"You're just trying to hook me up so you can ship me out of here."

"Of course not. If I wanted rid of you, I'd have thrown you out a long time ago."

"You'd miss me and Nelson."

"Oh yes. Dear Nelson. I love having white cat hair on all my suits. Superprofessional in the courtroom."

"Stop. I see you sneaking him snacks."

Suddenly, Nelson comes meowing into the room. I'm pretty sure he knows the word "snacks."

"Whatever. Get out of here."

"Gladly."

I head to my room to change, Nelson trailing behind me.

***

"Come on, Miss Boring, it's the weekend. Get those buns on the dance floor," Shauni shouts in my ear. I close my eyes, the music pounding way too loud in my head. We're at Shauni's favorite weekend haunt, aptly called the Weekender. It's a rave-like atmosphere with a lot of twentysomethings shaking it as if Monday will never come.

It's not my favorite. But Shauni won't let me stay at home.

"You've got to get back out there," she's been insisting. From the first awful week, she's pulled me off my couch every Saturday night to ensure my weekend consists of more than my cat and Netflix. "You're young. Stop being a grandma," she's told me on more than one occasion.

To be honest, the grandma life sometimes suits me, especially in the past few months. Most weekends, I'd sort of rather curl up in my frumpy sweatpants with Nelson and gorge on ice cream.

I must admit, Shauni is right. Twenty-eight is a bit too young to completely give up just yet. So, most weekends, I find myself on a lonely barstool at the Weekender, avoiding eye contact with creepers while Shauni dances like a lunatic and tries to pull me on the dance floor.

Shocking, I know, but the introvert from high school surfaces at places like this. Dance moves? I don't have any. Charisma? It's still coming in.

Finding a perfect man at the bar, therefore, is more difficult than usual.

I down a single shot, knowing I'll need a lot of liquid courage if I'm going to go out and dance to Pitbull's latest song. Don't get me wrong—I don't make a habit of imbibing.

There are plenty of weekends when I volunteer to be the designated driver, alcohol not my closest friend. However, tonight, after the whole reunion scandal, a few drinks seems like a good plan.

Shauni helped choose my outfit, deeming most of my choices too dowdy. I'm in a very tight leather skirt—which, FYI, is making me sweat in all kinds of odd places—and a plunging neckline halter. In short, I feel ridiculous. Walking without needing a censor bar is a feat, let alone doing any type of dancing. But the shot warms my blood and muddles my brain. I strut a little bit, as if I could channel my inner Beyoncé. I feel a bit like a queen.

In the middle of the dance floor, I'm shaking it a little. Once I settle into my spot, I feel pretty damn good. I have this. I'm not *too* bad. So I dance as if no one is watching.

However, someone is watching. I can sense it. Soon, hands grab my waist.

"Hey, sexy mama. Want to come home with me?" His breath is hot in my ear. I get chills as his breath hits the tender spot on my neck. Shauni is dancing wildly—she's had a few shots and a few other drinks—so she doesn't notice. I grin in spite of myself. Oh yeah, my dancing has definitely improved.

I don't brush away what I'm imagining to be a sexy hunk. I just keep dancing. Maybe Shauni's right. It is time I get back out there. Screw Jeremy. I'm going to find someone better, someone more fun. Someone who will make me even better than the Maylee I was with him.

His hands are on my hips, and I, rather smoothly if I do say so myself, continue a Shakira-like shake as I twirl to face him. Mentally, I'm picturing an Adam Levine lookalike or a Channing Tatum or maybe even a Gerard Butler. But when I turn, I almost gasp in sheer surprise.

Actually, in sheer horror.

Let's be clear. I'm no shallow girl. I do not need a six-pack or a perfect jawline or perfect anything to be happy. Give me personality, give me a guy who makes me laugh, and I'll be fine—although, as stated, Gerard Butler or Adam Levine looks wouldn't be a strike against him, for sure.

Still, it doesn't take me long to note a few things about the owner of the hands on my hips.

1. By the looks of his hairline, graying whiskers, and potbelly, he's at least old enough to be my dad.

2. The wink he gave me when I turned around was not platonic or sexy. It was actually very creepy.

3. His humor and personality, judging from the scandalous, perverted phrases he whispers once I face him, are less than admirable.

4. This is not Adam Levine, Channing Tatum, Gerard Butler, or any semblance of the three.

5. My gut instincts are not telling me to go home with this man. Or stand near this man. Or take a drink sitting near this man. They are telling me to run very, very far away.

"Oh sorry, sir, I have a boyfriend."

"Too bad, sexy mama." Cue creepy wink again and an even creepier, raspy chuckle. I quickly run from the dance floor, grabbing Shauni's hand on the way.

"What's wrong?"

"Okay. I'm done dancing. Mr. Creepo asked me to be his

sexy mama tonight."

"Oh, sounds fun." She glances back to where we were standing. Beside creepy guy is an actual Channing Tatum lookalike. Figures. It couldn't have been his hands on me.

"Okay, if *that* guy asked me to be his anything, I'd be leaving the dance floor to go do some other kind of dancing. Not him, the guy beside him."

Shauni shifts her eyes. "Oh God, not the guy in the white wifebeater with stains on it?"

I nod. Shauni does what any best friend would do. She starts laughing hysterically. Tears rolling down her cheeks, knee-slapping laughing. When her hysteria calms enough for her to breathe, she wipes her tears. "I'm sorry, Mays. I am. It's not funny. But seriously. Ew."

In spite of my frustration, I manage to crack a smile. "Yeah. Not what I had in mind for tonight. But listen, maybe it was a good thing. I'm not ready for something new anyway. It's too soon."

"It's been five months."

"We were together for nine."

We are back on the barstools now. Shauni looks at me seriously. "You loved him. I know."

The buzz from the shot is starting to fade just enough to take me from Beyoncé dancing queen to feeling a bit sucky.

"I did. I really did." Tears form, to my chagrin. Everything was just so damn fairy tale-like.

The house.

The ring.

The plans.

It was perfect.

Until one day… it wasn't. I was happily jaunting along, playing out the tomorrows and the forevers in my head.

Then slam. Crash. Bang. It all went to shit, Jeremy deciding forever would only last nine months and three days instead of a lifetime. He decided the house, the ring, the plans, weren't worth it. He decided to trade them in on a cheap bottle of wine, some pink lingerie, and a girl named Ava.

"You know what, he's a fool. Seriously. Someday, you're going to look back at him and realize he was nothing but a complete moron. You're going to feel nothing but happiness he messed up like he did because you are going to find a man who actually deserves you."

I pat her hand. "That was actually quite beautiful. It may just be the shots talking."

"Stop, I'm elo… eloq… oh, whatever the hell the word is."

"Eloquent?"

"Yeah. Now stop being so sappy. Drink some more."

"I actually think I'm calling us a cab."

"The night is young."

"Exactly what Mr. Creep is thinking."

Shauni followed my gaze to see Mr. Creep heading straight toward us.

"Oh, goodness. You're right. Let's split. I do not want to run the risk of having his hot breath on *my* neck this time."

We leap off the barstools, almost taking a spill, and head to the ladies' room to call our cab.

CHAPTER EIGHT

The cab driver drops Shauni off first because her apartment is closest to the bar. I ride the last five minutes alone, but not really. I'm swirling in memories, in moments of Jeremy.

Shauni's right. He was a fool.

It doesn't matter. No matter how much I want to hate him, and be happy I found out before it was "too late," as everyone says, I can't. All I can think about is the life we were supposed to be living right now, the perfect two-car garage house, baby on the way, Cape May summer kind of life. The dinner with the family on Sundays, movie night Saturdays, and pizza Thursdays. All I can think about is how I, like so many times in my life, wasn't enough. Like so many times, I was just the mousey nice girl trampled on by some outgoing, overtly sexy woman.

I was the girl left behind in the dust of someone better.

When we pull up to the apartment, I clear my throat so my voice doesn't come out all scratchy when I say, "Thank you." The shot has definitely worn off. I'm definitely not feeling like a dancing queen. I just feel like shit. The grandma life sounds wonderful right now. Or the lonely cat lady life. Whatever you want to call it.

I trudge up the steps, my head leaden from bad memories. I smell the nasty mix of alcohol and sweat on my skin. Man, I need a shower.

When I get to our landing, I rustle in my bag for the key. Mitch said he was going out tonight, I'm sure with Josephine. I'm actually thankful though—not for his choice of date but for the fact I'll have the place to myself. My head is pounding a little. I need some solitude.

I fling open the door, and Nelson greets me. I blink a few times, trying to adjust to the lack of lighting. That's funny. I thought I left the lamp on.

I hear some rustling in the living room, but my muddled head takes a while to catch up. What the hell is going on? Nelson is at my feet.

My heart quickens a bit as the rustling continues. I hear a male voice say, "Shit."

Oh my God. There's a robber.

In my confusion, I don't run out the door or call 911. It all is happening so fast. You know how you watch those crime shows and you're like "Wow, what an idiot. Call 911, bimbo."

Well, I get it now. Because in the moment, you're like *holy shit, what do I do?*

So I do the thing any college-educated twenty-eight-year-old would do.

I flip on the light.

I so, so, so wish I hadn't.

***

There are screams from my mouth. There's an Oedipus-like moment where I think I might gouge out my own eyes. There's a moment where I slam myself into the corner by the door, desperately grasping for the doorknob.

Nelson keeps meowing.

The male voice keeps screaming, "Shit."

The female voice is screaming, "I thought she wasn't going to be home."

My inner bitch voice is screaming, "It's my damn house, I'll come home when I want."

Instead, though, I stand, practically rocking myself in the corner, trying to unsee what I just saw.

But when your high school archenemy and your brother are in a… well… compromising position on the sofa—the one you, ew, eat ice cream on and nap on—you can't unsee it. Even when your eyes are shut.

There's more rustling. Again, I wish I could Dorothy up out of here. To Oz. To the Underworld. To freaking anywhere. I consider dashing out the door, running away and potentially never facing my brother again.

Then I hear the words. The fighting words. The words challenging the quiet, mousey Maylee from the inner recesses of my being.

"You know, you could knock next time," the familiar voice says.

The quiet, mousey Maylee would have burst into tears. Sorry, sister, but that girl's long gone. I spin around, hoping as I do that they're decent. They are.

"Excuse me?" I stomp toward her, pointing a finger. "You're screwing my brother like a skank on my sofa, in *my* apartment, and I'm the one who should knock?"

"Ladies, let's chill, okay? Calm it, please."

Mitch is fifty shades of red. I'm pretty sure this isn't what he had in mind for the night.

"I'm sorry, but walking in on you two on our sofa. Our sofa. The one I, you know, used to sit on, relax on, eat ice cream on, it's a bit over the top, don't you think? I mean, first of all, you do have a thing called a bedroom. With a lock on it. Down the hall. Ever think of that one?"

Josephine twirls her hair, her fiery eyes staring me down. She smirks. "Oh, we just couldn't make it that far. You know, chemistry."

Oh my God, really? This woman is disgusting.

"Okay, second, the woman you choose to fornicate with on our sofa is… that?" I point wildly. All pretenses of calm, polite Maylee are already out the window. Might as well go all-in.

"Okay, Maylee. Enough."

"Third, you live with your sister. I get that's a little weird. But you know, this never happened with Dina because she wasn't a slut. She wasn't all about throwing herself around. She was respectful of our living arrangement."

"You know what, maybe if you didn't mooch off your brother, maybe if you had your own place, this wouldn't be happening," Josephine retorts. I throw my hands in the air. Good. The real Josephine is surfacing. Now Mitch will see she hasn't changed.

"Okay, both of you, enough."

My jaw drops. "You're going to let her talk to me like this?"

"Maylee, you're both being ridiculous. Look, I'm sorry, I really am. This was just…. God, this is weird and embarrassing. I wasn't thinking. I just got caught up."

I throw my hands up. "TMI."

"Look, we're all just flustered. This is all my fault. Let's just cool down and try to forget about this."

"Sure. When my eyes stop bleeding."

"Stop being ridiculous," Josephine retorts, leaning on Mitch's arm. "Listen, let's be adults. We'll go get a hotel room for the night so Maylee isn't uncomfortable."

I scrunch my nose, glaring. "I'm sorry your sexcapades are cramping my style. You know, of living in my own home."

"Well, from what I understand, this is Mitch's home."

I pause, hurt creeping in. This woman knows how to cut. Deep.

"May, no, it's not like that. You know I don't mind you living here."

I fight back the tears. I will not cry in front of her. I will just let it sink in what a bitch she is.

True to Josephine's style of warfare, though, she starts tearing up. She plays victim. She wins my brother over. "Maylee, I'm sorry, honey. This is just so stressful and so uncomfortable. I didn't mean any of it. Mitch loves having you here, he's told me. I know you went through a tough time with Jeremy and with the house and everything. You shouldn't feel bad about living here. I'm sorry. I feel like such a bitch."

Now Mitch is telling her about Jeremy? What else is he confiding in her about? I want to tell her she freaking should feel like bitch because she is. But I know what she's doing.

She's getting back on Mitch's good side. It's working. Because he just wraps an arm around her as if she needs comforting.

"Whatever," I say flippantly. Mitch gives me a look.

"I'm sorry again."

"Whatever."

"We're leaving. The place is yours," Mitch says, searching for his keys.

"I hope you know you're buying a new sofa."

"Stop being dramatic."

The two leave arm in arm, flirting the whole way out.

Gag me.

I sigh, staring at the couch, still considering gouging my eyes out. Nelson meows, waiting for our couch time.

"Well, Nelson, there's only one thing we can do for now."

I stomp to the kitchen, grabbing some garbage bags for a makeshift tarp to cover the sofa. There's no way in hell I'm sitting on the floral print after the things it and I have seen.

No way in hell.

***

When Shauni answers the door at ten the next morning, she looks pretty much like I feel. Except maybe even worse. Her hair is matted to one side of her head, a weird halo shape on her left side. Her eye makeup, glitter of course, is running down her face, settling into the crevices and cracks in an unflattering way. She is gray, she is squinty-eyed, and she is sluggish.

Plus, she's still in her dress from last night.

"What are you doing here?" she asks, her voice scratchy like a worn old man's.

"Coming to get you for some coffee."

"Are you crazy? It's early."

"It's ten."

"It's early."

I push back her door to lead myself into her one-bedroom.

"Go get some clean clothes on. Let's get coffee."

"You're crazy," she says, holding her head and yawning. "But coffee does sound good."

"Last night wasn't such a grand idea, huh?"

"Are you kidding? It was awesome."

I raise an eyebrow. "Looks like it."

She groans and trudges off to her bedroom. She emerges five minutes later wearing a wrinkled Led Zeppelin T-shirt and a pair of holey jeans. Her hair, still a matted pile of frizz, needs some work, but she'll pass.

"Let's go," I say. "I've got quite the tale for you."

She winks. "Oh my. Did you take someone home?"

As she pulls her door shut—not locking it, of course, as is her unsafe custom—I sigh. "Do you not remember last night?"

"I remember the shots."

"No, I didn't take anyone home. It's not that kind of tale."

"Then what is it?"

We walk down the block, Shauni squinting at the bright rays of sun as we head toward Coffee Barn.

"A terrifying one. An 'I walked in on my brother in a compromising position' one."

"Oh, shit. Please don't tell me he was with the blonde."

"Of course he was with the blonde. Of course. The snooty witch had the nerve to complain to me, as if it was my fault."

"You're kidding."

"Wish I were. The image has been carved into my brain."

"Maybe we should head to a hypnotist. Get that shit removed from your head."

"Trust me, I've thought about it."

"God. So what did you do?"

"After having a brawl with her?"

"Physical, I hope?" Shauni grins. She was always one for a good fight.

"Verbal. After she played the manipulative, I'm-so-sorry card, my brother took her to a hotel."

"Ew."

"Tell me about it. Then Nelson and I spent the rest of the evening binging on Netflix."

"You did cover the couch, right? I mean, after all of those activities?"

"Please stop. I don't want to think about it." I cover my ears. I do not want to think of the… activities… and last night.

"What? It's a reasonable question."

"Yes, I covered the couch. With a garbage bag, all right? God. I definitely need a hypnotist now." We arrive at Coffee Barn, and head through the door to our regular spot. The bells on the door jingle as we walk in.

We order the usual, although more perfunctorily this time since Matt isn't working. As we meander toward the corner booth, our weekend booth, Shauni nudges me. "Maybe you won't need a hypnotist to make you forget about last night." She tilts her head to our left.

My heart flutters a bit.

Just a bit.

To our left, his laptop and a cup of coffee nearby, Benson types away. He adjusts his glasses, peering out the window in a moment of thought before returning to his computer.

I put my head down, suddenly feeling like my eighth grade shy self.

"Where are you going? Go talk to him," Shauni hisses, taking my coffee from me.

"I don't have anything to say."

"How about hi, how are you? Want to go have hot sex with me?"

"Shauni," I practically shriek. Benson looks up.

Smooth. Real smooth, Maylee.

He smiles as soon as he sees us. "Hey, how are you two?"

"We're fine," Shauni says, smiling. "I'm going to get our booth. Take your time." She winks at me and trudges off, abandoning me. I consider just following her, running away. Seeing Benson here in his element, writing, looking all scholarly, it unnerves me. I'm not even sure why.

"So, you two been scheming lately? I almost didn't recognize you without your wigs."

I shrug. "I decided a flapper bob didn't suit me. No scheming today. Not really. Not yet, anyway."

"Sounds promising," he says, lifting a cup to his lips. He motions to the seat across from him. Not sure what to do and realizing I'm awkwardly standing in the way of other customers, I oblige.

"What are you working on?"

He swallows his coffee and looks down at the keys before returning his gaze to mine. "A new novel."

"How many have you written?"

"This is my fourth."

"Really? That's great."

"It would be, if any were published. Kind of silly, I guess. I just… I don't know. I just can't stop, you know?"

"What do you write?"

He bites his lower lip, tension on his face, as he sets his coffee cup down. He's unnerved, too. This is the first I've seen him like this. Of course, every other time I've seen him, I've made a complete ass of myself.

"Romance," he says, practically coughing.

I wasn't expecting this. I don't know what I was expecting. I don't have oodles of writer friends or anything. Actually, I don't have any. I guess I pictured, I don't know, *Lord of the Rings*-style stuff. Fantasy. Manly. As I inwardly chide myself for being sexist, he exhales.

"You think it's weird."

"No, no. I don't." I throw my hands in front of me to reassure him, to try to convince him he's incorrect in assuming I think his romance writing is unconventional even though I'm thinking exactly that. Then, cue awkward, unnerving moment three. Yep, predicable, I know.

My hand flies into his coffee cup.

Coffee cup dumps.

On his laptop.

Sizzle. Scream. Shit.

"I am so sorry. Oh my God, I'm so sorry. Did I ruin it?" I haphazardly toss some napkins on his laptop. Coffee is dripping down onto his lap. Benson reassures me he's fine, it's all fine, but he's wincing in pain.

"Oh God, did I burn you? Oh my God, are you hurt?" I eye the coffee. It's dripping down his leg. It's oozing very close to… well, some sensitive areas.

"I'm fine. It's fine," he reassures, dabbing his leg with the napkin. At this point, Shauni, apparently seeing the scene I'm making, dashes over. Despite her hangover, she's practically gliding.

"What happened?" She assesses the dripping coffee, the sizzling computer, and Benson wincing.

"Oh my God, Maylee, did you freaking burn his manhood?"

Benson freezes, and I cover my mouth with my hands.

Benson, despite the obvious pain, manages to chuckle. "My manhood? All this, and you ran over to worry about my manhood?" He shakes his head. "Rest assured, my manhood member is fine."

"Phew. I was worried for you, Maylee. God, that would be disastrous. We can replace a computer. But that, well, can't really replace that. I mean, you could, but it would involve—"

"Shauni!"

"Right, right. I'm talking too much. I'll stop now. You two okay?"

I close my eyes, again wishing I could disappear. "We're great."

"Yep. Never better," Benson teases.

Shauni walks away, and I feel my face cool down from embarrassment. "I'm sorry. For everything. For the leg burn. Are you sure it's okay?"

"It's fine," he says, tossing a hand in the air.

"And for Shauni's embarrassing comment."

He shakes his head. "Again. It's fine."

"And the computer. Is it ruined?" I get closer to the computer, sort of leaning over him to get a better look. It has a screen looking far from okay, and there is still a sizzling sound.

Benson eyes me. "Well, I think the laptop has seen better days."

Tears well. "Oh my God, I'm such a disaster. Your book. What about your book? Is it gone now?"

"No worries." Benson pats his shirt pocket. "I always back it up."

"Oh thank God. I promise I'll pay for this. I'll get you a new one."

He waves it off. "Honestly, it's fine. I needed an upgrade anyway."

"You're lying." I feel like an absolute idiot, a huge piece of crap, and worse than Shauni's hangover. Why am I such a freaking klutz around this man? Why can't I catch a break?

"No, I'm serious. Plus, I needed a rest from it all anyway."

I look over at Shauni. She may as well have binoculars out spying on us, she's craning her neck so hard to observe. She's also smiling at me.

"Listen. I'm probably going to regret this because I'm sure she'll say inappropriate stuff. But do you want to join us over there? We're just sort of recovering from last night, getting some coffee. Nothing exciting. But you're welcome to join us."

He stares at me for a seemingly eternal moment. "One condition."

"What's that?"

"You think we can get coffees with lids, please?"

I laugh, shoving his shoulder. "Well, now you know without a doubt that I'm a complete klutz."

"Never really doubted it," he says, again showing me his huge, toothy grin.

I shrug. "I guess you're right."

"And I also know for sure now that you do, indeed, think my romance writing is weird."

"I do not."

"Listen, it doesn't take a sizzled computer and some dumped coffee to realize romance writing isn't quite what most men are up to."

"I think it's cool, really. I'd love to read your work sometime."

He shrugs. "Yeah, maybe."

"Will you two stop flirting? The coffee is getting cold," Shauni bellows from across the coffee shop. Martin, the owner, glares at her. He should be used to Shauni's boisterous behavior by now, but I don't think he is judging by the glare. From my coffee spill to her obnoxiously loud laugh, I'm a little concerned we're going to get banned from here for life.

"I told you this might be a mistake."

"I'm okay with it. Mistakes are sometimes good things," he says. I offer him my hand and help pull him from the booth.

When his fingers skim mine, I notice two things.

One, they're still kind of damp from the coffee spill.

Two, there's a heat when our hands touch that isn't coffee-based. It's a deep, sensuous heat I didn't expect, so much so I almost jump back.

I've fallen in front of him twice. I've dumped coffee, sizzled his computer, and come dangerously close to singeing off his manhood. Now, as I lead him to the table with Shauni, I realize there's something even more dangerous brewing, a disaster waiting to come crashing down. Something about this nerdy writer in Ray Bans with his blond, spiky hair has me feeling restless, clumsy, and crazy.

HIGH SCHOOL SOPHOMORE YEAR

I readjust the straps on my navy swimsuit, letting go and hearing them slap against my wet skin. I'm wearing my hot-pink swim cap, and my goggles are firmly in place. I waxed my bikini line twice just to be sure. I also did some extra yoga this weekend.

I don't feel quite like a supermodel. I'm still nervous as heck to get in the pool. I'm terrified for Eric Sentsa to see me in my bathing suit. I'm afraid I'll drown or look like a flopping fish in the pool or fall behind on the laps.

Glancing in the mirror as Mrs. Karlson blows her whistle and orders us out of the locker room, I realize I have no choice but to be ready. The first day of swim class, a mandatory spring semester physical education requirement tenth grade year, is about to begin.

It's a coed class. It's the talk of the tenth grade. The hot girls, mostly the cheerleaders, are ecstatic about the chance to flaunt around their perfectly tight bodies—they even started a petition to allow bikinis as appropriate swim uniforms. The heavier girls started a petition to ban swim class, calling it sexist and noting how unfair it is for the boys to get to glimpse their bodies.

Then there are the in the middle girls. Me. The not so tight, baby pudge girls who aren't quite hot but aren't quite terrible in the bathing suit. We're just at the point of lacking self-confidence but wanting to try to find it.

"Race you to the pool," Josephine yells as Ariel and I trail behind. Like me, Ariel is tugging on her swimsuit, readjusting, reaffirming everything is in place.

Not Josephine.

Her blonde curls sway down her back—she vowed she didn't need a swim cap. Her hair looks perfectly fine, she'd announced—as her hot-pink suit hugs her curves. She laughs gleefully, skipping ahead of everyone to be the first in the pool area.

The rest of us hunker back. We know as soon as we step into the pool area, we can't hide anymore. The boys will all be there. Eric will be there. His perfect abs, his golden locks flowing. His tight, tanned body.

Not long ago, Adam was the guy who had my eye. Then Jo caught his, and I moved on.

I'm going to potentially vomit—not a good way to catch Eric's eye. But it's all good. I'll be fine.

"God, I'm nervous," Ariel mutters.

"Me, too."

The confident girls, Jo in the pack, strut right in, their hands on their hips like models. Ariel, a few other girls, and I hang back.

When we get to the area, we're told to line up alongside the pool. The guys are across from us. I can feel their eyes on us. I try to forget I'm practically naked.

There he is. Right across from me. Eric. He looks perfect. I feel my cheeks warming. I'm probably blushing. He smiles at me.

"Okay, ladies and gents, get in the pool. We're going to start with some laps. Each lady will be paired with a gentleman. Ladies, you will swim across the pool and tag your partner in. Then the gentleman will swim his lap. The first couple to complete their laps wins. Everyone line up. Find a partner."

My stomach flutters. I'm across from him. I'm nervous as heck, but this is my chance.

We all climb into the pool, a splashing, fluttering mess of arms, legs, and bathing suits. There's a shuffle as everyone switches around to pair up with their choices. Eric doesn't move. He motions across the pool, asking if I want to pair up with him. I smile, probably too wide. I nod.

Just then, Josephine makes her way from the other end of the pool, swimming a perfect breast stroke. Of course.

"Hey, Eric, want to be my partner?" she asks, acting as if I'm invisible. I sigh. Ariel catches my eye.

We've been chatting lately about this, about how Josephine has been a bit competitive with me. I thought it was just me, but several other girls have noticed it too.

I've tried to ignore it. Josephine is always doing so many nice things for me. Just when I feel like I'm going to walk away from our friendship, just when I feel like she isn't really my friend, she does something nice for me. She calls me to come over for a sleepover and we spend the night eating popcorn, bonding over our love for Friends. *Or we head to the mall to shop, her telling me how good I look in a skirt she picks out. She's a walking contradiction. Nice and supportive one moment, sneaky and manipulative the next.*

This is one of those moments I question her motives.

Josephine smiles sweetly. I look across the pool. I figure I'm done, I'm a goner. I can't compete with the hot-pink bathing suited, perfect skin Josephine. How could I?

Then something happens that surprises even Josephine.

Eric shakes his head. "I'm already with Maylee," he says, smiling. Josephine turns to me.

For the first time, I see a look in her eye that says it all. A jealous look. An evil look. An angry look. It's ridiculous. What the hell should she be jealous for? She doesn't even like Eric, hasn't shown any interest in him. Plus, she can honestly have any guy she wants.

Except right now. Except for Eric.

"Fine. I'll find someone else." Josephine brushes past me, kicking her feet as she swims to the other end to find a partner. She ends up paired with Sampson, the new boy who just moved here. He is currently picking his nose.

Eric and I don't win the swimming contest, but in a way I do win because I get to slap his hand.

And it is the most glorious hand slap I've ever experienced.

When we head back to the locker room at the end of class, I'm not feeling as bad about myself. I don't strut back, but I don't slink back either. I wear my bathing suit a little bit easier, a little bit more assuredly.

Josephine, though, doesn't. She stomps back to the locker room, a scowl on her face. She doesn't speak to me the rest of the day.

"The girl is psycho," Ariel whispers to me.

I don't agree, but I don't defend Jo as I usually do, either.

I'm starting to see that maybe the sweet, loving act is just that.

The next day, I get verifiable proof it is.

CHAPTER NINE

"Never gets any easier, huh?" Mitch says as he pops a packet of popcorn in the microwave.

"Never." I swipe at some leftover tears. My nose is stuffy, and my head throbs as if it's been clobbered with a ton of bricks.

I stare at the picture on the stand by the television, picking it up to get a closer look. Mom and Dad are gazing at each other, a decrepit cabin in the background. Dad has his arms around Mom, who is wearing a skintight white dress that stops well above her knees. She's popping a foot up behind her, laughing as the sun sets perfectly behind them, gleaming off the fresh-fallen snow. Her hand caresses his chest. A few wisps of daisies are in her hand, probably fake since it's December. Their breath is visible in soft puffs of clouds above their heads. My mom must be freezing, but there's nothing except warmth radiating through the photo. Smile lines punctuate their faces, and the only way I can describe the connection between them is love, a love so strong it is palpable even on this piece of photo paper.

It's my favorite picture of them. It's unconventional yet gorgeous—the love between them is obvious. My only hope is some day, I'll have my own wedding picture like this one.

I set the picture down, swiping away a tear. This day never gets easy. We've survived the part I hate the most, though, the part reminding me just how much we're missing. We left our customary white daisies, Mom's favorite, on the joint grave. We sat pressed into the dirt, Mitch rubbing his hands over the words we hate to see, the words that make everything so permanent.

Five years have gone by. Five August sixths. Five visits to the cemetery, five days of chest-pounding, heart-aching moments. Five years of remembering we're orphans.

But at least I have Mitch.

Mitch and I were always close. Call it the twin thing. Even though we were so different in high school, we still had a bond. Ever since the life-shattering phone call, though, Mitch and I've been even more inseparable. The hospital morgue moments, the funeral home moments, and everything after that… we've drawn closer knowing we're all we have left.

The first year was undeniably the worst. We were two lost fish in a sea of memories, of uncertainty. We were two twenty-three-year-olds still trying to find our places in the world and now we had to navigate it without any parental guidance. At a time when most twentysomethings are trying to break free from parental overseers, we were closing our eyes, wishing for nothing but that.

We were two lost souls missing two of the greatest free

spirits we knew. Our advisors, our mentors, our fan clubs, our support systems were ripped to shreds the night the truck slammed into my parents' SUV. With the crashing of metal came the crashing of our lives.

We muddled through the first anniversary, a heaping mess of tissues, regrets, apologies, and wistfulness.

We purposefully walked through the second. There were still tissues and regrets, still a blanket of grief. However, it was on the second anniversary we decided we were doing things all wrong. It was on the second anniversary our tradition began.

Mitch had started it. "You know, Mom and Dad would make fun of us, sitting here bawling around."

"Well, what are we supposed to do?" I'd asked between tissues.

Mitch looked at me. "Remember them. Celebrate them. Live."

"And how do you suppose we do that?"

He had grabbed my hand, pulling me away from the grave. "Follow me."

That's when our unconventional memorial ceremony began. We vowed that night we would never miss one, that we would always spend the anniversary of the most tragic day of our lives together, doing just what Mom and Dad would want.

"You got the movie?" Mitch says now, snapping me back to the present.

"Of course," I reply, heading to our shelf where *V for Vendetta* is displayed.

It was my parents' favorite movie and, thus, the movie we watched as a family way too many times.

"You got the M&Ms?"

"May, it's not my first freaking rodeo. Of course I do."

He settles onto the couch, the movie previews starting as he hands me the bag. I dump them into the popcorn bucket, stirring it around with my hand.

We dig in to Mom's favorite movie treat as we watch the movie. We've both memorized it. We know every word, we know the V monologue by heart. We could skip it, say we're tired of it. Hell, we could say it's disrespectful to be eating popcorn and watching their favorite movie on today of all days.

But we don't. Because we know this is what our parents would want. They'd want us to celebrate the good times, to remember all of our family memories. They'd want us, most importantly, to be together, brother and sister, the last remnants of our family.

We mindlessly eat our snack, both lost in a world where Mom and Dad are on the couch beside us, Mom yelling to pass the popcorn, digging to the bottom for the superchocolaty bites. Dad yells at Mom to move her gross feet, so she naturally shoves them in his face, giggling wildly. They both sing out the beloved monologue in dramatic voices, their words echoing dramatically in an odd duet.

Mom and Dad aren't here, no matter how much I want them to be. There are no feet. There will be no popcorn digging or name calling.

They're gone.

Before I get swept up again by the still raw emotion, I hear the door. Startled, I turn to see who it is, who could possibly be dropping by today. All of our closest friends and family know what today is, and they know we prefer to spend it alone.

Then I see it. A flash of blonde hair. An infuriating smile. A bag of groceries.

Her voice, which sounds like a belt skipping on a car to me, screeches, "Hey, guys. I'm here."

I turn to Mitch. "What the hell?"

His face turns red. He knows I'm going to be pissed. So he does what any intelligent, perceptive male would do.

He hits Pause on the remote, shoves the popcorn bucket at me, and plods to the kitchen to greet my nemesis, avoiding eye contact and me altogether.

***

"Maylee, do you think you could find a vase for these, sugar?"

Josephine has quite literally taken over our kitchen, strewing groceries for a, in her words, "delicious pasta dinner to make us forget all about today" on the counter. She clacks around in her ruby high heels, playing housewife. Worst of all, Mitch is following her like a lost puppy, trying to ignore the scowl on my face, the obvious rage bubbling inside.

The nerve of him to invite her of all people today. The nerve of her to prance into our house today, to insinuate we need to forget today.

"I'm good, thanks," I mutter from the couch, shoving popcorn in my face. She looks over to me, her heels stopping for an instant. "Dinner will be ready in about an hour. Are you sure you want to shove all of the popcorn down?"

I turn to stare at her, to see if she's serious. She is, as evidenced by her gleaming white smile.

"As delicious as tofu pasta sounds, as much as it will probably make me forget all of my problems, I think I'd rather drown in the saturated fat in the popcorn in hopes my arteries clog in the next fifteen minutes."

The smile on Josephine's face turns to a frown. "Oh, honey, I know it's a tough day. It's your grief talking."

I leap from the couch, the popcorn flying to the floor. "No, Josephine, it's me talking, Maylee, you know, the girl you tortured in high school? The girl you single-handedly tried to ruin, the girl you thought nothing of? Now, here you are in my kitchen on the anniversary of the hardest day of my life, intruding on our family traditions because, what, you have the hots for my brother for five minutes? Don't act as if you care about my family. You don't get that right, not after everything."

"Maylee, calm down." Mitch is standing between us, perhaps afraid a catfight is going to ensue. His face is pained. I can tell this is a messy situation he wasn't really looking for today.

I want to take a breath, to calm down, to let this whole thing slide. Today's not the day to get into it with Josephine, or Mitch for that matter. Mitch is having just as shitty a day as I am. While I want to choke him for inviting this she-devil into our home, I know grief works in strange ways. Maybe this was what he somehow needed for today, although it gags me. But he doesn't know. And he can't. It would kill him.

I exhale dramatically, eyes squinting shut. I try counting to five, try to remind myself this doesn't matter. Today's not about tofu queen. It's not about high school arguments. It's about a whole lot more important things.

Just when I'm ready to extend a temporary, one-day olive branch to my high school adversary—and apparently my current adversary as well, since Mitch has brought her back into my life—it happens.

Josephine does what Josephine does best. She clacks over close to me, passing right by Mitch.

"Maylee, I'm so sorry." She says these words all breathy, pausing between each dramatically. She's probably picturing dead puppies or a tofu shortage or something, because she's working up some huge crocodile tears. I fight the urge to roll my eyes. But then she continues. Of course.

"I'm *so* sorry." She reaches for my hands. I fight back vomit. *Be mature,* I remind myself. At least she's apologizing. Maybe we can put this in the past. Maybe she has changed.

"I had no idea our silly high school times had such a deep, psychological impact on you. Listen, one of my friends in college had a bit of a psychotic break a few months ago, and she saw this amazing therapist who really helped. Maybe I can get you his card?"

I stare, a long pause heightening the tension in the room. I wait for her to laugh, to show some sign she isn't serious. She lasers those crystal eyes, leaking with tears, into me. I start to laugh because I have no idea what else to do.

"You think I need a therapist? Are you out of your mind?"

The signature pouty frown is back. Tears flow for real. "I… I don't know what to say. Oh, this is such a mess. I should just go." Tears are now flowing as if she's the victim. Yet again.

I look to Mitch. Certainly he sees her for what she is now.

Then he does something more shocking than Josephine's ridiculous statements. He wraps her in his arms.

"Hey, this is just a bad day for all of us. I know you came here with good intentions. It's my fault. I should have checked with Maylee first." They embrace.

I rush to the living room, grab the popcorn bowl—which only has a few pieces left in it—and head down the hallway to my room. I slam the door like a ridiculous teenager.

Josephine's back in full swing, her manipulative attitude, her prying ways.

Worst of all, though… Mitch has totally fallen for her.

CHAPTER TEN

"Okay. Enough is enough. Jo is a part of my life. You are a part of my life. You two need to sort out this ridiculous, immature crap from high school."

I glance up briefly from my magazine. I roll my eyes—yep, not ready to let go of immaturity yet—and then return to my article on smoothing eye wrinkles.

"Hello?"

I continue flipping pages very… well, flippantly.

Mitch tosses my magazine across the room. "Maylee, I'm serious. I was wrong to let her come over yesterday. I know that now. I just… I thought it would be okay, I thought it was a nice gesture on her part. I really don't think she meant to say the things she did."

"So you're still defending her after she basically called me a psycho?" I still don't make direct eye contact with him. I'm tired of this argument.

"I just… I think it was a bad situation the whole way around. As I said, it's all my fault. I'm sorry. But, I like her, okay? If you took some time to get to know her, you might like her too."

At this, I'm off the couch faster than a raccoon scrambling in the night. "Are you kidding me? I might like her? This isn't some random girl you picked up at the supermarket. This is Josephine Crawford. This is the girl who made my life hell. This is the girl I *hated* with a passion. By senior year, we couldn't be in the same hallway, let alone the same room. Now you want me to be besties with her because you've fallen for her act?"

"Maybe, Maylee, she sees something in me. You ever think of that? Maybe this is the real deal. And maybe she's changed."

"Yeah. Botox changed maybe."

"You know what? Maybe Josephine hasn't changed. Maybe she was never the problem. Did you ever think maybe you're the one who was the issue?"

I grit my teeth. I remind myself this is my brother. I remind myself I love him.

But I just about explode.

"You *bastard*. You know the shit she put me through. Do you recall the pictures? The ones that, I don't know, Mitch, made me burst into tears in front of the entire auditorium? Do you remember how for days, weeks even, I didn't want to get out of bed? Or how about all the rumors. Or the swimming pool incident. Or all the other nine million ways she made my life hell. Yeah, I'm clearly the problem."

I stomp toward my room, prepared to slam my door like an insolent teenager.

Mitch follows me, putting his hand on the door before I can slam it in his face.

"Wait."

I try to slam the door anyway, but he's strong. Apparently I need to do a few more push-ups at my boot camp class on Thursdays.

"May, I'm sorry. I'm just… I'm just frustrated with this whole thing. I know this sucks for you. I didn't plan on falling in love with your archenemy, I didn't. It's just… I haven't felt this way, not since…."

"I know." I sigh, softening. I let go of the door and head to the edge of my bed. "I know. I see the way you look at her. A huge, huge, huge part of this is that I hate her. I don't want to be near her. I'm not going to lie. But another part of it is I don't trust her. The Jo I know is manipulative, selfish, and scandalous. I'm worried you're just going to get your heart ripped out."

"Wouldn't be the first time," he says, leaning on the wall.

His last relationship truly did do a number on him.

"Look, I get it. You two aren't going to be besties. I wouldn't want you to be. But please, for me, will you just give her a chance? Be the girl I know? The girl who isn't afraid to open her heart, who isn't afraid to see the good in people? Can you just try to let go of this idea of who she used to be? I'm not asking for best friend bracelets or manis every Monday. Will you just go to dinner? The three of us? And be open-minded?"

I collapse backward on my bed, studying the pattern on the ceiling.

Dinner. With Jo. My brother's girlfriend, Jo.

It won't kill me.

At least I don't think.

"Fine." I mumble the word so it is barely audible.

"Did you say yes?"

"I said fine. Big difference. 'Yes' implies I want to. 'Fine' implies I will but I'm pissed about it."

"Okay. How about six tomorrow?"

"Fine. But you're buying me anything I want. And we're going to Gigi's."

"Deal."

I exhale loudly, sitting back up. Then I grin. "Did you use the word manis?"

Mitch shrugs. "So what if I did?"

"Ridiculous," I say, striding across the room to fiddle with the perfumes on my dresser. I shake my head, wondering what I've just done. So there's going to be yet another reunion. And this time, I haven't had time to do my starvation diet.

Round three… or four… or whatever we're on, here we go.

***

In my favorite Levi's, I trudge into Gigi's Diner beside Mitch. I probably should've picked somewhere more expensive since he's paying, but I can't help it. It's my favorite. Low-key, low prices, supergreasy foods. It calls to me.

Mitch wasted no time in planning our third-wheel date— me being the third-wheel, of course. He was probably terrified I was going to back out. Truth be told, I thought about it. But Mitch has done a lot for me over the years. He was there to help me through Mom and Dad's loss. He was there to pick me up after the Jeremy debacle, letting me cry on his shoulder, helping me work out the logistics of a life torn apart. He's always there.

I guess it won't kill me to do this for him. I'm sort of hoping it might kill other parties, though.

"Can you at least pretend to not be miserable?" he asks as we walk into the diner. Josephine is meeting us here, coming straight from her yoga class. Maybe she'll get stuck in traffic.

"Oh, I'm sorry. Should I plaster on the fake Josephine smile? I'm not sure I've mastered it. How's this?" I smile so wide, I'm sure I have a double chin. I blink ninety times, and give him a wink. He shakes his head.

"Please just…."

"Try not to kill her? No worries. I'm not in the stabbing mood tonight."

Mitch sighs. He's probably thinking this is a bad idea.

I have promised myself to try to be open-minded. I'm not an insecure seventeen-year-old anymore. She doesn't have the pull over me she once did, over our family. I can stand up to her. She's a yoga instructor, not the First Lady. Besides, I don't need to compete with her anymore. I know. It's going to be fine. I just have to make it through this dinner, make it through a few weeks until they break up, and then I can whip out the "I told you sos."

I'm getting ahead of myself, though. Dinner first.

We claim our corner booth, Mitch pulling out his phone to see if he has any texts. I play with a straw on the table, deciding whether I want the double cheeseburger or hot wings and pierogis.

"Hey, guys," a voice calls from across the restaurant. I turn to the door to see Josephine, the glittering vision of her.

And yes, I'm being serious. Glittering as in she's wearing what could probably pass as a black prom dress. The bodice is covered in a million glittery sequins. Her hair is done in an Audrey Hepburn style updo, and her makeup is perfectly airbrushed. She looks as if she's ready for a ball with the president.

She looks freaking ridiculous in a 1950s-style diner serving $5.99 cheeseburger meals.

"Did you tell her we were coming here?"

"Of course."

I scowl. Mitch just ignores me, getting up to greet her as she sashays over to the booth. They kiss for an eternity before sitting down across from me.

"Hey, Maylee. How are you? You look gorgeous."

I look down at my outfit, which is suitable for a summer carnival. I'm not wearing a speck of makeup. My hair is in a librarian bun.

"Thanks. So do you," I manage, a somewhat genuine—or at least convincingly genuine—smile plastered to my face.

"Oh my. I'm such a mess. I only had fifteen minutes after yoga class to throw this on."

I raise my eyebrows. Mitch kicks me under the table. "How was yoga?"

"Wonderful. Relaxing. You guys should come sometime. It's so good for the body and spirit."

"Sounds really fun. I love Twister, so I'm sure I'd love it."

Josephine smiles. I smile. There's a whole lot of smiling.

"So, anyway, what's good here?" Josephine asks.

"You've never been here?" Mitch asks.

"No. I mean, I know it's so close to where I lived, but Mom never liked this sort of place. Too greasy. Guess I get my penchant for health foods honestly."

I think of ninety-eight sassy remarks I could make. I make none of them, instead just nodding.

"So do they have chicken marsala?"

"Oh, let me see, I think it's right between the chicken cordon bleu and the bacon lover big burrito," I say.

"What page?"

I laugh at her gullibility. I can't help it.

"Well, they don't have those, but I think they have salads?" I flip to the salad page. They do have salad. As in one.

"Oh, yes, perfect. I'll just have that."

For the next twenty minutes, we place our orders, and Mitch and Josephine swoon over their date last week and their date next week and basically pretend I'm not there. I play with a straw paper… and pretend I'm not there.

Not that I mind. At least I don't have to come up with conversation.

Our food comes. Josephine daintily plays in the iceberg lettuce, probably horrified Gigi's doesn't use spinach leaves and organic tomatoes. She eats the salad without a speck of salad dressing, croutons, or anything worth eating. When the waitress brings her bread to go with her salad, she asks if they have gluten-free—apparently she's "allergic." The waitress looks at her like she's from another planet. I bite into my double cheeseburger, bacon grease dripping down my chin. I chew loudly, hoping to horrify Josephine. She ignores me.

After a few moments of awkward chewing, Josephine decides to try to break the ice.

"So, Mitch, I know Maylee's name is from her grandparents, May and Lee. Where did your name come from? Who are you named after?" She sits blinking her huge eyes expectantly. I think she thinks it is sexy. I think she looks like Dora the Explorer awaiting an answer with her purple backpack.

I smirk. Oh, this is perfect. Well played, Josephine.

Mitch looks at his plate. "No one, really."

"Liar," I say. I turn to Josephine to proudly detail the answer. "Mitch was my mom's favorite poodle growing up."

Josephine starts laughing, thinking I'm telling a joke. Mitch looks at her very seriously.

"I'm not kidding," I add. "And Mitch doesn't really like to talk about it."

A part of me lights up with sheer glee as the smile on Josephine's face melts into a frown. "Oh dear, I'm so sorry," she murmurs over her salad.

"It's fine," Mitch says, trying to smile. I know it's his fake smile.

"Hey," I say, swallowing a huge chunk of burger. "Could be worse, buddy. Could be named after Snazzy."

Mitch smiles now. It's his real smile. "God, do you remember the time he ate the fish?"

"I think he's going to choke on the scales," I say, mimicking my mom's voice. Mitch starts laughing.

Josephine awkwardly looks at us. "Wait, what?"

"Long story. Inside joke from when we were in high school," I say calmly, not a hint of snarkiness in my voice. Josephine just nods.

This sparks an entire conversation about the summer we went camping with our parents, a conversation Josephine isn't really privy to. She tries to be polite, to laugh at appropriate times, but I can tell she feels out of place. I can tell she realizes she doesn't know Mitch as well as she pretends to, that she isn't as close as she wants to be. I can tell she's uncomfortable. I can tell I've reminded her of how out of place she is in our family.

Best of all?

Mitch hasn't even noticed. He thinks I'm giving it effort.

Maybe I've taken a manipulation card out of Josephine's deck, but that's okay. Whatever it takes to shoo this woman away from my brother, out of our lives, and most of all, out of Mitch's heart before she poisons it, cracks it in half, and stomps it into cinders like I know she will.

HIGH SCHOOL SOPHOMORE YEAR

I saunter into the school ready to get Friday over with. I'm tired of books, of studying, of swim class... I'm ready for the weekend.

When I walk in, I notice a few chuckles from a group of preppy girls. I feel a little self-conscious, looking down to verify my fly is up, my shirt isn't tucked in weird, and there's no toilet paper on my foot. Everything looks fine.

Walking down the hallway toward my locker to find Ariel, I notice another group laughing as I walk by. Okay, it's not just coincidence or my imagination. Something's up.

Thinking maybe there's something on my face or my hair is a mess or God knows what, I speed up my walking, needing to find either Ariel or a mirror. Like right now. When I get to my locker, I stop. I freeze in place, no idea how to react. My stomach wrenches, clenching tight. I cover my mouth.

A group has gathered around me, but none of them friends. Mostly they're just onlookers, trying to see if anything even more exciting is going to hit the high school.

On my locker is a huge, almost life-size picture of me.

In a bikini.

It's my face, my mousey hair, my smile.

But the body is quite off.

Someone's photoshopped my head onto the body of a rather large, rather unattractive woman. A picture of me in a bikini would be humiliating enough. A picture photoshopped to make me look even worse than I am is unrecoverable. I blast to the bathroom, tears forming in my eyes. I don't bother to rip the picture down. I know it's made its way around school. I'm sure I'm about to become an Internet sensation.

When I get to the bathroom, though, it's even worse. All the stalls and the bathroom walls are practically wallpapered with pictures of me.

My high school career is over. I can't possibly go to class. I can't recover from this.

Who would do this to me? Why?

Without a doubt, it hits me. Ariel's words come back to me. The niceness is just an act. Deep inside is a jealous, vengeful girl. And this is her first act to undo me.

CHAPTER ELEVEN

"So wait, you're telling me after all that, the ball gown, the salad, everything else, he still likes her?"

I nod.

"What is his problem? She's so not his type. Mitch is such a sweetheart, so down-to-earth. What the hell is he doing with a tofu-loving yoga instructor? They have nothing in common."

"Tell me about it. But yes, he still likes her. Sadly, as much as I want to puke, I think it might even be more."

"Oh my God, don't tell me he's falling in love with her?"

"I think so." I frown, scrubbing down the tables with a Clorox wipe a few days after our diner escapade. It's the end of the day, and I've filled Shauni in on the Josephine situation. Sadly, I've admitted to myself she might not be going anywhere, at least not for a while.

"So what does he see in her?"

"Well, if he's like most guys, he probably sees a tight body, perfect makeup, and the sweet, innocent, frail woman act. She's mastered the whole "rescue me" act. Mitch is a rescuer.

Plus, he says she understands him, listens to him. Whatever the hell that means."

"Probably means she's good in bed."

"Let's not go there, okay?" I grimace, not wanting to remember my encounter a month ago.

"So what are you going to do about this?"

"What can I do? It's his choice."

"You mean to tell me you're going to accept the fact she's in your life, your brother's falling in love with her, and you're going to have to deal with her in your life, after everything?"

"What can I do?"

"Whip out the big guns. Tell him the whole story."

"I can't do it, Shauni."

"Why not?"

"Because it would kill him. It almost killed me."

"Maylee, this is ridiculous. He thinks this is all about some childish high school rivalry, but it's so much more."

"I know. But I can't. For the same reasons I couldn't tell anyone then."

Shauni puts her arm around me. She's the only person I've trusted with the whole truth. It's too painful. I've let go of it. It's all so irrelevant now. There's no reason to bring Mitch more pain.

So much of my issue with Josephine is just childish high school rivalry. But a part of it is about something so much bigger, something unforgivable, even now. It's certainly not her fault. She tied herself up in the situation, however, to a point where I can't help but associate her with it.

If Mitch knew the truth, he'd probably feel the same way.

Shauni's right. If I want rid of Josephine, this would probably do it. But I can't do that to my brother. I just can't.

"I can't do it, Shauni. We need to find another way."

She scratches her chin. She thinks about it. "I think I may have it. I doubt you're going to approve of it."

I sigh. "As much as I won't approve of it, I bet my abhorrence for Josephine will help me accept it. Let's hear it."

When she's finished, I say, "You're right. It's terrible. Let's give it a try."

So mission break up Mitchephine is a go.

***

I sit in the coffee shop, my phone glued to my fingers. I'm waiting for the text, the success text, the text saying that against all odds, Shauni's succeeded.

I feel crappy about this. I feel like a manipulator, like Josephine. I don't care.

It's not as if we're totally bluffing. Shauni's always had a thing for Mitch, and I've always felt they might be good together. Just a fling, enough of one to throw Josephine into the ex pile. As I push the button on my phone to make sure I haven't received any texts, Shauni blows through the coffee shop door. The bells hit the glass so hard they almost shatter it.

She slumps into the chair, resting her head on the table.

"Hey, what happened?"

She lifts her head to shoot me a dirty look. "What do you think happened? This was a stupid idea. I should've never let you talk me into it."

"Me?" I ask incredulously. "*You* came up with this brilliant plan."

"You should've stopped me. What the hell were we thinking? That I'm going to charm him with my womanly prowess, convince him to run off into the sunset with me?"

"Hey, don't be so hard on yourself. You're gorgeous and funny. I've seen Mitch look at you a time or two in a lascivious way. I thought there was a chance, if we just pushed him along."

"Well, no. No chance. He practically laughed in my face, asked if you sent me, and said he's in love with her."

"Wait, he admitted it? He used the L-word?"

"Yep. It's official."

"I knew it was coming. Well, look. I love you for trying."

"God, I knew this wasn't going to work. But I didn't expect to be so mortified afterward."

"Can I buy you a coffee?"

"No way, sister. You can buy me a real drink after this whole scenario."

"What happened anyway?"

Shauni stands. "Let's get out of here, get somewhere where they serve something a bit stronger. I'll tell you all the sordid details on the way."

I grin in spite of the situation. "Deal."

On our way to our new favorite haunt, I blush a little at the horrible details of Shauni surprising Mitch at work, her pickup line—which was cringeworthy—and all the details. I also wince a little as we get closer to the bar because I realize I've only been half listening to Shauni's rant.

All I've been able to think about is the fact I might be seeing Benson again. It doesn't matter. There's no chance for us.

Inside though, I feel a little tingly, the telltale sign that I do in fact care, and it does in fact matter.

***

As soon as we burst through the door, I see him. He's wiping down the bar, and there are a few stools left in the vicinity. Before I can tell Shauni we should grab a table, she prances right over to the open seats, slams herself down, and orders two martinis.

Benson looks up and smirks. "That kind of day, huh?"

"You have no idea."

I join Shauni by the bar. Benson smiles at me before getting to work on our martinis.

"With you two involved, I'm sure I don't."

I sigh, wishing we'd gone to any bar except this one. Shauni winks at me. When Benson slides our drinks to us, Shauni says, "Put them on our tab. I think it's going to be a long night."

He nods. "How have you been, Maylee?"

"Good. How about you? How's the writing?"

"So-so. Trouble finding inspiration." Just then, a lady from across the bar called to Benson using some provocative terms. I grin.

"Duty calls?" I ask.

Benson rolls his eyes. "Mrs. Garrity is in here at least four times a week. Her husband died last year. She likes to remind me he was a bartender too."

"Oh, I see. Well, don't keep her waiting." I smile as he walks away.

Shauni looks at me with very judgmental eyes. "Don't

keep her waiting?" She laughs. "You're so transparent."

"What?"

"You like him."

"No, I don't."

"Come on. I saw it since the first time in here. Stop being coy. Go out with him. Get some already. How long has it been anyway?"

I feel my cheeks warm. "Stop."

"Why? What's the problem? He's gorgeous. He's funny. Seems like a nice guy. A little dull for my taste, but for you, well, he seems like the appropriately nerdy type."

"Even if he is sexy, smart, and sort of my type, it won't work."

"So you admit he's your type and you're into him?"

"It doesn't matter."

"Why?"

"Really?"

"Yes, really. Why not?"

"It's pretty obvious. The clothes. The perfect hair and glasses. The quiet, reserved nature. His romance writing. He's obviously gay."

"No, stop. First, you're stereotyping. Stop it. Second, I have excellent gaydar. He's not gay."

I raise my eyebrows. I've been thinking about this quite a lot. I mean, he has made some slight innuendos. But a guy like Benson—quirky, sexy, funny, seemingly sweet—he just has to be gay. I don't luck into a guy as great as him without some kind of baggage or hurdle.

A few hours pass. We chatter about mindless things—

Shauni's new mani, the guy she likes at the coffee shop, whether Alexander Skarsgard is actually as sexy in person as we both think. We keep the drinks coming, and Shauni makes sure my tab is going to equate to full payment for her embarrassment with Mitch. She outdrinks me two drinks to one, which is fine by me. I'm a terrible drunk. Cranky. A bit paranoid.

Benson keeps working the whole time, stopping to chat when he can. I catch him eying me though, even when we're not talking. I squirm a little at the thought.

Maybe Shauni is right. But how will I ever be able to tell without a totally embarrassing, awkward conversation? Just as I'm thinking about how to cleverly figure it out or do some Facebook stalking, Shauni comes to my rescue—which is never a good thing.

She jumps off her stool out of the blue. "Benson?" she asks.

"Yeah?"

"Are you gay?" Her question is quite loud and, thanks to a gap in the music playing, quite audible. Some patrons nearby gawk, mouths open. I audibly gasp and then bury my head in my hands.

"Uh, last I checked, no. Not gay. On the contrary. Why?"

I try to keep my head down, hoping I can use some Harry Potter-style wizardry to float out of the bar. My head is spinning a bit, but I haven't had nearly enough to drink to deal with this in any sort of calm way.

"See, Maylee, I told you. He's sexy and perfect for you and, best news, he's not gay! And he's using words like contrary.

Jump his bones."

My face burns so much I think I might light the napkin on the bar on fire. I just wave my hand, praying acknowledgement will shut her up. I hear Benson's chuckle. It's a sexy chuckle. Not one of those snorty, geeky chuckles, but not one of those tight-ass manly chuckles either. It's comfortable.

Not that it matters now. Pretty sure my chances are sort of ruined.

I hear footsteps, uneven ones first. Shauni.

Then I hear some confident footsteps. I glance up from the bar. Benson is right in front of me.

"So," he says, hands in his pockets. "Since we've established I am in fact interested in women and not men, can we go on a date now?"

I just stare.

"Maylee?"

Shauni elbows me, snorting a bit.

"You want to date me?"

"Last I checked, yeah."

"You don't want to check again, after this whole scene?"

"Not the first time I've been asked if I'm gay. I think it's the whole writer aura thing. Not the worst thing in the world to be called. Unless the girl you've been crushing on calls you gay. Then it can present some issues. Thanks to your friend, we've traversed the hurdle."

"Oh, dear Lord! Traversed? Who are you people? Use normal words." Shauni puts her head on the bar as I chuckle.

Who are we?

We're perfect for each other. Or at least perfect enough to

go on a first date.

"Okay. You're on."

"Tomorrow at eight?"

"Sounds great."

Shauni groans. "Now you're rhyming. Okay. Enough nerdiness for one night. Let's go. Eight is perfect. Pick her up. You know where she lives. She'll try to wear a dress that keeps her boobs in. Or, well, maybe not, since you're not gay."

Benson laughs. I shake my head, leading Shauni out the door.

"I'll call the cab," he says.

"He's a gentleman, too," I whisper as we smile and wave.

"Oh God. You two are going to make the nerdiest little glasses-wearing babies someday."

"We haven't even gone on a date yet."

"I know. I'm already getting visions of these little nerd children running around using words like corpuscular."

"Let's just see how tomorrow goes."

And with that, Shauni barfs all over the sidewalk.

CHAPTER TWELVE

"You didn't seem like the flowers type," Benson says, handing me a box of chocolates.

"Should I take that as a compliment?" I ask.

"I think so."

He's dressed in trendy jeans, a button-down checked shirt, and Converse sneakers. He looks like a trendy high schooler stuck in the body of a farming man.

But the hair. The perfect eyes. The dimples. It works. God does it work. My heart flutters.

"So are you ready?" he asks, and I realize I've been just staring at him, chocolates in hand.

"Oh, yeah, just let me put these on the counter." I plod over to the kitchen, my ballet flats not really helping me move gracefully.

I went through eleven outfits to get to the one Shauni deemed worthy of a scholarly man like Benson. In the end, we settled on a black pencil skirt, a red bow blouse—*Cosmo* says they're in again, according to Shauni—and some ballet flats.

She wanted me to go for six-inch heels, but I vowed I'd end up in the ER if I did. We compromised, settling on ballet flats.

I slap a sticky note on the chocolates, scrawling, "Touch and you die" on it. Mitch will probably still eat them all. He's working late, mercifully. I didn't want to have to go through the whole "hurt my sister and you'll feel my wrath" routine Mitch is famous for. He's a nice guy, a levelheaded guy. But he gets this false sense of bravado when I bring men home.

Benson's standing in the doorway. I notice he's the one staring now. "You look gorgeous," he says as I walk out the door.

"Glad you think so," I say, sounding a little more flirtatious than I intended. As he pulls the door shut behind us, I realize how out of practice I am. It's been so long since a first date, so long since any date really. Ever since Jeremy....

Stop. I am not going to do this. Not tonight. Tonight, I'm just going to think about Benson, about whatever this is, even if it turns out to be nothing. I'm just going to have fun, go out, and forget about Jeremy.

"So," I say, turning to him as we wait for the elevator. "Where are we going?"

"Well, I thought we'd go to one of my favorite places. It's pretty low-key, but that's sort of how I roll, if you haven't noticed."

"Anywhere I know?"

"Gigi's Diner?"

I smile wide. "It's my favorite place."

"Really?"

"Since high school. Man of my own heart." The words fly

off my tongue before I can swallow them. Ew, that sounded weird.

He doesn't seem to notice. "Glad to hear it. Not hard to win your heart, huh? Some greasy burgers at a cheap diner?"

I shrug. "What can I say? That's how *I* roll."

We head to Benson's car, which is quite impressive, just like last time. He opens the door for me—a true gentleman, a mental check on my imaginary man-qualities list—before climbing in. Some country tunes blast through the stereo.

"Oh no, country?" I ask. I shrivel my nose as a cowboy crooner sings about his tractor. "This might be a deal breaker."

"What's wrong with country?" he asks.

"Everything?"

Benson sighs. "Get out of my car."

I laugh; he doesn't. He looks at me. "Get out of my car."

The smile melts off my face. Is he serious? He looks serious. Shock creeps in. Things were going so well. He seemed so perfect....

As I'm debating on what to do, as my fingers search for the handle, he starts to laugh.

I punch him in the arm. "I hate you."

"Sorry, I had to. But geez, I'm getting a complex here. First you think I'm gay. Then you think I'm such a country fan slash asshole I'd kick you out of my car for dissing the song? Ouch."

"Well, hey, I've dated some assholes in the past," I admit, hands up.

"Same here."

"Okay, Mr. Comedian, can we just go get some burgers now?"

"Let's do it," he says, shifting into Drive and belting out some country tunes on the way. Although I hate the song, I have to admit two things.

First, he's a pretty good singer. I have visions of him serenading me someday. I quickly realize how creepy it is to be picturing that on a first date. Scratch the serenade.

The second thing I realize is Benson isn't the quiet, reserved guy he seemed to be. He is witty, he is funny, and he is zealous. He's even more than I thought he was, which in this case is turning out to be a really, really good thing.

***

"So you're obviously not a calorie counter, huh?"

"Never. I love food too much."

"Thank God. The last girl I was with was an obsessive low-cal, marathon runner who wouldn't eat anything unless it came from the earth. Which became quite a problem when she started believing I should follow her strict food manifesto."

We had an amazing dinner at Gigi's, both getting burgers, shakes, and fries. We'd already covered the first date rituals, discussing parents, childhoods, jobs, and dreams.

Now Benson is leading me on a walk, heading to a cute little park where there's a clear view of the sky and the numerous constellations. It's a perfect night to just breathe in the autumn air.

We saunter along, laughing about our food choices and how annoying health nut tendencies can be in a significant other. Things get serious, though, when I ask him what happened with his last relationship.

He sighs as we come to a park bench. We sit down together,

leaning back to look up at the sky.

"She was everything I thought I wanted in a woman. Besides the health nut part, of course," he notes, looking at me, and then returns his gaze to the sky. "Kate was in med school, so I moved to be with her, knowing I could do my writing anywhere. Things were going well. We were planning on a summer wedding, and I saw this whole life set before us. House, kids, careers. Kate and I were going to have it all."

I sober at the pain in his voice. She must've done a number on him. I can hear it.

"And then, one day, I come home from a late shift at a bar I was working at. She was home but not alone. A guy she was supposedly in a study group with was there. Another med student, a pretty cocky guy. Basically everything I wasn't."

"Sounds like a prick." I study his face. He looks despondent, even if he doesn't want to be. I know a thing or two about having your heart screwed over.

"Well, she didn't think so. Because there was really no way to explain how their studying for the exams involved being naked. She admitted she loved him, admitted I wasn't enough for her. Case closed, heart broken, relationship burned."

"Oh God, Benson. I'm so sorry," I say, reaching for his arm. He nods, shrugging.

"It sucked. I was heartbroken. But, well, I did what I had to do. I picked up, moved back home, and tried to move on. Tried to focus on my writing."

"How's it working?"

"So far, so good. I mean, it's still a shock. I still think about her sometimes. When you're away from it all, when you realize it wouldn't have worked, you start to see the cracks you couldn't before. You see the weaknesses in your relationship you didn't want to see. I think maybe it's for the best. Kate wasn't everything I wanted, not when I sat down and thought about it."

I nod, getting where he's coming from. "I get it. Same thing happened to me. Pretty much exactly the same thing. Except Jeremy was a painter, not a doctor. I found out through text messages, not actually catching them."

"Still hurts, huh?" Benson asks.

"Yeah. There I was thinking we were ready to walk down the aisle. But not even close."

"How long ago did you break up?"

"Five months ago."

"Dated anyone since then?"

"Nope. You?"

"Nope."

We sit for a moment in silence, looking at the stars, hands in our pockets.

"Well, we're quite the pair, huh? Two ex-nerds recovering from two horrible exes."

"Who says we're both ex-nerds? I think one of us still qualifies," I tease, elbowing him.

"You have me there."

"Life is so much messier than I thought it would be," I say, sort of to myself but also out loud.

"Life from a high school vantage point seems awesome, like it's nothing but dreams and wishes coming true."

"When you grow up, you realize it kind of sucks

sometimes."

I look at Benson now as he looks right back. His eyes pierce mine. We stay locked on each other for a long moment, our conversation connecting us in ways we hadn't expected. Here we are, two people experiencing very similar issues, very similar emotions, very similar pain.

"Sometimes, though, you realize it doesn't completely suck, huh?" he practically whispers.

I nod. "I had fun tonight. I like hanging out with you."

"Me too. Can we do this again?"

I just nod.

We stay locked on each other. My heart flutters, my palms start sweating inside the pockets of my coat. I fidget with a straw paper in my pocket. I am sure he's going to kiss me. I'm sure Benson Drake is going to lean in on this adorable park bench and give me the picture-perfect kiss under a starry sky.

He doesn't.

He runs a hand through his hair. "Well, we should probably get going, huh?"

I smile, trying to mask the sinking disappointment in my chest. I sense some confusion in him, some nervousness, too. It's not annoying or frustrating or a turn-off. It's actually kind of adorable. I love the fusion of confidence and self-assurance with his introverted, geeky ways from high school. They've melded together into this man who is a perfect balance of confidence and hesitancy.

"Probably. Thanks for tonight."

"Thank you."

As we head down the sidewalk back to his car, I turn to

him, hands still in my pockets. "Oh, and Benson?"

"Yeah?"

"I'm so glad you're not gay." I smirk.

CHAPTER THIRTEEN

"Maylee? Hi, it's me, Josephine Crawford."

I knew when I saw the unrecognized phone number that I should've ignored it. As fate or stupidity would have it, however, I had picked up. I shake my head at the fact she has to tell me her last name. As if I wouldn't know who Josephine is.

"Yes?" I answer, not sure what she could possibly be calling me for.

"Hey, if you have a minute, I have a favor to ask."

A favor. From Josephine.

"Of course, whatever you need," I say, slapping on some extra sarcastic sweetness.

"Well, Mitch's birthday is on Saturday."

"Uh-huh." Does she think this is news? He is my brother. And, oh yeah, my twin.

"I really want to do something special, you know, like a surprise party?"

"Okay."

"So I was wondering if you could help?"

Help with my twin brother's birthday. On my own birthday. Clearly not weird.

I decide to humor her. "So what do you need?"

"Well, the thing is, my apartment is so far away for all of Mitch's friends and family. So I thought maybe we could have it at your apartment?"

"And how will that work?"

"Well, I was thinking I could take Mitch out on a date on Saturday. You could get the party ready. I'll pay for everything and do everything. Could you just help with some setup?"

I sigh. So I'm supposed to do all the crap work for her surprise party. Sounds wonderful. I remind myself I'm trying this whole be nice to Josephine, give her a chance thing. If nothing else, then for my brother.

"Sure."

"You'll do it?"

"As long as we keep it kind of small."

"Of course. I'll take care of everything."

I shake my head as I hang up. That's sort of what I'm worried about.

***

Later, I get a notification on my phone for the surprise party. It's entitled "Shhhhh, it's a surprise!" on the Facebook event. I think there were too many *h*'s put in the word shh, but I bite my lip and accept.

Josephine has listed the menu for the party... which includes things such as Tofu jerky, gluten-free pizzas, and quinoa. I make a mental note to buy some real party foods before Saturday.

Something else catches my eye, though.

The guest count.

It cannot be right. It must be a mistake.

I text Josephine.

Me: Hey, the Facebook event must be messed up. It says there are ninety-eight people invited.

Josephine: Oh, yeah. I still have a few more to invite.

What in God's name does she mean? Where the hell are ninety-eight people going to fit in our place? And what makes her think this is a small affair? I fight the urge to type back WTF. I tell myself to breathe. I'm sure it will be fine. They won't all come. There's no way.

***

"Shauni, I'm going to freaking kill her. Do you know any chemists who can whip me up a batch of poison?"

At the end of the day on Thursday, two days until the party from hell, as I'm now calling it, I'm in an even bigger rage than yesterday.

"Now what?"

"Well, besides the fact eighty-two people have RSVP'd yes to the party? Oh, and seventy-two of them are her friends, people we don't even know? Oh, and the fact I have to now make quinoa and gluten-free pizza because she just doesn't have time, on top of cleaning the apartment, all on my own birthday?"

"Tell her you can't do it. Tell her no."

"A little late, don't you think?"

"Yeah. You should've told her hell no on the first day. But

seriously, she's being ridiculous. Blow her off. Let's go have drinks. It's your freaking birthday, too."

"I'll look like a bitch."

"You *are* a bitch." Shauni grins.

"Maybe I'm just overreacting."

"No. I think this chick's crazy."

"Listen, I'm just going to get through this weekend. Will you help?"

"You want me to come to this tofu party? With Josephine's friends? And be shoulder to shoulder in your apartment in what is clearly going to be a fire hazard?"

"What if I tell you there'll be Jack Daniel's?"

"Fine. It better be the kind with honey."

"Deal."

"And can't we just buy regular pizza and pretend it's gluten free? She won't know the difference."

I tap my chin. "I think you're onto something."

"Well, at least I'll get to witness her in action firsthand. Maybe the party will be a disaster resulting in Mitch calling off the whole relationship."

"We can only hope."

So I put my metaphorical party hat on, plaster on my birthday smile, and go home to start cleaning.

***

"Where's the Jack Daniel's?" Shauni asks as she parades through the door. Guests have already started arriving. My apartment is already brimming with yoga addicts and health freaks. Oh, and snooty business professionals. And girls who think they're supermodels—and sort of look like they are, if

I'm being honest. Needless to say, I'm a bit out of place in my own apartment.

"I already drank some. It's in the linen closet," I whisper. I stashed it there knowing I'd need more.

Soft classical music is playing… one of Jo's "best friends" was put in charge of entertainment. Wow, thrilling. Josephine just texted to tell me they will be here in thirty minutes, so we better get our surprise voices ready.

The doorbell rings again. I prepare myself to feign enthusiasm for another party guest and fling the door open. I pause, my eyes not quite resolving the sight before me.

"Benson?"

"These aren't gluten free, but I thought you could make an exception." He hands me some chips with a grin as he heads in.

"I…. How did you…."

"Shauni."

"Oh, of course." I nod.

"Sorry for party crashing."

"No, you're not. I would've invited you. Just didn't think this was your scene."

"Are you kidding? Beethoven? Yoga discussions? Healthy foods? This is a dream. I've been practicing my tree pose all morning." He proceeds to do a sad interpretation of a tree pose. Some of the guests actually look at him with disgust. I laugh.

"I'm glad you're here."

"Me too. Oh, plus I have a little something something with me, too, just in case." He points to his pocket where the outline of a flask is clear. I wink at him.

"I knew I could count on you."

"What can I say?"

The doorbell rings again, but this time, I don't have to really fake enthusiasm. I have a smile on my face already just from the mere presence of Benson.

***

"Surprise!" we all yell half an hour later. Mitch does actually look surprised. Josephine literally jumps up and down, clapping her hands.

"Did you do all of this, baby?" he asks her.

I wait for her to say, "It was my idea, but Maylee did all the work. She's who you should be thanking."

Instead, Josephine just nods, saying, "Yes. You deserve it, honey."

I should've seen this coming. Benson, sensing my frustration, hands over the flask.

"Thanks."

"No problem. A few more drinks of this stuff, and the Beethoven music might actually inspire you to get on the dance floor."

"If I can find a patch of floor to even move on."

"Truth. But listen, it's kind of warm in here. Hopefully people will start leaving soon."

"Yeah right. They'll probably start doing hot yoga."

"True."

Mitch continues to thank Josephine and smile. There are more laughs and "oh mys" and discussions of how she pulled it off. I take some more drinks.

Josephine leads Mitch to the kitchen through a very intricate path through the crowd. "Let's get some snacks. All gluten free, of course."

Shauni, who is across the room talking to some rather sexy yogi, catches my eye and snickers. What she doesn't know won't hurt her.

The party painstakingly carries on, loud, polite chatter making me want to drown myself in the punch bowl. A few hours later, I hear some panic coming from the kitchen. Someone says, "Should we take you to the doctor?"

I shove through the crowd, worried for a moment something is wrong with Mitch. It's not him, though. It's Josephine.

She's hunched over and looks kind of green. Hives dot her skin. "No, no. Just get me to the bathroom. I'm going to be sick."

Mitch parts the crowd like Moses on a mission and leads Josephine to the bathroom. Shauni gives me a questioning look, but I just toss my hands up. Maybe the tofu is bad.

Twenty minutes later, Josephine makes her way out. The party has pretty much cleared out now. Apparently puking hazards will disperse a crowd. I'm fine with it.

"Maylee, you did make sure everything was gluten free, right?" Josephine asks.

"Well, pretty much. Except the pizza. And one bowl of chips."

Josephine stares at me. "What?"

"I ran out of time. So it's gluten. It thought it would be okay."

"I'm allergic to wheat, which is why I'm so adamant about

gluten free."

"What? I thought you just liked gluten-free stuff because you're a health nut."

"Obviously not," Mitch retorts, glaring at me.

I feel sort of bad now. Just a little. Then the anger from this stupid party comes out. "Well, maybe if I didn't have to prepare for a party for a million of her friends on my own birthday, I would have had time to make fucking gluten-free cardboard pizza."

Everyone stares at me. "May, I'm sorry. It's your birthday too. You're probably feeling shorted."

"I am not jealous over your birthday party. I'm angry because this witch manipulated me into having this party, made me do all the work, then complains when it isn't going as planned."

Benson tugs on my arm. "Hey, let's go for a walk," he says, trying to calm me down.

Mitch turns back to Josephine, comforting her and asking if she is sure she doesn't want to go to the doctor.

"Well, if you ask me, a few hives never killed anyone," Shauni retorts before sauntering to the door. "See you, Maylee. Happy birthday," she adds in a sweet voice. Mitch just shakes his head.

I storm out after her, Benson behind me.

He grabs my arm. "Hey. It's okay. No one died, right? Plus, you're right. It was crap for her to expect all of this from you."

I lean into him. "Thank you."

"For what?"

"For being on my side."

"Of course. Give me a gluten-only girl any day over a gluten-free yoga girl. Plus, who likes blonde yogis anyway? Honestly, I always thought she was a jerk in high school."

I laugh. "So you're discriminatory against blondes and yogis?"

"You can't trust them. Obviously."

I look up at him, happy he's here. For a second, I forget about Josephine, Mitch, gluten-free pizza, and the party. It's just me and Benson, standing in the somewhat smelly hallway of our apartment building, Beethoven music still audible from down the hallway.

I look up into his face, toe to toe with this man who blasted into my life from the past. I feel tension, but it's no longer the tension of Josephine and the whole crappy party. It all slides right off, the resentment melting away, giving way to something else.

A good kind of tension.

Benson senses it, too. It's not the romantic scene of the movies, with the park bench and the stars. There's scuffed-up lime-green carpeting in the hallway and a weird smell consisting of part smoke, part urine, part fried food. Down the hall, a neighbor is yelling at her cat. A car alarm is honking outside.

It is in this atmosphere, at this moment, Benson gingerly leans down, taking my face gently in his hands. I prop myself up on my tiptoes, prepared to meet him halfway. My hair glides down my back. When my lips meet his, every sensation in my body sparks to life. His fingertips graze over my cheekbone, and I drink in the sensation. Electricity floods from our lips through my veins, down to my fingertips, my toes. His cologne wafts up toward me, wrapping me up in its earthy, woody scent. His breath, warm and energetic, caresses my cheek as our lips continue to entwine.

When we pull away carefully, I'm breathless. I'm stunned. I'm misty-eyed.

I manage a smile, and Benson mirrors it. "Happy birthday," he says.

"Thanks."

"Oh, I almost forgot." He reaches into his back pocket now to pull out an envelope. It says "Happy Birthday" in a beautiful calligraphy.

"What's this?"

"Open it."

I'm still unnerved from the kiss. My hands are a bit unsteady, but I manage to rip open the envelope.

Inside, I find two things. A gift certificate to Gigi's.

"For your burger addiction," he says, hands now in his pockets.

"Thanks."

There are also some folded sheets of paper in the envelope. I pull them out.

"What's this?"

He looks at the floor before looking back at me. "Chapter one."

"Of your book?"

He nods. "I mean, you don't have to read it or anything."

I sense his nervousness. This is a big deal. I know he doesn't share his work with just anyone. I know he's a bit self-conscious. This is a huge step. A big moment.

He trusts me.

"I can't wait," I say, reaching up to kiss him on the cheek.

He turns his head, catching my lips again, pressing me against the wall.

I don't worry if we're making noise outside of apartment 5B. I don't worry he has me pressed up against the mystery stain on the wall or how my foot is squishing in some food residue.

All I worry about is that Benson's lips are on mine, he's given me a chapter of his book, and I'm falling in love with a spiky-haired scholar who just gave me the first kiss of a lifetime.

HIGH SCHOOL SOPHOMORE YEAR

"Why don't I come into school and take care of it?" Mom asks as she hands me a cup of hot chocolate and some M&Ms. Because clearly chocolate will take away the mortification from today's incident.

"That's not going to help." My eyes are swollen from crying, and my nose is so stuffy my voice is distorted.

"How about if I tape some pictures up of her? Ben is pretty good with photoshopping. We could give her a run for her money," Mitch offers.

I shake my head. "Also not going to help."

"Fine. Let's slash the tires on her mom's car. Or toilet paper her house." This is also Mom.

"Guys, just stop. None of this is going to help."

"So you're going to let this bitch get away with this?" Mom is incredulous. So is Mitch.

"I can't prove she did it."

"Come on. Ariel heard from Joanna she did it. She was bragging about it in the locker room," Mitch adds.

"In Principal Shoeman's eyes, there's not enough proof. She's going to get away with it."

I'm cried out. No more tears will run down my face. I'm the laughingstock of the school, and she's going to get away with it. Story of my life.

"Well, let her have her fun. She's obviously just jealous."

I grimace. "That's something a mom would say. Of course she isn't jealous. Look at her."

"She is. I've dealt with enough bitches like her in my day. She's jealous. And insecure. But don't worry, she'll get hers. Someday, some stud is going to break her heart, make her feel as if she's one centimeter tall. She'll get hers. You just wait."

"I doubt it. Girls like her never fall. Even if she does, I won't be around to see it."

I sigh. Tomorrow is going to be tough. But life goes on, especially in high school. I've seen enough scandals to know in a few days, the bulging photo of me will be history.

So will my friendship with Josephine. If anything has come out of this whole ugly scenario, it's that I now know who my friends are.

CHAPTER FOURTEEN

"Remind me again why I agreed to this?"

"So you could spend some time with me."

"Remind me again why you agreed to this?"

"So, in your words, I could stop being a creepy, introverted hermit."

"I changed my mind. Let's hermit it up."

"It's going to be fine. Hell, you might even have fun," Benson says as he shoves me toward the bowling alley door.

"Me bowling is never fun. Me bowling with Josephine is deadly. You're really going to give me a ten-pound ball and let me throw it near her?"

"Oh, stop. I thought you agreed to play nice."

Benson holds the door as I walk into the bowling alley, a wave of nacho cheese, cheap cologne, beer, and sweaty feet hitting me in the face. Appropriately enough, I haven't been here since high school. Couple the nostalgia of the alley with the not-so-rosy nostalgia of Josephine, and we have the setup for a disastrous night.

Things have, to my surprise, been going okay in the past few weeks. By okay, I mean:

1.   I haven't killed Josephine with any gluten since the birthday party… although it is

tempting.

2.   I have been overly friendly with Josephine when she stops by. As in, I give her a

slightly less derisive glare and sometimes nod a hello at her. I know, I'm pretty ambivalent.

3.   Mitch has been genuinely happy with the progress Josephine and I have made.

Things in my life have also, to my surprise, been going great… mostly because of Benson. We've been exploring this whole thing for the past few weeks, seeing if the kiss was just the beginning of something amazing. Seems like it could, in fact, be something amazing. We're both toting baggage, as we've established. But we've also got a heck of a lot in common. Plus, the chemistry. Oh, the chemistry. I haven't been this excited over chemistry since organic chem when I blew up the lab. This is a way better excited. Seriously.

We order our bowling shoes—so sexy. Pretty sure Benson is going to want to take me right on the waxy lane. Not that I'm thinking about Benson "taking me." Okay, so maybe a little. Or a lot. That's not something I want to think about as I prepare for a battle of the bowling balls with Josephine.

"Nachos?"

"Only if they have gluten." I smirk. Benson shakes his head. "And only if they come with a side of Long Islands."

"Deal. I think we all might need a few drinks to get through this encounter."

"Now who needs to think positively?"

We head to the snack bar, where Peggy waits on us rather angrily. She is not happy about my order—she lets us know this is the seventeenth nacho she's made tonight. Apparently it's nacho night in our town. I apologize for the nacho craving before also ordering our drinks. She is really not happy now.

As we're heading to our lane, chatting about our bowling stats, I hear the voice I've come to dread—even though I'm being "nicer."

"Hey, hey, hey, guys! You ready for some competition?"

I take a long, hard swallow of my drink before eying Benson. He clinks our plastic solo cups before turning to greet Mitch.

"Hey, how are you?"

The two do some weird handshake thing as if they're old friends. Which they're not. Mitch was way too cool for Benson in high school. He was way too cool for me, too. But this was Mitch's idea, so he is totally friendly. They start chatting a bit about cars and work while I stand guzzling my drink.

Being a man seems so easy. So chill.

I try to just plant myself in the middle of their conversation as a silent observer, ignoring the fact Josephine is standing pretty close in her perfectly curled 1950s-style ponytail and flouncy dress.

Who wears a dress to go bowling?

Silly question. Josephine does.

She has pucker-pink lipstick on, which accentuates her perfectly blended eye shadow. Her winged eyeliner is, of course, runway perfect. She's also still sporting high heels.

I turn to her. "Nacho?" I ask devilishly.

She just chuckles. "I brought my own snack."

"Let me guess. Celery sticks." Sarcasm drips from my voice.

She pulls out a ziplock baggy of celery from her purse. Even sarcasm can't get me through tonight... because she actually is carrying celery in her purse.

"Want one?"

"Tempting, but I'll stick with alcohol for now."

Benson puts a hand on my shoulder. He rubs as a bit of a warning. In case I'm not quite getting the message, he coughs a bit.

"Um, do you want a Long Island?" I decide to be genuine this time in my offer. Mitch is lacing up his bowling shoes, and Josephine has finally followed suit, kicking her slutty heels to the side.

"Oh, no thank you." She looks as if I just asked her if she wants to kick a puppy.

"You sure?" I inquire.

"Josephine doesn't drink," Mitch answers matter-of-factly.

I guffaw loudly. Maybe the Long Island is kicking in. "Since when?"

"Well, it's just so toxic for your bloodstream. I don't believe in dumping poison into my body."

"Why? Is it a temple?" I joke, elbowing Benson. He exhales. I warned him tonight was going to be a disaster.

"Why, yes, we all are. But also, I just think it's so immature."

I turn to Mitch, waiting for him to grimace. He's a rule follower, and he's a bit of a stick in the mud since law school. But he's also a partier on the weekends. He likes to get his drink on.

He doesn't make eye contact.

"Well, more for us, then," I say, clinking glasses again with Benson.

"You sure you shouldn't slow down?" Benson whispers. I glare at him. He shrugs.

"Your call," he says. So we go back to Peggy, who is even angrier this time, and order another round of sanity to deal with yoga girl.

***

"Strike!" Josephine yells, shuffling her way down the lane to jump into Mitch's arms. She's grinning so widely I think her face might crack in half.

I toss back the rest of my drink, grimacing. Of course Miss Goody Two-shoes would be a pro bowler.

"You're up," Mitch says to me. I slump down the lane and toss the ball haphazardly. My score is already pitiful. There's not much to lose now.

The ball rolls so slowly, I think it might actually stop in the middle of the lane. We all stand for an eternity watching my ball crawl toward the pins.

Then it veers to the right. Straight into the gutter.

Again.

I do the walk of shame down the lane. Everyone is just staring at me. Benson is sort of smiling. I give him a scowl.

"It's okay, Maylee, nice try," Josephine says, clapping

for me. Yes, she's clapping for my gutter ball. All with her signature sweet smile.

I glare at her, the booze pumping through my veins making me sluggish.

"You know, I think my yoga is what really helps me here. I just have so much more flexibility and concentration. Maybe you should come sometime," Josephine says, turning to me.

I stare in silence. "Oh, that sounds amazing, Josephine. I would just love to twist myself into a pretzel. How glorious."

"Maylee," Mitch and Benson say at the same time. I'm getting frustrated. Why does everyone protect her?

"Well, I was just suggesting. I didn't mean anything by it."

"Of course not. You're never at fault." I stare at her, walking slowly toward her. I really don't know what's going on in my head. I look like a crazy person. She actually just takes a step back.

"May, come on. Don't," Mitch says, grabbing my arm.

"I might have had a drink or two, but I'm sober enough to know she's not right for you."

"Okay, we're done here," Benson says, coming to grab my arm now. He leads me toward the back of the bowling alley. Jo stands there, sullen, as if I've just stabbed her in the heart.

"What are you doing?" Benson asks me, a bit forcefully.

"She's being a bitch."

"Maylee, she didn't really do anything."

"Oh, now you're on her side too?"

"No, I'm not. But there isn't a side to be on."

"Of course there's a side. She's just doing this to get to me. The dress, the perfect hair, the yoga comments. I'm tired of her throwing it in my face she's better than me."

"Maylee, this isn't a competition."

"It's always been a competition with her. You don't know her like I do. You don't know the kind of person she is."

"I don't care to know her. There's no competition with you. Because you don't need to compete with her. You have your own life. You're happy. You're beautiful. So what if she wants to prance around in ridiculous high heels and flaunt her yoga skills? You're better than that. So let her make a fool of herself."

I look up at him and, despite my hatred for Josephine, I can see superclearly. I see a man in front of me who gets me, who calms me, who makes me better.

Although I don't completely buy what he's saying, it doesn't matter. So Josephine insinuates I'm out of shape. So what if she has better hair and flaunts herself. It doesn't matter.

Because I have everything I want right in front of me.

I lean in to kiss Benson. It's a little sloppy at first, but soon, we're grounded in each other. Our kiss is natural, energizing. It's calming.

When we pull back, I smile at him. "So, you agree her high heels are ridiculous?"

He shakes his head. "We just kiss like that and you want to talk about shoes?"

I shrug.

"Okay, yes, they're freaking ridiculous. And her yoga talk is annoying. But who cares. Let her go. It doesn't matter anyway."

"You're right."

"So, shall we go finish our game?"

I eye the alley. Mitch and Josephine are snuggled up at the table by our lane.

I shrug. "Or we could ditch this joint, go somewhere?"

Benson's eyes are smoldering. "I think it sounds like a plan."

I smile like an eighteen-year-old about to break curfew. We toss our shoes on the counter, ignore the fact our bowling balls are still in the lane, and run out of the alley like a bunch of delinquents.

I'll probably hear about this later from Mitch, but I don't care.

Sometimes you just have to go with your gut and do what makes you happy. Right now, the thought of being alone with Benson makes me gloriously happy.

CHAPTER FIFTEEN

"So did you guys… you know?"

Shauni and I are, you guessed it, at the Coffee Barn. She's been grilling me about last night.

"Shauni," I retort, eyes averting to my coffee.

"Oh my God, you did. I knew you were glowing this morning! Details, please."

I grin. "Let's just say it was wonderful."

"Wow, good thing you snagged him up at the reunion, huh? Who knew nerds would be such a catch?"

"Seriously. I see why he's a good romance writer." I wink, probably creepily, at her.

"So where is nerd boy this morning? Why aren't you still lavishing in his killer good bod?"

"He had some writing to do. He's under deadline for some articles for a big blog. Plus, I didn't want to seem too clingy."

"Oh, please. He wants you to cling."

"I know. I just don't want to mess this up. I don't want to scare him away."

"Listen. He's not Jeremy. So get it out of your head. It wasn't your fault."

My smile fades a little. As much as I want to take the leap with Benson and push all my fears aside, I know, even after an amazing night like last night, I'm still holding back a bit. I'm still a little nervous to throw my heart back in the ring. Before I can delve too deeply into my self-psychoanalysis, though, Shauni breaks into my thoughts.

"Well, you're not the only one getting lucky these days." Shauni returns my creepy wink.

"What? Who?" My smile is back. This is news.

"Someone I've had my eye on for a while."

"Oh my God, Matt? Coffee Matt? Are you serious?"

"Yes," Shauni says, bursting. I haven't seen her this excited about a man… well, ever really.

"How?"

"He finally asked me out last week."

"And you didn't tell me? You jerk, holding out details on me."

"I didn't think it was a big deal. I thought it would be a one-time thing. Then we really hit it off and went out again last night."

I squeal. "This is amazing. How was it?"

"Glorious."

I stamp my feet a little under the table. "Look at us, falling in love, everything falling in place."

"I know. We're getting old and boring. What's wrong with us?"

"We're growing up."

"Speak for yourself." Shauni scowls. "Now finish your coffee. Let's go get manicures. I want to look good for tonight."

"Are you going out again?"

"Yep."

"Me too."

We smile like two teenagers who just received a note from our crush.

Maybe we're not growing up so much after all.

***

"Your rating?"

"Hmm… I'd say four out of five stars."

"You were practically spitting out your drink the entire time."

"He was a little too clean in his jokes for my taste."

Benson looks across to me, scrunching his eyebrows. "Since when are you all into raunchiness?"

"Okay, I didn't say it needed to be rated R or anything. But he used the phrase 'for Pete's sake.' Sometimes a four-letter word fits better, you know? You have to be a little edgy. The element of shock."

Benson shakes his head. "You are so peculiar."

"So are you. But hey, for a hometown comedian, I thought it was pretty good."

We've just left comedy club night at our local VFW. Benson had bought us tickets, deciding it was time for us to do something a little different. I'd actually put on a dress, he'd put on a tie, and we'd gone out for dinner and comedy.

Besides the fact the comedian wasn't too bad, I was pretty stoked about tonight. It was one of our first official, big couple events together. I found out I liked being the girl on Benson's arm.

"So when will I be getting the next chapter?" I ask.

"I'm sort of stuck right now."

"Oh no. Writer's block?"

"Yup."

"Maybe I can do something to stir up your creativity," I say, slipping a hand on his leg. Benson smiles, loosening his tie.

"Worth a try, I suppose."

"Seriously, though," I say, moving my hand back to my lap. "It's really good, Benson. You need to finish it. I want to find out what happens to Maria now that she's back with Sam."

"So you would tell me if you thought it sucked, right?"

"Obviously."

I mean it, too. I know my literature. When I say Benson is a good writer, it's the truth.

"I can't wait until I can say I'm dating a famous author."

"You and me both," Benson says, smiling. "Even if it doesn't happen, I'm okay with it. The fact you like it is all that matters."

"Really?"

"Really."

"So you don't want to be a best seller or anything?"

"Well, it would be a nice fringe benefit." He smiles.

"My mom would have loved this book," I say, looking out the window now, staring at the starry night.

There's a moment of silence between us. "Did she read romance?"

"She *loved* romance. She was more into those supersexy romance reads, you know, the ones with the ripped abs guy on the cover holding a woman in an 1800s-style dress?"

"Really?"

"Yep. The racier the better, she always said. My mom was not conservative in her reading material." I smile at the thought. I can still picture her in her lime-green lawn chair, bikini top, and cut-offs, with her book in her lap. Mitch and I would be playing in the front yard in the sprinkler while she sat, feet propped up, engrossed in her man of the day.

"You must miss her like crazy," Benson says.

"Every minute. She was my best friend. She went through so much."

"Were you close to your dad?"

I pause. This is a hard question. "Yes and no. There were some things between us. Thankfully, we pretty much settled them, had basically let them go when the accident happened." My stomach plummets a little bit just thinking about it all. I loved my dad. I still do. But sometimes, when my mind starts to go to that place, it makes it tough.

"I'm sorry. I shouldn't be interrogating you about this," Benson says, pulling the car into the parking spot. We're in front of my apartment building.

"No, it's okay. I don't mind talking about them. It feels good to talk about them, actually. Most people find it uncomfortable, so they avoid it. The only person I can really talk about them to is Mitch."

"Well, it's good you two have each other. You two probably have so many memories to talk about."

I nod. "We do."

It's true. It's good to have someone around to remember with, to cry with. Someone who understands what a loss we've suffered.

But it's hard too. Because there are some things we don't share, some memories I can't talk to him about. There are some burdens I've had to carry alone, burdens I'd like to say don't affect me anymore.

With Josephine back in the picture, though, they're back in full swing.

"So what about your parents?" I ask, wanting to change the subject, wanting to stop my mind from traveling the dark road.

"My dad left when I was young, so I never really knew him. My mom's pretty much a free spirit. I think I always held her back a little bit. Once I moved out, she headed down to Florida. She always wanted to waitress by the beach. So that's what she's doing. I talk to her once or twice a month."

I study his face, look for signs of sorrow or depression over this. He looks okay. He's strong. He's independent. His mom made him that way.

I squeeze his hand.

"I'm so glad I went to the reunion," I say, and mean it.

I went to the high school reunion looking for revenge, for comfort in other peoples' suffering. Instead, I found something else.

I found a man from my past who turned out to be the best thing for my present.

"I think I'm falling in love with you," Benson whispers as

he leans in across the center console.

"I think I'm falling in love with you, too," I reply into his lips.

We kiss for a long time, the pain of our pasts swirling together and helping us float away to a better place.

HIGH SCHOOL
JUNIOR YEAR

Ariel and Gina by my side, I stroll into the school wearing my comfy boots and puffy winter coat. Winter break was glorious, but now it's back to the grind. It's time to get my nose back in those books and get back to work. After all, I have my eye on some pretty prestigious colleges, so I need to get the grades.

We're giggling about the new movie we went to see last week when she stomps in front of us.

"Excuse me," Josephine practically spits at me, two of her little cronies on either side of her. Ariel, Gina, and I stand our ground in the hallway. The cronies cross their arms, and I can't help but laugh. It's like a scene out of Mean Girls, *except they're not all wearing pink—today.*

"Can I help you?" I spew back. I don't know what she could possibly want with me. After all, we haven't really spoken since the whole situation last year. She made it known she wasn't my friend. Despite her denial of the incident and the pictures, I know the truth. Her jealousy, her manipulation, is so clear to me now. I don't know why it took me so long to see her for what she is.

"There's a rumor going around I slept with Joseph McIntyre."

Gina snorts beside me. I just stare at Josephine, eyebrows raised. Joseph McIntrye is a bit odd, even for my nerd tastes. A true science devotee, he talks incessantly about black holes and the theory of relativity. By incessantly, I mean he literally doesn't stop. To even say hello to Joseph is to open up a wormhole of discussions about theories, space, and the time space continuum. Yeah, not exactly light Monday morning material. Joseph is so into space, he often sits alone in the cafeteria, a social outcast by choice.

However, for a girl as popular as Josephine to even sit with Joseph McIntrye, let alone sleep with him—talk about social suicide.

"So is it true?" I prod, grinning at Josephine's annoyance.

"Of course it isn't, you witch. But someone has spread it around. I can't even talk to any of the guys without them chuckling and asking me about black holes or Einstein or some other ridiculous scientific theory."

She is so angry, I think steam might come out her ears.

"Although entertaining, I don't see why this is quite my problem," I articulate. I notice students flowing around our little encounter, eyes wide, wondering if there is going to be a smackdown.

"Because I know you started it."

I laugh out loud in astonishment. "You think I started the rumor?"

"Well obviously you're jealous I'm dating Eric."

"Really? You think I'm obsessed with your love life so much that I'd spread a stupid rumor around like that?"

"Well, who else hates me enough? Honestly, Maylee, I thought you were better than that."

"First, I wouldn't stoop to your level. Second, I have better things to worry about than who you are or aren't sleeping with. Finally, I think Joseph is way, way, way too good for you. I would never spread a rumor like that. It would just hurt his reputation."

The Josephine cronies' jaws drop open. I am quite proud of myself for standing up to her. Despite my stomach burning from anxiety, I feel strong. I stood up to her. It's about time someone did.

"You'll pay for this, Maylee. You'll pay," she shrieks before pivoting on her high heel to stomp down the hallway.

Ariel and Gina turn to me, wondering what I'm going to say.

"Who wears high heels in snow?" I ask, shrugging and heading to my locker. "So anyway, can you believe those guys behind us at the movie on Saturday...?" I pretend we didn't just have a ridiculous showdown with Josephine over Joseph McIntyre.

Although I spend the rest of junior year waiting for Josephine to "attack," not much happens other than a few snide comments about my hair, a fake Facebook page about my horrible fashion sense, and a few mild note-passing encounters.

By the end of junior year, I feel like Josephine has certainly lost her touch, like there will be no climactic finale to our battle.

CHAPTER SIXTEEN

"I can't believe you brought me here," I say, jumping and squealing like a little kid. "I haven't been here since high school."

"Me neither. I thought it would be good for some nostalgia."

I leap out of his car, settling my sunglasses in place. It's a cool October day, but the sun beams down on us like a sign from the heavens.

"Let's get a picture," I say, holding my phone out as Benson gets in selfie position. I maneuver my hand so the Kennywood sign is perfectly in the background.

As he leads me to the ticket booth, I stop for a second. "So, I love, love, love it here. I do. But just so you know…."

"You don't like roller coasters. I know."

I give him a quizzical look. I thought I was telling him big news. "How?"

He turns to me in the middle of the parking lot, a car beeping angrily because we're in the way. It finally goes around us. "You know, you weren't invisible in high school.

I did notice you, even if you didn't give me the time of day."

"Wait, what?"

"I had my eye on you, Maylee. I just didn't think you were interested."

"I gave you the time of day."

He raises his eyebrows.

"Okay, okay. So not completely. I just… I thought you were quiet. I thought you didn't want to be bothered."

"Truth. Fair. But I wouldn't have minded being bothered by you."

I drop my gaze to the ground, surprised by his words. In all honesty, I barely noticed Benson in high school. It kind of blows my mind he noticed me. To think, all this time, we could have….

"Hey, no regrets. Maybe the time wasn't right for us then," he says, lifting my chin and kissing me. "Let's focus on the now."

"Yes. But one more question. If you know I hate roller coasters, why the hell did you bring me here?"

"You need to break out of your shell, don't you think? Live a little."

"The last time we were here, I burst into tears when my friends tried to shove me on the roller coaster."

"I know. I was in line behind you guys."

"So you understand the depth of my fear."

"Yep. That's why the first ride we're going on is the Exterminator."

"No way in hell." I plant my feet, my body going rigid. Just the thought of stepping on the roller coaster makes me want to puke.

"Come on. I'll hold your hand."

"And I'll break it."

"Let's go. New memories."

"No way."

Benson sighs. "Okay, I didn't want to have to resort to this, I didn't. To be fair, remember you made me do it."

I stare at him, wondering what he's going to say.

"All I know is Josephine Crawford rode the Exterminator twice. Twice. From what I hear, she didn't shed a single tear."

I know what he's trying to do, play on my petty sense of competition. I tell myself it's not going to work, that I'm not some insecure eighteen-year-old who worries about Josephine.

Who the hell am I kidding?

"Let's go," I say, exhaling as we head to the entrance. "But afterward, you are buying me a delicious funnel cake. Plus, we're going on every lame, childish ride I want."

"Deal."

I try not to think about how much I want to pee my pants as I am whisked toward what will either be an amazing memory or cardiac arrest.

***

I'm wolfing down the funnel cake, slapping Benson's hand away when he tries to steal a bite.

"This is mine. I earned it."

"You did. Although I don't think the parents of the kid behind us appreciated you yelling the F-word the entire time."

"It was better than peeing myself."

I had made a complete fool of myself, verging on sobs on

the damn roller coaster. I have to admit, it did help having a steamy guy's bicep to squeeze. It was still awful, though. Backward loops in the pitch-black awful.

"So, where to next?" he asks as I slide him a hunk of the powdery fried cake.

"Right here. I need my feet on steady ground for a few."

We're sitting on a bench, watching kids and parents alike practically skipping through the park. It is a special place, even if a few minutes ago it was a special kind of torture.

"Did you like amusement parks growing up?" I ask after taking a gulp of lemonade. Hey, if you're going to eat park food, you might as well go all-in. I've been eying up the cotton candy and ice cream, too.

Benson shrugs. "Yeah. We didn't go to a lot of them. Mom really couldn't afford them, and when she could, she had plenty of other things to do."

I see hurt in his eyes, but he shrugs it off.

"Were you guys close?"

He shrugs. "So-so. I think Dad leaving just always impacted her."

"When did he leave?"

"I was three."

"I'm sorry."

"Yeah. I don't talk about it much, other than with you. Writer's turmoil brewing, I suppose."

"Do you wish your mom lived closer?"

Benson is quiet for a moment, seemingly contemplative. "I don't begrudge her. I get it. She loves me. She needs a life on her own, though. She has a boyfriend now, Ricardo. I think it's pretty serious."

"Maybe sometime we could visit? I'm always up for a trip to Florida." It's a pretty heavy suggestion over fried amusement park foods. It's basically asking to meet his family. It's a more than one-night trip. It's a solidification of our relationship, an admission this thing is getting pretty real.

"I'd like that," he says, bumping my shoulder. "Now, enough stalling with depressing family talk. What do you say, another roller coaster next? You a fan yet?"

"No way, unless you want puked-up powdered sugar on your snazzy shoes."

"Did you just call my shoes snazzy?"

"I don't want to hear it. You used the phrase 'on the contrary' when they asked if you wanted strawberries on the funnel cake."

"You've got me. I'm just a word sophisticate."

"Whatever. I'm voting for the bumper cars next. I feel like kicking your ass."

"Watch who you're threatening. I happen to be a mean bumper car driver."

"Well, you're on."

We head off to the bumper cars, laughing like two children.

Benson pushes me to be different, to be adventurous. In a weird way, he also helps me keep in touch with the girl from high school. It's a perfect balance of being who I am and striving to be who I want to be.

I don't know what the experts say, but it seems like a pretty good foundation for a pretty good romance.

Plus, I mean, he's got snazzy shoes and buys me funnel

cake. What woman couldn't appreciate that?

***

"Let's make a bucket list," Benson says as we're driving home.

"Why, are you planning on killing me or something?"

Benson eyes me suspiciously. Right. Probably not appropriate for a girl who lost her parents in a car accident to make jokes like that. I've learned in the past five years that jokes about death don't change things, better or worse.

"No. But look, we crossed off roller coaster from your bucket list. Let's expand. Let's keep it going while we're on a roll. We could use adventure, especially me. I mean, some mornings my biggest adventure is going to the grocery store for more coffee."

"Okay, let's clarify. Roller coaster was not on my bucket list, not at all."

"Fair enough. But what is? Go. Name one thing."

"Get a tattoo."

"That's such a cliché."

"Well, what's on your amazing, unique list then, huh?"

"Learn to fence. Oh, and wear an actual suit of knight's armor."

"Okay, you win. Definitely unique… but also weird."

"There is nothing weird about fencing. It's a tough sport. And knight's armor is just cool. Okay, your turn."

"Um… well, I've always wanted to own a hairless cat."

"Are you serious?"

"Yeah, they're adorable."

"God, they're disgusting. Ew. We'll put that one at the bottom."

"Your turn. So far we're getting inked, fencing, being knights, and buying Hairy."

"Wait, did you say Harry? Really? Talk about clichéd."

"It's H-A-I-R-Y, not H-A-R-R-Y. It's ironic."

"It's ridiculous."

"You know, for being a proponent of the bucket list thing, you certainly are being a downer."

"Okay, fine. Next. I want to go somewhere where the water is crystal. Completely see-through with a beautiful girl." He turns to wink at me. I roll my eyes at him.

"Cheesy. But, if I'm being honest, same. Other than the beautiful girl thing. I've never seen any ocean water except the Atlantic, which is pretty murky. I've also always wanted to go to Baltimore to see Edgar Allan Poe's grave. Especially around Halloween. I know it's all touristy, but I've just always wanted to go."

He looks over at me, grinning.

"Go ahead, call me a freaking nerd."

"No. I mean, it is nerdy. But that's seriously on my list, too."

"Get out of my head."

"Not a chance."

"So does this mean we're pretty perfect for each other or what?" I tease. Deep down, there's a seriousness to my words.

"I think so," he says quietly. "I mean, between the bucket list and the fact you love funnel cake, it's all systems go."

"Most men like a girl who eats healthy."

"Most men didn't date my ex. Or well, maybe they did."

"Well, if it makes you happy, I'll keep eating all the funnel cakes you set before me. Just to make you happy, of course."

"Of course. So, when do you want to get started on the bucket list? I think there's a sketchy tattoo shop up ahead."

"Um, I think I'll pass for now. Maybe someday."

I don't tell him the tattoo I have picked out is for a very distinct spot.

As in a left ring finger.

I also don't tell him as I gaze over at him in the driver seat of his sexy car, I'm actually picturing the same tattoo on his left hand.

CHAPTER SEVENTEEN

"This better be important," I say, blowing the strand of hair from my eyes and putting down my red hood.

Josephine and Mitch are in our kitchen dressed as normal people. I feel a little silly in my Little Red Riding Hood costume. I was just at an early Halloween party with Benson. We decided to be adventurous and go to a party with Shauni and Matt, part of our "let's stop being nerds" together routine. It's the overall theme of our bucket list, which we've expanded since the Kennywood trip a few weeks ago.

We were doing a good job at not being nerds, actually socializing with new people. We even did the "Thriller" dance together. Near the end of the night, though, I received a text from Mitch asking if I could come home soon. Benson dropped me off, having some writing to get done anyway.

I'm all alone for this "super important" occasion. I can only imagine.

Mitch leads me to the sofa, handing me a glass of wine. There's a huge smile on his face. I instantly know this isn't good. As much as I wanted things to fall apart between them, as much as I've been waiting for the bombshell to drop, for Mitch to wake up, it seems like these days, they just keep getting closer. The googly eyes have increased tenfold.

Shauni still keeps prompting me to tell him the truth. A part of me wants to, a part of me wants to shatter this whole mess, to tell him the truth behind who this girl is. The truth about how she's not the sweetheart she claims to be.

The truth about what she tried to do to us.

But I can't. Because as much as I'm afraid she'll hurt Mitch, I know the truth will hurt him even more. There will be no recovering from it. Once it shatters his view, once it's out, it'll change everything he thought he knew.

I can't do that to him.

So here I sit in my Halloween costume, awaiting what is certainly going to make me rethink my stance on the whole issue. Mitch jumps right in.

"We have some news."

Josephine is, of course, grinning ear to ear. She plays with the hem of her bright yellow dress. Apparently she hasn't read the memo that fall colors are now in.

They look at each other, and I know this is going to be life shattering. As in, Josephine isn't leaving my life anytime soon kind of news.

"We're getting married," Josephine explodes. I inhale deeply.

A part of me knew this was coming. The past month, I've seen the telltale signs of a relationship growing stronger. In actuality, I think a piece of me knew this was coming from the moment Mitch and Josephine made eye contact at the reunion.

Damn the ten-year reunion. I should've listened to Mitch and this wouldn't have happened.

I don't move from the couch. I don't leap up to hug my soon to be sister-in-law or my brother. I sit, motionless, melting into the couch. I know my face is neutral. I can't make myself care.

"Congratulations," I say, trying to feign an ounce of enthusiasm. My eyes travel to the rock on Josephine's left hand. It's gorgeous. My brother has good taste—in jewelry, at least.

"I know this is probably shocking. I mean, I didn't expect this so soon either. It's just… when you know it's right, you know it's right." Josephine giggles, looking at me, probably waiting for me to leap up to ask her about wedding dates, colors, and dress styles.

I remain motionless. I look over at Mitch.

He stares back, expectantly.

"If you're happy, I'm happy for you." It's the most I can muster.

"I *am* happy. Josephine and I are so happy. I know I probably should've told you first so it wasn't so shocking."

"No. It's good. I get it. You don't have to ask for my permission. I just want you to be happy."

More smiles ensue. A piece of me wishes my Red Riding Hood costume was real so I could turn into the big bad wolf and chew Josephine into little pieces.

Okay, I've gone too far. I know. But seeing her fake smile and her fake sunshine dress, knowing what this woman tried to do to our family… it's too much. Every birthday, every Christmas, every random Sunday family dinner, I will be looking at her fake smile at my dinner table. I'll be an aunt to her children. I will never, ever be rid of her.

Worst of all, though? I know without a doubt she's going to ruin my brother's heart. She tried to ruin me in high school. She tried to ruin my family. Now, she's going to win. She's going to break his heart.

There's nothing I can do, not tonight anyway. I have to approach this carefully, in the right way.

This has gone on for too long. I didn't want to hurt Mitch. But I know I can't let him go through with this, not without knowing the truth.

"So, Maylee, while you're here, we have a question to ask."

I snap back to reality, although reality isn't very comforting.

"Will you be my maid of honor?"

And now I truly wait for my wolf-like claws to come out.

HIGH SCHOOL SENIOR YEAR

It's senior year, and things are falling into place, at least in the romance department.

Josiah Morefield has asked me to be his girlfriend, and I'm ecstatic. He's a top football player, but he doesn't have the jock arrogance about him. He's sweet, his brown eyes and brown hair complementing his soft personality. He makes me laugh. He puts his arm around me in the hallways.

I still can't quite believe he's my boyfriend. From the moment we sat across from each other in Chemistry, I knew I wanted to be with him. But, I figured there was no way in hell. He was popular; I was not. End of story.

Not quite.

Because one month into school, he asked me to help him study for Chemistry. From there, he asked me to go to a movie with him.

A few weeks ago, he asked me to be his girlfriend.

I find myself smiling a heck of a lot more. I find myself thinking what he would look like standing at the end of a church aisle waiting for me. I know, I'm getting crazy. We're only seventeen.

But in his eyes, I can see myself, I can see love, and I can see forever.

Not everyone, though, is on cloud nine about us being together.

And her name happens to be Josephine. Apparently, word is she's had her eye on Josiah. I suspect it's probably because we have our eyes on each other. I've seen her trying to talk to him in the hallways when she thinks I'm not around. She suddenly drops her books in Chemistry when she's near his desk. She's constantly trying the "damsel in distress" move.

It isn't working.

It's hard to believe there was a time that girl and I were friends. Because now, we're known as the school's most vehement enemies.

So I know, all happiness aside, I'd better watch my back. Josiah and I are strong and in love. We'll have to stay that way to repel the vile, envious girl known as Josephine Crawford.

The sooner I get out of this high school, the better. Because the sooner I get out of here, the sooner I can be rid of Josephine and all of her scheming ways.

PART II

CHAPTER EIGHTEEN

"Isn't this so fun?" Josephine asks as the nail technician massages her feet.

"A blast," the other two girls, redheads, say.

I sit silent in the pedicure chair, seriously questioning why I didn't bring a flask as Shauni suggested. Today is the first of what will, if Josephine has her way, be many bridesmaids' activities.

If I have it my way, it will be the last.

I didn't want to say "yes" when Josephine asked me to be in the wedding. I wanted to tell Mitch right then and there. I wanted to blast this woman right out of our lives.

Then I saw the way Mitch was looking at her, the sheer joy in his eyes. I thought about how lost he'd been since the breakup with Dina. I thought about how bad this would hurt to have not only his relationship but the picture-perfect image he has of our family shattered all at once.

So I decided to put it off. I know—it's a recipe for disaster. It's like one of those anguishing movies where you're shouting at the screen, "Just freaking tell him already!" I didn't say it was the wisest choice.

With much prodding from Mitch, I said "yes" to the one thing that is simply too much to ask. I said "yes" to being maid of honor.

Of course, it was halfhearted because in my mind, this wedding… well, it's not going to happen. If Mitch can't see what a witch she is, I'll out her. I'll do what I have to do to make him see the truth. With each passing day, I know the clock is ticking. I know, rationally, waiting is only going to make this harder, make it hurt more.

I guess I've just been hoping she'd screw up enough, he'd see her true colors, and then I won't have to ruin Mitch's view of everything he thought he knew.

"I'm so glad you could make it today," Josephine says.

"Me, too. This is so much fun."

Josephine smiles. She has no idea what's coming. Or maybe she does. She sure as hell should remember the horrible thing she did to me, to us.

***

We've dropped off the other two girls—both also gluten free and yoga instructors, in case there was any doubt. It's just me and Josephine in the car.

Now is my chance.

"So, listen. We need to talk." I am staring at her as she drives. She furrows her brow.

"Okay."

"You need to tell him the truth."

Josephine pales. Or maybe it's just my imagination.

173

"Tell him what?"

"Don't pretend you don't know what I'm talking about, you bitch. This is me you're talking to."

Josephine pulls the car over. She puts on the four-ways. She, to my surprise, looks a little teary. Turning slowly to me, she seems to weigh her words.

"Maylee, I'm sorry. I thought this was all behind us. You haven't mentioned anything, so I just thought it was in the past, that we were over it."

"Of course you did. Because you're in love with my brother, or so you say. You want this swept under the rug because you know if he knew the truth, he wouldn't forgive you."

"So you never told him?"

"Of course I didn't tell him. It would've killed him, with everything happening with Mom. After they died, there was no point. Why should I shatter his image of them, confuse him, taint the memories? It was pointless."

Josephine sniffs, trying to hold back tears. This angers me even more. She is definitely not playing victim on this. "Why didn't you tell him once we started dating?"

"Because I thought there was no way in hell you'd last. I know you, Josephine, know who you really are. You don't deserve him."

There is a long pause, the tears flowing down Josephine's face only making me angrier. Finally, between sniffles, she speaks. "May, I'm sorry. You're right. I was a witch then. I was selfish and stupid. I was a jerk of a teenager. What I did was wrong. But I didn't do it. It wasn't my fault."

"You were sure willing to rip my family apart just to get to me, weren't you? You were willing to go to whatever length it took to destroy me."

"You're right. I was. I'm a different person now, though."

I laugh, scoffing at the idea. "Different? Sorry, but I don't buy it."

She pauses, again seeming to weigh her words. She blinks. She's definitely trying not to cry.

"Maylee, I'm sorry. I was wrong. But I want you to know I mean it when I say I love Mitch. I don't want to hurt him, or you for that matter. I want to make this right. Please give me the chance."

I nod. "I can do that."

"Really?"

"Yep. Tell him the truth. Tell him the real reason I have such an issue with you. See, right now, he thinks I'm just holding on to a petty high school catfight. Which may be true. I do hate all the things you did to me. But he doesn't know it's so much deeper. Tell him the truth. Then walk away."

"But—"

"Tell him the truth, or I will."

At this, I get out of the car. Josephine is yelling after me, but I ignore her pleas. I have a few blocks to walk to get home. It's raining, and I'm already soaking wet, but I don't care. I trudge forward, feeling riled up but also feeling at peace. I've finally let her know she's not getting away with it. I'm doing what I should've done a long time ago.

I'm telling Mitch the truth about the girl she used to be and, in turn, the woman she is now. I'm going to make sure he doesn't fall for her traps. Because that's what I do. I protect my family.

HIGH SCHOOL
SENIOR YEAR

"So, how are things with Josiah?"

Josephine and I are alone at my locker. I had to stay late for the Reading Competition. Josiah has football practice. There's no one around.

"Great, why?" I ask. I try to ignore my desire to shove her or make a snide remark. I grab my jacket and try to head out of the school.

"Not for long."

I spin to face her, staring at the scowl on her face.

I raise an eyebrow, insistent I will not play her games.

She pulls something out of her folder and hands it to me.

It's a picture.

"What's this?"

"Look at it."

I do. My stomach plummets. I feel sick. I feel sure this is fake. She must have photoshopped it.

In the picture is my father. He's standing beside a car.

Josephine's mom's car. The redheaded Ms. Crawford is standing beside my dad, leaning toward him in a friendly embrace.

"What is this?" I demand. There must be an explanation. Or she's just messing with my head. But why would my father

be with her mother? When was this? Where?

"Are you an idiot? You mean you don't know about this?"
Her matter-of-fact attitude just makes me angrier.

"You made this up."

"Really? Don't be naïve. Look at it."

I can't stop looking at it.

"So maybe her car broke down or something."

"Try again. This has been going on for a long time." She
smirks as if it's hilarious.

"What has?"

"Your dad. Cheating with my mom."

"How long?"

"Six months."

Tears brim in my eyes, cascading over as I realize what
this means. I suppress the thoughts, pushing them to a dark
corner of my mind.

This is a lie. My dad is crazy about my mom. They're so
in love. My dad's such an amazing man. Sure, he works a lot
of hours sometimes. But it's to make a better life for us. My
mom's amazing. He would never be interested in some stiff,
snobby woman like Josephine's mom.

But the picture. The embrace. The late nights. I want to say
it isn't true. I want to chuck this picture back in Josephine's
face.

I can't. Because what if she's right?

I remind myself to breathe, to calm down.

"Why are you showing this to me now?"

"Because."

"I'm not playing this game. Tell me."

"Because. I want Josiah."

"Well, he's with me."

"Not for long. Break up with him or I'll show this to everyone."

"Why would you?"

"To get what I want, of course."

"And why would I let you do that?"

"Because you don't want your family's reputation ruined. Because you don't want to hurt your mom by making this public."

"And you would hurt your mom?"

Josephine shrugs. "She's never around anyway. What's it to me?"

Tears flow now. I want to crumple to the ground. I want to throw up. If this is true....

It can't be.

"I don't believe you."

"You've got two days."

She turns on her heel and prances out of the school like she's off to tea or to the mall. Meanwhile, I slump to the ground, staring at the photograph in my hand, wondering how this could happen or if it is really true.

***

"We need to talk. Now," I demand, stomping into the garage where my dad is alone. I'm sure I look like a disaster. I cried the whole way home, coming in the side entrance of the house to avoid Mom, who is in her studio.

"What's wrong?" Dad asks, looking up from the car he's working on.

I don't speak, simply slamming a picture down in front of him. "This. Is it true?"

I want to scream the words, to shriek. But I don't want Mom to hear.

My dad pales. I know without hearing a word it is true. He stares, probably thinking of ways to explain, wondering how I found out. Wondering how he got wrapped up in this. It's too late. His face says it all.

"How could you? What the fuck?" Rage now fills my heart where hurt, doubt, and confusion once were. The man I trusted, the man I thought was the ultimate family man—he's a lie.

"How could you do this to Mom?"

My dad slumps to a stool near his workbench and buries his head in his hands.

"I'm sorry, May. I'm so sorry."

The tears are now unavoidable. I cry too. I cry because my family is falling apart. The beautiful, witty, charming family I belonged to is now nothing but a façade. The man before me I admired, I idolized, is a lie. The wind is kicked out of me at the realization, as if I'm swirling in a murky swamp of muddy water, my lungs craving the clean air from the moments before I realized my dad is not who he claims to be.

Everything around me crumbles.

"May, I'm sorry. I didn't mean for it to happen. I'm an idiot."

"Yeah, you fucking are. I hate you. I hate you for what you've done to Mom, to us."

"I hate me too. But it's over. I ended things. I love your mother."

"That's real apparent."

"I do. I really do. I messed up, May."

"Well, you have two days to tell Mom everything or I will. I hope you know you're going to kill her with this news."

I turn to run out the garage and dash up the stairs to my room, slamming the door.

I lie on my bed, staring at Thoreau's quote above my television, my mom's favorite quote.

"This world is but a canvas to our imagination."

In my wildest imagination, I would have never imagined our family's canvas would look like this.

*****

Two days later, my life changes again. Mom's mammogram results come back with bad news, and our family spirals into a downward tailspin of despair.

The doctors say it's breast cancer. Stage three.

Dad's affair might not kill her; breast cancer could.

Looking at each other across the table as Mom cries her eyes out on Dad's shoulder, we both silently agree.

She can't know what happened. She can never know. As much as it hurts me to keep this secret from her, it's for the best.

Sometimes loyalty means being selfless. Sometimes being selfless means keeping things to yourself.

CHAPTER NINETEEN

"So, I did tell you I'm not the best cook, right?" Benson asks. Pasta sauce stains his collared shirt, and I'm pretty sure the noodles are boiling over. Oregano and garlic permeate the air. No vampires will be attacking us here tonight.

We're at Benson's place, a retreat in the middle of nowhere, or at least what feels like nowhere. We're really only five minutes from town, but you wouldn't know it. It's secluded, it's peaceful.

It would be the perfect place for him to kill me if he were one of those psycho writers.

Luckily, he's not.

I hope.

"I'm sure it'll be great," I say. I dance around his kitchen as a new Meghan Trainor song blares from the radio. I've picked the radio station this time. No country tonight.

He puts down the salad he's been whipping together, to take my hand. We dance around the kitchen, him twirling me in place. It doesn't go with the beat, but that's sort of how we are. It's beautifully symbolic.

"So you're in a great mood," Benson says, leaning in to kiss my cheek.

"Yep. I mean, I'm in a woodsy retreat with an adorable writer."

"Last we talked, you were in quite the mood about the whole wedding situation. Dare I bring it up?"

I smile. "I don't think there's going to be a wedding," I say.

Benson pauses, his grin melting. "What are you and Shauni up to?"

"Nothing except the truth. I've decided not to keep it to myself any longer."

Benson reaches to turn down the radio. "Okay, spill."

"How about first we get the pasta off? I think it's beyond done."

"Oh, shit. You're right." Benson scrambles to the burner to strain the pasta. "I think it's kind of waterlogged."

"It'll be fine." I head over to help him assemble our dinner. Once the food is plated and on the table, we sit down.

"Okay, now spill," he says.

I bite into the pasta. It *is* a bit waterlogged, but pretty good. Benson's effort was adorable, if nothing else. "This is good. And okay, I'll tell you."

Benson settles back, chewing on his food.

"So you know I hate Josephine."

Benson smiles. "Um, yes. I think that's clear."

"You don't know the whole reason why. Yes, a huge part of it is girl rivalry. I was the mousey girl, as you know. She was the flaunty, showy girl. Plus, you were there for the whole swimsuit debacle, the auditorium debacle, and every other stunt she pulled."

"I know. I remember. I thought you'd moved past it all?"

"No. No way. Partially because, well, girls never forget stuff. But partially because of the thing she did no one knows about."

"I'm listening."

"She threatened to reveal my dad's affair if I didn't break up with Josiah."

Benson looks at me confused, practically choking on his pasta. "Affair? What affair?"

"His affair with her mom."

"Wait, slow down. What?"

I close my eyes, exhaling. This is harder than I thought it would be. "So, my dad had an affair with Josephine's mom. Josephine caught on and snapped a picture. She threatened to reveal it to everyone if I didn't break up with Josiah. She wanted to be with him."

"Are you sure?"

"Yep. I confronted my dad about it that day. He admitted to it."

"Oh, shit. How awful. The whole way around."

"Yeah. So first, it was awful I had to find out that way. Plus, there was the blackmail."

"So what happened? What did you do?"

"I threatened Dad to tell Mom or I would."

"Did he?"

"No. Because eventually I changed my mind."

"When your mom got breast cancer?" Benson asks,

everything clicking into place.

"Yeah. A few days later was when she was diagnosed. I couldn't do it to her, not with everything happening. We thought she was going to die. I didn't want to dump it on her. As much as it killed me, as pissed as I was at Dad, I couldn't do it to Mom. I went to Josephine and begged her not to do it."

"Did she listen?"

"Nope. She told me to break up with Josiah and she'd keep her mouth shut."

"So you did. I remember senior year. It was quite the gossip for a while."

"So now you see why I have such harsh feelings?"

"Well, it makes sense. Why is Mitch even with her then?"

"He doesn't know."

Benson raises his eyebrows. "Wait, you never told him?"

"No. I didn't want to shatter things for him. Once Mom recovered, we were all so happy. I didn't think there was a point to telling him, or Mom for that matter. I felt awful about harboring Dad's secret. We had some serious issues those few years. I was so pissed at him. But I just couldn't do it."

"So why didn't you tell Mitch when he first started dating Josephine?"

"Protection. I guess I'm still protecting him. He's still under the impression our family was perfect. Don't get me wrong, it was in so many ways. But I think this would just be hard for him. I didn't think he and Josephine would last. I thought it would be a nonissue."

Benson takes my hand. "You're selfless, you know?"

"I don't quite think I'd go that far."

"I would. You dealt with her just to keep your brother happy, to keep him from hurting."

"Yeah, so all those times you told me I was being awful, I was actually being pretty mild, huh?"

"Yes. So what are you doing now?"

"I told Josephine she has to tell him the truth. Because when they were just a fling, I could let it go. But I will not let my brother marry her knowing what she did or threatened to do to our family."

Benson moves his pasta around on his plate, apparently deep in thought. "Can I ask you something?"

"What?"

He looks at me. "Don't freak out. But do you think maybe she *has* changed? Maybe she feels bad?"

"Oh no. Not you too. You're falling for her crap now?"

"No, I'm not. But listen. It was a long time ago. Maybe she's a different person now. People change. You've changed. And what if she really does love your brother?"

"She almost ruined our family."

"Maylee, it wasn't her, not really. Your dad was the one who had the affair."

"But she's the one. She did it." I try to fight back the tears. I can't cry, not now.

"Hey, I'm on your side. I'm just saying. Once you tell Mitch, you can't go back. You've harbored this secret all these years. Don't you think you had good reason to?"

"Yeah. Because I thought she'd never be in our lives again."

"What if he forgives her?"

My tears turn to rage. "He wouldn't. He's loyal to our family."

"Sometimes, though, living life means letting things go. You have to learn to let the past go sometimes. Maybe not forgive, but at least try to make the best of a situation, to move on."

"I don't want to talk about this anymore."

"Me neither. Let's talk about us. I like that topic better."

He rubs my hand, and I smile. I let go of the whole Josephine thing. I try to push it out of my mind.

Benson's words keep coming back.

Am I doing the right thing? Is this really what's best?

HIGH SCHOOL SENIOR YEAR

She sits on the edge of her bed, nausea written on her face. She hasn't put her wig on yet, her patchy, balding head slapping us all in the face with the fact she may die.

Dad sits beside her, stroking her back. She leans against him, tears falling. "I don't think I can do this," she says, her voice weak with the strain of the cancer and the chemotherapy.

"You can, love. You can do this. I know you can. We have so much to live for. I don't want to live through it without you."

There are tears streaming down my father's face, too. Genuine tears.

I stand in the hallway, taking it in. They don't notice me, are too absorbed in their moment.

They keep embracing for a long time, Mom leaning against Dad, just like always.

I should be pissed about this. I should run into the room and scream, "Liar," to my father. I should tell her what he's done. I should want to spit on him, to tell him to screw off. I should hate him.

But in this moment, I can't hate him. I can't feel anything except love.

Because seeing him with my mom, seeing how he's been

her rock these past few months as she goes through the worst stage of her life, I can't feel anything except forgiveness.

The way he looks at her, the way he sits with her, the way he hasn't left her side. The way he tells her she's beautiful, the way he wraps her in a warm embrace every second he gets. The way he sits through You've Got Mail *and* Something About Mary *and all her other favorite movies on repeat when she's at chemo.*

It's all of these things and all of the moments from before.

Despite what I know, despite what he's done, I can't help it.

When he says he doesn't want to live without her, I believe him. I completely believe him.

So, for the tenth time, I reassure myself I'm doing the right thing.

I've done the right thing.

CHAPTER TWENTY

"Game night!"

Josephine bursts through our apartment door with several board games, what appears to be Twister, and some snacks.

Gluten free, obviously.

"Oh, goodie," I say, and Benson nudges me.

Let's be clear. This game night… not my idea. Mitch kind of spewed it at me this afternoon.

***

"What are you doing tonight?" he asked as I painted my nails lime green.

"Going to Benson's."

"Can you have him come here? Josephine and I kind of wanted to hang out, the four of us. Since we're going to be close and all soon."

I turned to look at him. "So anything new with you two?" I waited anxiously. Certainly he wouldn't be this calm if she'd told him. But what is she waiting for? She was supposed to tell him by today.

"We've picked a date."

"When?" I curtly asked, realizing she had no intention of telling him.

"We'll tell you tonight."

I had sighed. I had thought about turning him down.

But then I realized tonight would be it. Tonight would be the perfect night to make her tell him. Tonight would be the end of this whole charade.

So I'd agreed. And having Benson here will only make it so much easier.

***

Josephine welcomes herself in, kissing Mitch before setting up shop for our game night. Pretty sure game night isn't going to happen, not completely.

"So, what do you guys want to play first?" she asks. Mitch and Benson turn to each other. I just stare directly ahead.

"Let's play truth."

"What?" Mitch asks.

Josephine stops dead in her tracks, playing with a piece of her blonde hair. She knows what I'm getting at. She just stands, staring at me.

"Not now. Please." She practically whispers it.

I take a step forward. "Why? You think this whole thing is going to crash down like a Jenga game? Pretty sure it will."

"What's going on?" Mitch asks, approaching us. We all stand in a circle, awkward tension between us.

"Will you tell him, or should I?"

Josephine starts to tear up. She turns to Mitch. "We need to talk. I haven't been honest with you."

Mitch looks from Josephine to me. "What is this?"

"Um, yeah, so maybe I'll step out," Benson says.

"No. Stay," I demand. It's selfish, but I need him here.

Josephine sighs. "The reason your sister hates me… well, it's more than just girl drama. I did something awful, something unforgivable. I don't know if you're going to forgive me."

Mitch is clearly nervous. His face shows shock. "What is it? Just tell me."

"I blackmailed your sister in high school."

Mitch turns to me, confusion on his face. I stand stoic. "What?"

"I blackmailed her with a picture. I threatened to expose your dad's affair with my mom if she didn't break up with her boyfriend."

Mitch stands, frozen, for a long moment. He is rubbing his hands on his face. "What? This doesn't make sense. What the hell are you talking about?"

I decide this is my time to jump in. I tear up now, too. "Dad was cheating on Mom. Senior year. With her mom." I point maliciously to Josephine. "Josephine took a picture of them. It's true, Mitch. I confronted Dad about it. This witch threatened to reveal it to everyone."

Mitch stumbles into a chair.

"I don't understand. Why? When? Why didn't you tell me?"

I sit down across from him. "It was right before Mom found out about her cancer. With everything going on, Dad and I decided it was best she didn't know."

Josephine is crying now. Full-blown crying. Of course she is. "And Maylee came to me. I was so different then, Mitch.

I was a different person. Because I said it didn't matter and I blackmailed her anyway."

Mitch isn't saying anything. He isn't looking at either of us. He's staring at the center of our kitchen table, deep in thought. I notice, though, that his fist is balled up.

"So, about me leaving," Benson says. I forgot he was here. I turn to him.

"I'm sorry about this. Maybe I'll call you later?"

Benson nods. I do feel stupid for wrapping him up in this. I thought it would be better for him to be here. Now I realize it probably wasn't.

"Get out." These are Mitch's words now. He's looking at Josephine.

"Mitch, please, I—"

"Get out. Now." Mitch is red with anger. I haven't seen this look on his face for a long, long time.

Josephine is full-blown sobbing now—ugly, snotty tears.

"Mitch, please. I'm sorry. I should've told you."

"You heard him. Get out." I stare at her, no pity in my eyes.

"You, too."

I turn to look at Mitch. I realize, heart sinking, that the rage in his eyes isn't just aimed at Josephine. It's aimed at me.

"What?"

"Get out, Maylee."

"Mitch, I didn't do anything."

"Are you kidding? You knew about the affair and you didn't tell me? You kept this from me, playing this stupid little game? You think you're all high-and-mighty, but you're just as bad as her."

My mouth drops open. He can't possibly be pissed at me. This is all her. She did this. I'm the victim here, too.

"I didn't do anything. I protected you."

"From the truth? Yeah, thanks a lot."

There's more silence, more standing.

"Come on, let's give him some space," Benson whispers into my ear. I just stare. How could this be happening? How could I be Josephine's victim again?

I let Benson lead me out. Josephine is in front of me, still crying. We all three head down the hall, outcasts.

"This is all your fault," I spew at Josephine.

She wipes away her tears. "I told you we shouldn't tell him."

I fight the urge to rip out her hair, to toss her down the stairs.

Looking at her, I start to feel something else.

I feel what Mitch was just saying.

Maybe I'm not the innocent one. Maybe I got exactly what I deserved. Because maybe, just maybe, I'm not as perfect, as pure, as blameless as I think.

This wasn't all about telling the truth or protecting Mitch. It was about hurting her the way she hurt me all those years ago.

Except now I'm old enough to know better.

CHAPTER TWENTY-ONE

"I love you, you know I do. I don't mind having you here. But remind me again why you're not staying with your hunk of a boyfriend?" Shauni has her hair wrapped up in a towel, turban-style. She's in short shorts and a camouflage print top.

It's Saturday. It's been a week since the board game night gone rogue. Mitch has refused to speak to me—by text, by phone, in person. I was lucky he didn't change the locks so I couldn't get in and get a bag of clothes for the week. It's been pretty ugly.

"I don't want to rush things."

Shauni smirks. "If I had a man like that, I'd be rushing all the way to the altar."

"You have a man like that, remember? So why aren't you and Matt living together?"

Shauni winks. "Don't rule anything out, Missy."

"Seriously? Things are that good?"

"Better."

"Look at this. Miss Play the Field is thinking about settling down?"

"Don't get carried away. Moving in together is not settling down, not in my book."

"Whatever."

"Seriously, why are you holding back with Benson? You're crazy about him."

Which is true. The man makes me smile. He is amazing.

"Wait, don't tell me," Shauni interrupts. "I think it may have something to do with a dick named Jeremy. Is that right?"

I sigh. "I don't know. I just… I don't want to rush into it. I mean, I thought things with Jeremy were perfect, and look what happened."

"Benson's not Jeremy," she says.

"I know."

"Then stop treating him like he is. Take a risk."

"You just want me out of here."

"Well, you do take really long showers. I'm pretty sure my water bill is going to be astronomical."

"I'm hoping Mitch lets this whole thing go soon and I can move back in."

"He will. He just needs time."

"It's been a week."

"Look on the bright side. At least she's gone."

I frown. "I feel sort of bad though. It's my fault."

"Snap out of it. It is not your fault. She's the witch who did it."

"I'm the one who hid it from Mitch."

"For his own good."

"I don't know."

"Anyway, he's going to let this go. It's ancient history."

"We'll see." I head back to my suitcase to pull out some clean clothes. "I think I'm going for a walk."

"Ew. A walk? Now? I think I'm going to watch some soap operas I DVR'd. Want to watch?"

"No, I need to clear my head."

"Right. Well, I'll be right here," Shauni says, plopping on the sofa. I go change, thinking about everything, wanting to think about nothing.

As usual, my life is one giant ball of problems.

***

The fall leaves float around us as we sit on our blanket in the grass, Benson's arm around me. He's wearing Ray Ban shades, worn jeans, and a T-shirt. He looks scrumptious. I'm donning my favorite leggings, a long-sleeved shirt, and some riding boots. November means boots and leggings time, no matter how warm the weather still is.

I take another sip of my champagne, watching a dog catch a Frisbee in the distance. I recognize him. It's Henry, the mastiff that lives down the street from our apartment. The dog could double for a horse, but somehow he manages to be agile with the Frisbee. It's sort of breathtaking.

"This is wonderful," I say, meaning it. "Thank you."

"Well, it's not quite the romantic picnic I had in mind," Benson says. A child screams at the swing set nearby. We had peanut butter and jelly sandwiches and Doritos for lunch. With champagne. The movies always make it look better. But I'm on cloud nine. Jeremy would've never taken the time to do something so sweet.

"It's perfect," I say. "You just have high standards because you write romance. Which, by the way, why haven't you given me any more chapters? It's been a while, and I'm dying to know what's happened. Did you quit writing?"

"No," he says, smirking, wrapping me tighter.

"Then why are you keeping me in the dark? I thought I was a pretty damn good beta reader. I even took notes."

"I don't want you to read any more just yet."

"Why not?"

"I want you to read it when you have an actual paperback between your hands."

"I want to know what happened. I don't want to wait any longer."

"Well, it should only be about seven more months. I think it'll be worth it."

"Wait, seven?"

Benson's literally bursting out of his smile. "Yep. I signed the contract yesterday. I'm officially a published author. Or I will be."

"What?" I squeal, tackling him to the blanket and kissing his cheek. "Oh my God, this is nuts! I mean, I knew it was good from what I'd read. I knew it would happen. But so soon? This is amazing, huh? I'm so happy for you! Why didn't you tell me sooner?"

He shrugs. "I wanted to wait for the perfect moment."

"So you're making me wait, though, until the general public has it? Where are my girlfriend privileges? Why date an author if you don't get special access?"

"Pretty sure you get special access." He winks.

I scowl. "Not like that, you pervert."

He tickles me, and I squeal. I'm beaming for him. I'm seriously thrilled to the core. It feels like I'm getting a book published, I'm so freaking happy. That's when it hits me, looking at Benson, soaking in the sunrays in the middle of a crowded park with the smell of peanut butter on our breaths.

This thing we found at the high school reunion, it's not a rebound. It's not about Jeremy or Kate. It's not about desperation.

It's about the fact we're better together. It's about the fact he's become so much a part of my life in the past few months I feel like it's one life. His triumphs make me just as happy as if they're my own. We put each other first, think of each other, support each other.

We're a good pair.

I kiss him passionately then, perhaps a bit too passionately for a park full of children and onlookers.

"I love you," I say.

He grins. "Do you love me because I'm going to be famous?"

I shake my head, nudging him with my nose. "I love you because you're you, my nerdy writer who is freaking sexy as hell."

He kisses me back before replying, "Good. Because I doubt I'll be famous."

"You're famous to me."

"I love you, too, by the way," he says.

"By the way? What kind of add-on is that? For being a romance writer, you've got a thing or two to work on."

"For being a romance writer, I didn't have a lot of material in the past."

"You had Kate."

"It wasn't love."

I eye him now seriously. "Really?"

He shakes his head. "I thought it was."

"What changed your mind?"

He takes my chin in his hands. "You."

He kisses me again. This time, I melt into him, as if I've been swept out to sea. I might never come back in.

CHAPTER TWENTY-TWO

More days pass, and I don't hear from Mitch. He won't take my phone calls, won't answer the door when I try to stop in. So much for picking up more of my stuff—he's gone as far as to change the locks after all. I consider doing a karate chop move or some ninja warrior stuff to break in, but decide breaking down the apartment door is probably not the way to help Mitch right now.

A huge part of me is shocked he's this pissed at me. She did this, not me. Why am I being punished, as usual, for that jerk?

Then again, I guess I get it in some respects. I lied to him. I'm the one person he's supposed to be able to count on in this world.

I let him down.

Either way, I should be happy. I've accomplished the impossible. I've gotten rid of Josephine for good.

But I'm not celebrating with victory champagne. Hell, I'm actually quite miserable. Because as happy and in love as I am with Benson, I'm realizing how sad and miserable Mitch is right now. Benson said a few of his coworkers saw him at the bar on Monday… at three in the morning. It is so unlike Mitch to drown his sorrows in alcohol. Things must be bad. I feel guilty because I'm so happy and he's so… not. After the Dina debacle, this is pushing him over the romance cliff.

And I'm partly to blame.

Maybe it's best he found out now, before he gets too involved. I remind myself that he is involved. When he looks at that woman, whether I like it or not, there's nothing except love. Now I've shattered not only the image of the family he thought was perfect, but the woman he thought was meant for him.

I think about me and Benson, how good it feels to be with him. I think about how crushed I'd be if some secret from the past tore us apart.

It hurts just thinking about it.

I've succeeded in annihilating Josephine, obliterating her from the family.

I may have destroyed my brother in the process.

When did grown-up life become so damn complex? Are there ever any right answers?

***

"Things are such a mess, Mom," I say, standing in front of the gravestone. I kneel down, picking a few weeds from around the edges. I run my hand on the stone, still smooth. I trace the letters in her name, in Dad's name.

"I was just trying to do the right thing. Then again, maybe I wasn't. Maybe a huge part of me was just trying to show her I'm not that girl anymore, the girl she can push around. I wanted to take a stance. But I ended up hurting Mitch in the process. I think he really loves her. I'm an idiot."

"You are."

I turn to see my brother standing behind me, wearing his jogging gear.

"What are you doing here?" I ask.

"Same thing you are." He walks over and stands beside me. "Looking for some comfort."

We stand silently, listening to the birds chirp for a long moment.

"I'm sorry."

"I know."

"I was stupid."

"You were."

"Do you forgive me?"

"I already have."

I turn to face him. He looks calmer, more relaxed. I think this past week and a half has really helped.

He puts his hands in his pockets. "Look, Maylee. What you did was fucked-up. But I get it. I get it now why you kept it a secret from Mom, from me. I think Dad was an idiot. I can't be too mad at him. It doesn't matter now. I thought it changed everything. I thought it shattered everything we had, our whole family. It doesn't. What he did was an asshole trick, and I don't understand it. But I can't talk to him about it. I can't figure it out. I have to just let it go."

"I just didn't want to hurt you. I knew what it was like to have that image destroyed. I didn't want that to happen for you."

"I know. I get it. Josephine made me see this wasn't your fault."

I spin my head faster than a rocket. "What?"

"I talked to her yesterday. I needed some time to think about all this. At first, I thought you were right. I thought this changed everything. I thought I finally saw her true colors. I hated her for what she put you through before. But this, well, this was unforgivable."

"So the wedding's still off?" I ask, reassured.

"No. The wedding's back on."

"What?" I'm flabbergasted. "You just said…."

"I said I thought it changed everything. It doesn't. If I were eighteen and dating Josephine, this would change it all. But I'm not. We're older now. We've grown up. People change, Maylee. She was awful then, and she made some horrific choices. She hurt you. I'll never forget the girl who did that to you. She's not that girl anymore, though. I know she's not perfect, but neither am I. I love her, Maylee. Good and bad, I love her. She makes me happy. I'm forgiving her."

There's a pause as we both stare at the gravestone. Every time I come here, I realize how life's so fragile, how everything can shift so quickly.

"I can't just forget what she did. I can't trust her. I don't know how you can."

"I know. And I understand. I do. But Maylee, don't you understand? Can't you understand how sometimes love just takes over? I know when you look at her you see this manipulative, lying, scheming girl. When we first reunited, I thought I was going to feel that way, too. I don't. When I'm with her, everything makes sense. Life's so short, we both know that. I just can't see letting go of what makes me happy for something that happened in the past."

"Mitch, this is absurd. You realize what you're asking, right?"

"I do. I'm asking you to empathize. I'm asking you to understand people change. Look at you and Benson. You were never even close to being a thing in high school. Now look."

I soften. I still hate her. I still can't forgive her.

But I sort of get where he's coming from. I see what she must mean to him. I see his heart is in this for the long haul, whether I like it or not.

I exhale through my lips, a puff of air floating into the breeze.

"And really, she's the reason I can move on from this. She's the reason this isn't destroying me. She made me realize this doesn't change who our family is. Or at least it shouldn't. She made me realize I should forgive you. She took all the blame, Maylee."

We stand, staring at the gravestone again. What would Mom say about all this? What would she tell me to do?

"Well, I guess it was nice of her," I admit. It almost kills me. Boy, that would be ironic timing.

"Listen. I know you don't like her. I get why, even more now. But she's going to be a part of this family. So can you at least try to tolerate her? Because, Maylee, she's important to me, but you're my family. I don't want to live my life constantly assuaging warfare between you."

I nod. "I get it. And you're right. I still don't like her. But

I'll try."

He looks at me, eyebrow raised. "What's the catch?"

"There is none."

"There's always a catch."

"And maybe that's the problem. Maybe I need to change, too."

He puts an arm around me. "Love you," he says.

"Love you too. Now can I move back in?"

"I guess. Race you back."

He takes off like a flash, leaving me in the dust.

"This doesn't mean I'm going to like her, just so you know," I yell to him. He is so far away, I'm not sure he hears. But that's okay. I just needed to say it out loud.

I saunter along, thinking about how messed up this whole situation is. Thinking about how Josephine's wormed her way back in.

Thinking about how maybe, just maybe, I can learn to be okay with it.

CHAPTER TWENTY-THREE

"So that's it? She's forgiven?"

"I suppose," I say, stirring my iced tea as Shauni and I sit on the balcony of her apartment. We've decided 3:00 p.m. might be too soon to break out the wine, although the kids were beyond crazy today. We'll at least wait another hour.

"That's insane. How can he just forgive her? She was going to destroy your family."

"I guess he believes she's changed. I don't know, maybe she has."

Shauni laughs out loud. "Okay. Wow, Maylee, you're going soft here. I give it a few weeks, though, of dealing with bridezilla, and I think you'll see the light."

"It doesn't matter. She's going to be family now." I pretend to gag at the comment.

I may be trying to accept her. I still do not like her. Not at all.

"So what is the illustrious wedding date?"

"Christmas."

"No. She didn't."

"Yes. She did."

"So not only is she attempting to ruin everyone's holiday and claim her wedding day is as glorious as the birth of Jesus, but she's also...."

"Stealing my parents' wedding date? Yep. Of course she is." I stir my tea, grimacing at the prospect.

"What's Mitch think of this?"

"Oh, he's all for it. He thinks it's a sweet gesture. Of course."

"Well, on the bright side, at least they'll be on their honeymoon for New Year's." Shauni shrugs, giving me a knowing look.

"I guess. But I think this is crazy. They've been dating what, a few months?"

"She dug her claws in real deep, I suppose."

"Mitch is usually way more levelheaded than this."

"He's never been up against Josephine."

"Truth." She's right. Josephine's a different kind of woman, for sure.

"Maybe they'll divorce by next Christmas."

"Shauni! You can't say stuff like that."

"Of course I can. I'm your best friend. I say what you're thinking."

"I honestly don't want that. I want Mitch to be happy, no matter what."

"Even if it means having the wench in your life forever?"

I grimace. "When you put it that way."

"Well, I have some lovely news to cheer you up."

"Really? Spill," I say, taking a sip.

"Matt's moving in," Shauni sings, doing a little dance move to go with it.

"Are you serious? Things are progressing well then?"

"Oh yeah."

"So please tell me you're going to rush to the altar too, plan a Christmas wedding, and then I'll have to back out of my maid of honor duties?" I flash Shauni a grin. She punches me in the arm.

"Shut up. You know better. White dress? Till death do us part? No thanks. I'll take freedom with a side of hot sex, please. Once you get married, it all goes away."

I roll my eyes. "Whatever. Anyway, I'm happy for you. We should go out sometime soon, the four of us."

"How *are* things with the hot bartender?"

"Things are great," I say, looking into my iced tea.

"Just great?"

"Okay. They're freaking awesome. He's amazing."

"I smell love in the air. Maybe you're the one who'll be at the altar. Hey, hey, maybe you could have a double wedding? Wouldn't it be adorbs? I've seen the whole twin-wedding thing on television before. You could make the news."

"Bite your tongue. I will never share a wedding with the blonde. No way."

"But the wedding is a distinct possibility?"

I fiddle with my cup. "I don't think so. I don't know."

"What is it?"

"I just… what if we're rushing things? I mean, maybe we're just rebounding."

"Please. Not everything's a soap opera, Maylee. Don't make it complicated."

"I don't know. I want to take it slow."

"As long as slow involves some bedroom romps."

"Is that all you think about?"

"No. I think about wine too. So do you think it's time for some wine?"

"It's three thirty," I say, checking the time on my phone.

"Perfect. It's early evening. I'll go get the wine."

I smile at my flighty, crazy friend.

CHAPTER TWENTY-FOUR

I'm watching a rerun of *Friends* on a Sunday morning, handing Nelson a bite of my brown sugar Pop-Tart as I laugh. Crumbs fly out of my mouth onto my slouchy sweatpants and T-shirt, but I don't care. It's the day of rest, of reruns, of doing nothing, especially since Shauni couldn't make our coffee date this morning.

Mitch is out for a jog before he goes fishing with some of his friends. I've got the place to myself. It's quiet. It's peaceful. It's magical.

Until the doorbell rings.

I groan, dragging myself off the couch to answer it, hoping it's at least Benson. Of course, then I hope it isn't Benson because this isn't quite an outfit worthy of a visit from the boyfriend, no matter how comfortable I am with him.

I pull the door open, though, and glower.

It's her.

"Hey, hey, hey, Maylee, what's shaking?"

I raise an eyebrow.

She's decked out in a hot-pink dress and stiletto boots, her hair curled to perfection. Her bright red lips are nightclub-worthy.

She looks ready for a night out or a runway… at 10:00 a.m. on a Sunday.

"Mitch is out," I say, ignoring her annoying entrance.

"Oh, I know. I'm here for you." She traipses through the door carrying a huge box. I don't offer to take it from her. She's fit, after all. I'm not.

"What's all this?"

"Wedding supplies," she sings, clasping her hands dramatically after putting the box on the counter.

"Okay?" I still am not putting together why she's here.

"Well, we have exactly forty-three days until the wedding."

"Okay?"

"So we need to get crafting."

I stare at her, waiting for more explanation. "Crafting what?"

"Well," she says, pulling out some things from the box. "We have centerpieces. See, I thought we would make this little snow globe centerpiece, see here?" She hands me a picture of some complex Pinterest craft involving photographs of her and Mitch. We will then glitterize it, shove some red fluffy stuff in it, and call it a centerpiece. And then surround it by poinsettias.

"Oh, lovely." In actuality, it looks like something we could buy at the dollar store. "Can't we just buy them?"

"No way. This is my special day. I am going to have a hands-on approach to everything."

I continue staring. It's way too early for this.

"So what does your hands-on approach have to do with me?"

Josephine does her wide-eyed Dora blink. "Well, you're maid of honor. So I want to make sure I include you and the bridesmaids. It'll be fun, don't you think?"

No. Hell no.

"Yes, of course," I say. Living in Josephine's world isn't very hard, I suppose. You just say the exact opposite of what you mean. All the time.

"Oh, good," she smiles, wiping her forehead with her hand. "So that's project one. We've also got, well, let me get my list," she says. She pulls out a four-page document. Apparently all of the craft projects we must complete are written on this "sacred" list. I'm surprised it's not literally diamond encrusted.

"Well, we've got the snowman and candy cane favors, the candy bar signs, the 'We Wish You a Married Christmas' plaque with all of the hand-painted poinsettias, the bride and groom wine glasses painted with poinsettias, the ornaments for the tree we're putting up by the head table…."

Josephine continued to list about ninety other "fun" projects. And she continued to say the word "poinsettia" about eighty more times. I guess you're getting the idea of the theme.

"Wow, so did you say there are two hundred and eighty days until the wedding?"

"No, why?"

"Because I'm pretty sure we're not accomplishing all of it

before Christmas."

"Oh, no worries. I have a tightly written schedule here, see? The other girls and my mom will be here in about an hour."

"Wait, other people are coming? Today?"

"I didn't think you'd mind, being maid of honor and all," she says, giving me the puppy-dog eyes coupled with the signature Josephine pout.

So the whole accepting Josephine thing… it's getting harder by the minute.

"Well, the more the merrier, right?" I smile. I consider heading to change into something more appropriate, but decide against it. If I'm having a surprise crafting party, I'm going to be comfortable, especially if I'm going to have to face the woman who slept with my father.

I shove the thought quickly out of my mind. No sense going there today, at least not verbally.

"With my mom and the girls, I think if we stick to this schedule, we'll be fine."

She hands me a piece of paper. It is literally a schedule of crafting parties.

And there are seven more on the list—weekends, weekdays, you name it.

"Whoa, whoa, whoa, seven more parties?"

"If all goes well. We might need to tack one more on if need be."

"Don't you think this is a bit crazy?"

Josephine again gives me the eyes. "Why no. You only get married once, right? I want this to be perfect. I want to make sure we honor your parents' wedding date."

Now I'm the one doing the Dora blink. Honor my parents' wedding date? After she almost singlehandedly threw their wedding down the tubes with a single revelation?

I do some deep breathing. The doorbell rings again.

"Oh, they must be early! I'll get it," Josephine announces, tapping over to the door.

"Well, Nelson, get ready for some crafting fun," I say with sarcasm.

"Oh, baby! I'm so excited! I brought my glue gun!"

I squeeze my eyes shut. I recognize the voice.

It's Margaret. Josephine's mom. The woman my dad cheated with.

I turn around and have to cover my mouth with my hand so I don't audibly gasp.

She's wearing a zebra-print skirt suit, a hot, hot, hot-pink tank top revealing a lot of cleavage, and a bright red hat. Yep, I see where Josephine gets her fashion sense from.

"Hello, darling," she says to me, like we're in Queen Elizabeth's castle. She's probably waiting for me to curtsy.

"Hello, Margaret," I offer, keeping a neutral voice.

"Can you believe we're going to be family? I'm so excited to be getting two new children," she says, rushing over for a hug. I take a step back. The nerve of her. I seriously want to plug in the glue gun and burn her eyes out.

"Let's just focus on the crafting, okay?" I say between gritted teeth.

Margaret frowns. "Well, where are the mimosas? Let's get to this. How many crafting parties for your daughter's wedding do you have, after all?"

"Eight," I say, heading to the liquor cupboard to find the strongest alcohol I can. Sunday morning? I don't care. It's five o'clock somewhere… unfortunately it's not five o'clock here yet.

***

My hand has a ginormous blister on it. I think it's going numb, but I don't want to quit. Because the more I get done now, the fewer crafting parties I can attend. Plus, in a way, I'm picturing Margaret's face every time I slam my hand down. It's helping. I force my hand to keep hitting the stupid Santa hole punch on the red paper.

I have a mountain of confetti in front of me. This will be scattered at the bridal shower. Apparently I'm not crafty enough to handle anything of importance for the wedding, so I was delegated to confetti making duty.

I'm fine with that. Because I get a little table to myself, away from the tight-lipped, stuffy crafting table of Josephine, her mom, and her best friends. Despite alcohol, there is no laughter there. It's all about precision and perfection.

How the hell can things get so serious over a freaking snowman ornament?

An hour into the crafting party from hell, Mitch comes home, sweating and huffing heavily.

"Oh my, there's my future son," Margaret exclaims. She's taken off her zebra-print jacket at this point, so she's showing off the breasts in all of their former glory. She brushes up against Mitch, holding him for an uncomfortable amount of time. He gives me a look. I snicker.

215

"Hey, Ms. Crawford," he says. She takes his face in her hands. I can tell he's uncomfortable, especially with the recent developments. I wonder if Margaret knows we know. I can't imagine she'd be this comfortable if she did. Although, this is Josephine's mother. So who can really know?

"How did my Josephine snag such a handsome one?" she asks. Mitch isn't sure what to say.

"I think she bribed him," I yell. Everyone ignores me. I laugh at my own joke. "Or maybe it was blackmail."

At this, Josephine gasps a little, and Mitch gives me a look. I just put my hands up, almost spilling my drink on the confetti. Wow, that would be equivalent to a nuclear disaster, probably. Better be careful.

Mitch gives Josephine a kiss before heading to my table. "Confetti duty, huh? This one looks a little weird," he says, pointing to a Santa I cut out. It's missing half its hat.

"Fire me, please," I say. I grab his arm, hanging off it. "Say I can't be a part of this. Please," I whisper as the other ladies examine the carrot nose on a frosty ornament.

"Oh, stop. You're having a blast."

I hold a fake gun to my head and fire. Five rapid shots.

"Thank you for trying," he says to me.

I roll my eyes. "You still owe me."

"Fine. I'll pay half the rent this month," he jokes. I punch him in the arm.

"Oh, girls, girls, listen up, please."

She actually taps on her freaking wine glass as if there aren't only six of us in a nine-hundred-square-foot apartment. Really.

"We are going to be picking out our bridesmaids' dresses on Saturday! We'll be heading to Blushing Brides on Saturday at two, so don't be late."

Roslyn and Erica clap excitedly. I just stare. Well, there goes next Saturday. "Where is Blushing Brides?"

"State College, of course. It's only the best bridal shop in the state," Margaret exclaims.

Oh, how silly of me. How peasant-like of me.

"Can't wait," I say. I wonder if they can sense my sarcasm by now. I continue with my confetti punching, wondering how long this eternal hell will last.

Just when I'm considering texting Shauni or Benson to fake an emergency, the bridal bliss crafting party breaks up.

Margaret has a bikini wax to get to. *Thanks for sharing, Margaret.* I guess when you're tossing around the bikini line with married men, you have to keep it in line.

"Next week, same time, same place?" Josephine asks.

I'm ready to say no when everyone else says yes.

"Oh, Maylee, dear, do you think next week you could have stuff ready to make Bloody Marys? They're my favorite."

"Bloody. Sounds wonderful." I glare at Margaret, hoping she picks up on my sarcasm and potentially murderous plots. I don't think she does because she just grins.

For once in my life, I hope the workweek never, ever ends. Because next week, spending two days with this wretched family may, in fact, kill me.

CHAPTER TWENTY-FIVE

"This wedding is cramping my style. Have I told you that lately?" I sigh into the phone as Benson laughs.

"Hey, it's okay. I need to finish some editing this weekend. Rain check. We'll just make next weekend epic."

"As in, can we run away?"

"And who would be Josephine's crafting party hostess then?" Benson teases. I make a sound somewhat like a squirrel and a giraffe combined. Basically, I'm displeased.

"Look on the bright side," Benson says.

"Why does everyone keep saying that? There is no bright side."

"Well, at least you get to have an amazing date for this whole thing. We can drink our faces off, and then I can shred the dress you pick out into tiny pieces."

"I like it. Who knew nerdy bookworm from high school had such a wild side?"

"Same to you," he says. I laugh.

If you had told me at seventeen I would be flirting with

Benson on the phone at twenty-eight and talk about him ripping a dress off my body—and liking it—I would have scoffed at you. I guess sometimes it really does take age and wisdom to see what you couldn't before.

Of course, the fact his hotness has increased twentyfold doesn't hurt, either.

"Anyway, I better get going. I need to mentally prep myself for this weekend. Wish me luck."

"Luck. Try to have fun, maybe?"

"Not happening."

"Didn't think so."

"Love you."

"Love you too, by the way." We hang up, me silently ticking off the possible ways I can avoid this Saturday. Call me crazy, but a day of girlie "fun" trying on dresses just doesn't sound enthralling. Then, if that isn't fun enough, I get to spend the evening touring wedding venues with Mitch and Josephine. Apparently, the maid of honor just has to come. Although the best man, Mitch's best friend, Brad, doesn't have to come. Wow, that's fair.

***

On Saturday, I get in my car and jump on the highway, thankful at least for the forty-five minutes of silence until I get to State College. I blast some Ed Sheeran, think about what a pretty wedding song this would make, and then scowl because I've just internally said the word I'm trying to forget.

The car ride is over way too fast, and before I know it, I'm screeching to a stop in a parking spot in front of Blushing Brides. I think the sign is made of gold. It looks tacky.

Josephine is, of course, wearing white. A floor-length white gown. I would wear it as a wedding dress, not an afternoon shopping dress.

I get out and am greeted with a ton of estrogen, frilly dresses, and kisses on the cheek. Apparently I missed the memo. Everyone is wearing a fancy dress.

I'm wearing my good old Edgar Allan Poe T-shirt and jeans. I'm sporting second-day hair I spritzed with dry shampoo this morning, and I think I may have forgotten to put powder on my face. I'm basically a mess. Oops.

Oh well. If I'm going to be the outcast, I might as well play the part. I still don't know what the hell Josephine was thinking, making me maid of honor. Other than she probably just wanted to torture me. Even more, though, I'm wondering what in the hell I was thinking accepting the offer. I'm pleading temporary insanity or sister of the year, one of the two.

We scamper into the store—there is no walking with the Josephine clan. I remind myself I am doing this for Mitch. I am going to try to leave the sarcasm at the door, and I am going to be compliant.

"Oh. My. God. I can't believe it!"

Squeals at a decibel I cannot describe ensue. They go on for hours.

The saleswoman, a prim lady in a white pantsuit, squeezes Josephine and Margaret. The bridesmaid minions also join in. It's a huge, happy family hug. And I'm excluded. Thank goodness.

"When your mother called, I was floored! This is the most exciting thing that's happened since the royal wedding."

Well, I could think of a few more exciting things. No one is asking me, though.

The squeal fest continues. I smile. It's the plastered on smile I seem to only wear around Josephine events.

"Come, ladies, I've pulled some beauties."

We head to dressing rooms where an array of bright red gowns awaits us.

Don't get me wrong. I adore red. Love it. But this is Josephine. So yeah, I'm a bit annoyed we're wearing fire engine, blinding red. I think it wouldn't matter what she picked, if I'm being honest.

But the red gowns she has picked, God they are too flashy. We're not talking Eric Clapton's "Lady in Red" kind of gown.

We're talking red gone wrong, rogue, or just plain hideous.

They are made of the satiny fabric on every prom gown in a 1980s movie. It's supershiny fabric with an artificial, glossy sheen to it, the kind that isn't forgiving of a single lump, bump, or cellulite chunk. Yikes.

I could deal with the fabric. I cannot deal with the embellishments. They're all bedazzled with what are probably real diamonds, but so many I think the dress has to be a laceration hazard. A few of the choices also have feathers on them. I try not to snivel.

For the next three hours, I am jammed into at least twenty dresses. I am then paraded in front of Josephine's scrutinizing eye to see if I meet muster. This is more infuriating than I could've imagined.

"Um, I like this one, but Maylee's shoulders are so broad. It just doesn't look right. Next."

"Oh, looks like we don't have enough going on up top to fill this one," the saleslady says to me as she pokes at my chest when I squeeze into the next one. Awkward. And ridiculous. I refuse to come out.

"This is it!" Josephine exclaims nineteen dresses later. The other bridesmaids squeal with delight. I'm pretty sure at this point they're actually Stepford wives.

I look down at the dress, making sure I'm wearing the same one they are.

It's floor length with a train, of course. It's red, but not even a good red. It's an orangey-red, the kind you have to examine in different light to see what the heck shade it actually is. It has three different layers of tulle on it, making it scratchier than a wool sweater. It's strapless, so I'm already picturing all sorts of embarrassing wardrobe malfunctions, not to mention the fact it's not very flattering on me thanks to my lack of goods in the chest area. While it's loose in the boobs, it's stuck to my ribcage so tight I'm pretty sure I can't breathe. It's also covered, I mean covered, in bright red feathers.

The best part, though?

The sides are cut out, and the stomach is pretty much see-through. It leaves little to the imagination.

"Um, this is a bit revealing," I whisper, trying to voice my protest tactfully.

Everyone turns to stare at me. I can't be the only one thinking this. Erica is a bit heavier than me. She cannot be feeling confident.

Everyone looks at me as if I'm nuts, including the saleswoman.

"Oh sweetie, stop being so conservative. You look fabulous," Josephine says.

I wait for the punchline.

Then it comes.

"Besides, we'll tighten everyone up so they're feeling more confident at the classes starting next week."

"What classes?"

"I thought I told you. I'm sure I did. The bridesmaid boot camp yoga classes start this Monday."

"What?"

"We're all going to get fit for the wedding together." She does a fist pump. I stare.

"I don't think I can make it."

"But it's a bridesmaid thing."

"Don't you guys think this is getting out of hand? All of these events and parties and now yoga? Please." I look back at the other bridesmaids, hoping for some support. They don't even blink.

Definitely Stepford wives.

"Well, if you think you're good to go, you don't have to come to yoga, I guess. If you're okay with the way it fits." Her face says it all.

I want to say "screw you." I want to say I'll have my semi-beer gut hang out if I want to, if she's picking this awful thing. I want to tell her I'll just get some Spanx.

But the look in her eye, the look that says I'm inferior. Dammit, it gets to me.

"You know what?" I say, walking toward her. Margaret and the saleslady look alarmed. They give each other a look as if to say they need to watch the psychotic Poe-wearing one.

"I'll come to yoga, and I'll fit in this goddamn slut dress. But it's not for you. It's for my brother, because for some unknown reason, he loves you. So I will do all your stupid downward dog poses and your child's pose and I'll stand on my head. Because I can. You just wait. I'll own your class."

And then… I pause. What the hell do I do now?

I sort of make a drop the mic gesture—embarrassing the second I've done it—and spin to head to the dressing room.

Then, of course, I trip on the train. I fumble to the ground. I hear a rip.

Oh God. This can't be happening today. Benson's not even here to save the day.

I lie facedown on my dress. No one moves to help. Finally, the saleslady comes over and offers a cold hand. I take it.

Yep. There's a huge rip down the front.

She purses her lips. "You know you'll have to pay for this. And for the dress you order. So you'll be paying for two."

"Whatever. How much is it, fifty bucks? Big deal."

"Nine hundred."

I cough, choking on my own spit. "What?"

"It's on sale," Margaret says. "Lucky for you."

I stomp into the fitting room and rip the dress off. I stomp on it a little for good measure. I wipe the sweat beading on my forehead and make faces in the mirror.

Once I've calmed down and realize what a fool I've made of myself, I go all-in. Back in my regular clothes, I burst out of the fitting room, holding the ripped dress. I stomp toward the front of the store.

"You know what, I'm taking this with me. Maybe I can make a quilt out of it. Oh, or a bird's nest," I say as I slam it on the counter up front.

The whole store is quiet. Everyone is eying me like I need a straitjacket. Maybe I do.

"So I guess you won't be coming venue searching tonight?" Josephine asks me.

I see the twinkle in her eye, the look saying she's getting exactly what she wants.

I stand my ground. "Oh, honey. I'll be there. Don't you worry. Wouldn't want to shirk my maid of honor responsibilities. Unless you're firing me. I mean, you could always tell Mitch you just can't do it."

"Oh, no. Why would I do that?"

I nod, grab my frilly, feathery dress, get my burning hot Visa back, and march to the car, wondering how in the hell I'm going to pay for this debacle.

CHAPTER TWENTY-SIX

"I'm so glad you made it," Josephine squeals. She's wearing the tightest black yoga pants I've ever seen and a hot-pink tank top reading "I love yoga."

Of course she does.

She is practically bouncing around the room. Her enthusiasm is quite the foil to my clear lackluster attitude.

It's freaking eight at night. On a Monday. This should be illegal.

I have on some threadbare sweatpants from high school and a wrinkled T-shirt from a garage sale. My hair is in a frizzy ponytail, and my eyes are so bleary I feel like I'm drunk.

This is going to be awful.

The other two bridesmaids are already here. They're much more devoted. I don't know why she didn't make one of them the maid of honor. Maybe because they'd actually fight all *Hunger Games* style for the title.

They follow her like lost puppies, nodding at the right times, telling her how glad they are she came up with this idea to get fit for the wedding because, gosh darnit, they wanted to come to yoga anyway.

I yawn, finding a mat and a clear spot away from Josephine's shadows. This is probably against my maid of honor contract, but I don't care.

I glance around as everyone gets in their spot. There are five other people at this stupid late-night torture class.

I know, eight o'clock isn't very late. For me, though, it may as well be two in the morning. I should be in my pajamas on my couch with Nelson. Not to mention I have a forty-five-minute drive home after the class.

Two elderly ladies stand in the corner. They wear revealing yoga outfits clearly showcasing their saggy arm skin. I guess yoga doesn't do a heck of a lot for muscle tone.

Okay, I'm being rude. But hey, it's Monday. I'm at yoga. And I only had one cup of coffee today.

Beside the elderly women is one man, about my age. He's wearing hot-pink leggings and a purple shirt with Hello Kitty on it. Interesting.

Then, in front of me, are two clearly devoted yogis. They are already meditating, their tight little bodies underscoring the fact they live in the gym. I think one is actually making humming noises.

Oh Lord.

"Okay, ladies and gents, thanks for coming to yoga! I can't think of a better way to start the week, can you?"

"Sleeping?" I mumble. The two yoga experts in front of me turn to glare.

I shrug. Apparently yogis don't have a sense of humor.

"Okay, so we have a few newbies here. Let's start with you, Maylee. Why don't you introduce yourself and tell us why you're here?"

I stare at the eight sets of eyes on me. "Um, hi. I'm Maylee, just like she said. I'm here because my future sister-in-law is a yoga fanatic who is making me come so I can lose my baby fat for the wedding." I smile at the end, waiting for chuckles.

Instead, I get a few frowns. Wow, this is a tough crowd.

"Yoga fanatic has such a negative connotation," the woman in front of me says, her nose turned up. She's still sitting cross-legged on the floor.

"Yes. Most slugs on their sofas don't realize the enormous social, psychological, and physiological benefits of yoga."

I blink a few times. "And most yogis don't recognize the benefit of a few extra hours of sleep and of sitting in natural positions."

The two women in front of me huff.

"Okay, moving on," Josephine says, glowering at me. She remembers where she is very quickly, though, because she instantly paints on her fake smile as she introduces her other bridesmaids.

Class begins after Erica and Roslyn obnoxiously partake in Josephine-praising introductions. I find myself trying to contort into all sorts of impossible positions for the next twenty minutes. At one point, I'm convinced I pulled a muscle in my ass cheek somehow. I'll never admit it, ever. When Josephine asks how I'm doing, I tell her amazing.

In actuality, twenty-five minutes in, I'm lying on my back instead of doing the sea turtle pose. I'm trying to nonchalantly rub my ass muscle so I don't cry out in pain.

I watch the women in front of me expertly transition from pose to pose without missing a beat. Either they're both related to Gumby or they live in this yoga class.

The hour goes by so slowly, I think I must've heard the times wrong. She must've accidentally kept us longer. This cannot be a one-hour class. I lie still, thinking about how ridiculous this is I'm here. Shauni was right. I should've said no.

The weird pipe music she's playing softens, and it's finally the cooldown music. Josephine leads us through a cooldown routine. "You've earned it," she says.

Actually, I really haven't, but I oblige anyway.

She leads us through some weirdo meditation. I think about the ice cream sundae I'm going to buy on the way home.

"Now, let's go around and say what we gained from class today," Josephine insists when the lights softly come on. I sit up. Is she serious? Is this counseling now, too? Two for the price of one?

"I learned how much I adore coming to the gym and working out. I just… wow, so amazing. I love pushing myself." The yogi in front of me, in case you were wondering.

"Me, too. I can't imagine how I'd survive not coming to the gym. If I'm not here at least four hours, I feel so worthless."

I look around to the other participants, sort of giving them a, "Wow, they are weirdos" glance. No one seems to share my sentiment.

And now it's my turn. After the yoga experts. Thanks, Josephine.

"I learned… well, I learned my ass muscle isn't as loose and flexible as I thought."

The old ladies' jaws drop. Josephine sits tightlipped. The pink pants man sort of snickers. I put my hands up.

After everyone's left, the bridesmaids flock to Josephine, telling her how much they loved class and how much they want this to be a weekly tradition until the wedding.

I start flooding my head with hundreds of excuses I could use to get out of yoga. I am not coming back. I guess next week I'm going to be getting a really bad cold. Or have to take Nelson to the vet. Or maybe I'll just accidentally forget.

I waddle out to the car, hoping tomorrow I'm not at a doctor to get medical attention for my ass cheek muscle.

HIGH SCHOOL
SENIOR YEAR

Josephine hangs on Josiah's arm as the line to the auditorium crawls on. I see her catch my eye and wink.

It's been a few weeks since the breakup. Josiah claimed to be heartbroken, confused about why I would end things so suddenly. Josephine was there to heal his wounds and probably comfort him in all sorts of ways. I sigh. Ariel puts an arm around me to comfort me.

"It's going to be okay," Ariel says, not really knowing what all I'm dealing with. I told no one about it. Only Josephine and I know the truth.

I shrug it off, act like I'm fine. I hate how she's won. But I have bigger things to worry about.

As Ariel and I inch closer to the door for the senior awards presentation, an assembly to honor seniors and say goodbye to us, Josephine comes closer.

"Hey, Maylee. How are you? Josiah's doing great."

"Glad to hear it," I say through gritted teeth, not looking at her.

"It's a shame you two had to break up. I feel really bad about it."

"You've won, Josephine. What do you want?"

"Oh, nothing. Just wanted to tell you you're in luck.

You're winning a special award today for being top student. Congratulations. See, you don't lose at everything."

"Why are you telling me this?"

"Well, the good news is, since I'm Student Council President and adorable, they let me be the announcer today. So I'll get to give you the award myself."

I want to claw her eyes out, shove her to the ground.

I don't. She's not worth it.

"Whatever, Josephine."

"See you inside." She blows me a kiss, and I'm infuriated.

"She's crazy," Ariel says. "I always knew she couldn't be trusted."

"I just don't get her. I don't get her vendetta."

"Girls like her don't need one. They just run on jealousy."

"What does she have to be jealous about?"

"Stop, Maylee. You're pretty. You're smart. Guys value you. They care what you have to say. Plus, you have an amazing family. From what I've heard, Josephine's mom's a real piece of work. Runs around with tons of men, is never home. She has plenty to be jealous about."

I suppress the twinge in my stomach. It won't do to dwell on this now.

The awards last the afternoon. There are photographs, goodbyes from administrators, and then awards. There's a PowerPoint going with all of the awards being announced on the screen in the auditorium. Awards are given for attendance, for leadership, for everything that will never matter in ten years.

Then it's the highest GPA award. My award.

"And now it's time to announce the winner of the highest GPA award," Josephine's perfect voice enunciates in the microphone. "This girl, wow, I'll tell you, she's a really amazing girl. She's hardworking to a fault. I mean, she's just so cute, always studying, always geeking out. I mean that in a loving way, of course. At one point, we were practically family."

My face reddens. She's looking straight at me.

"We came so close to being family."

She can't possibly. She couldn't possibly do this here. She wouldn't risk her reputation, risk getting in trouble. Some people around us look at me, knowing she's talking about me. They look confused.

"But that's for another time. On with the award. The highest overall GPA award goes to Maylee Keagan."

I stand as the applause picks up. I'm ready to head up the aisle when I hear tons of snickers and laughs. The whole auditorium has erupted into laughter. I see the principal rushing toward the computer running the program, and I see the dean rushing Josephine, who is looking shocked and appalled.

I know she's not, though. This has her name all over it.

On the screen, two stories high for all to see, is a picture of me from seventh grade. It's the picture I've tried to forget.

I have on mom jeans and an ill-fitting tie-dyed shirt. I'm clearly wearing no bra. I have this awful, crooked smile that makes me look even worse than I feel right now.

And the hair. Oh the hair. It was the year I tried to let my pixie cut grow out but failed miserably. To make things worse,

I'm pretending to ride on a pink flamingo in the backyard. It's a picture from a sleepover when we were all just being silly kids. I don't even know where this came from, how she got her hands on it.

I'm not exaggerating. It is a picture I would never even let my mother see, let alone the whole school. Instead of my senior portrait being on display as I accept my award, this is there.

I can recover from a clearly photoshopped picture on my locker, or rude comments. I can recover from a lot of things.

But this, well, this is too much.

Kids are laughing so hard they're crying.

Josephine is shouting it wasn't her.

Mitch is running after me as I head out the doors of the school, tears flying.

"Hey, it's fine Maylee. It's not so bad."

"The bitch needs to pay," I shriek.

"We don't know she did it."

I glare at him and think about hitting him. How could he protect her?

That's the problem with girls like Josephine. No one ever believes they are wrong.

CHAPTER TWENTY-SEVEN

I settle into the comfy leather seat as Benson hands me the bucket of buttery popcorn. I shove my hand in the bucket and my fingers drip with grease. I may have overdone the buttery flavoring just a little. Tonight, I'm planning to eat myself into a food coma. Screw the bridesmaid dress. I hope my fat oozes out of it.

"This was the best idea ever," I say to Benson. Mercifully, there were no wedding duties tonight.

Even if there had been wedding events, I think I would've passed. The dress shopping was enough for me. If I spend one more hour doing anything revolving around the wedding, I might snap. I think even Mitch understands. Last night, he and Josephine worked on centerpieces. I think he was ready to stab his eyes out with the end of the poinsettia.

"I'm glad to have you to myself. It's a tough feat these days."

"Trust me, I'm glad to be with you and only you."

"Ah, don't you even. No Josephine talk tonight, remember?

No wedding talk. Nothing. This is about you and me."

"And some Alice," I say, doing my best Mad Hatter impression. We, the book geeks, are both stoked about the release of *Through the Looking Glass*. We're both wearing our Mad Hatter T-shirts. Yeah, we're adorable.

As we watch the commercials before the previews, I pass him the Coke. "This is seriously wonderful. Jeremy would've never come to see this with me."

Benson gives me a look. "Now you've done it," he says, throwing his hands up in the air—after he puts the Coke down, thankfully. "All *J* names are off-limits. No Josephine. No Jeremy. No, no, no."

"Shh, people are looking," I say, glancing around at some angry elderly people in the row behind us.

"Off with their heads, then," he shouts. I bury my head in my hands, unable to stop laughing. He is such a goofball.

"You know, in school, I thought you were such a quiet nerd, so delicate."

"Delicate? Really? You jerk, I was masculine. I was stoic."

"You hid in the corner and ignored everyone."

"Maybe no one was worthy of my great intellect," he says, talking in a Morgan Freeman type of voice for dramatic effect. And then he starts laughing. "Okay, you're right. I was a weirdo. But aren't you glad you got to see how different I am now?"

"I mean, I think I'm different too. A bit more sarcastic."

"And a lot more sexy," Benson says, kissing my cheek.

"I guess people can change, huh?"

"Yes they can. Now quiet, the previews are starting."

I smile and nod, turning my attention to the movie.

***

Hours later, tucked away under the gray flannel sheets in Benson's bed, I've realized quite a few things.

The Mad Hatter never gets old.

Popcorn before sex is never a perfectly great idea, especially when you drown it in butter. Popcorn kernels in your teeth and buttery breath aren't exactly a turn-on. Then again, it's not like Benson complained at all.

Finally, I've realized yet again that Benson is way more sexy than high school. He might still be nerdy, but if nerdy moves like that, I'll take it.

I roll into him, running my fingers through my tangled, messy hair.

"I love you," I say into his neck, kissing him softly. I lie back, taking in the view of his cabin-like room. It's lacking a bit in the décor area, but I like it. It has a rustic, simple aura.

"I love you, too, by the way," he says, smiling. "And by the way, I have an idea."

"What's that?"

"Well, you see, while you were ignoring me back in my nerd days, I was noticing you."

"Stop it, you weren't," I say, playfully hitting his chest. "Were you?"

"Of course. Give me some credit. Oh wait, I forgot, you thought I was scoping out the men."

"Well?" I playfully put my hands up. Benson tickles me, sending me into shrieks.

"Anyway. I recall something you said when we were

reading *The Crucible*."

My grin widens. I'd forgotten Benson was in my English class that year. It was my favorite play. "Go on," I say. Butterflies surface at the thought maybe he isn't lying. Maybe he did notice me back then.

"I remember you telling Mr. Skarsgen the one thing on your bucket list was to go to Salem."

I cringe a little at the memory. I was a bit dark the year we read that book. I was very into Poe and witchcraft.

I wasn't a creeper or anything. Don't get me wrong. I preferred to think of it as a dark, brooding phase.

"So did you ever go?" he asks me.

"No. Never made it. I seriously did want to go. I don't know why, but the whole thing fascinated me. Still does, if I'm being honest."

"Well," Benson says, taking my hand and locking his fingers around it. "It's sort of been on my bucket list too."

"Really?"

"Yep."

"Wow. I think we were made for each other. Two witchcraft weirdos."

"I'm going to think of it as writing research."

"You're writing about witches in your romance novel?"

"No. But hey, one never knows what research will come in handy. So, I'm thinking, we should do it."

"Really? You want to go to Salem?"

"Why not? Let's road trip it."

I bite my lip, thinking about it. Looking at Benson, though, I see a sparkle, a "go get it" attitude. I like the dichotomy in him. He's rational, quiet, brooding. He's also spontaneous. He makes me want to be spunky and a little bit wild.

"Well, let's do it then. Road trip. I will warn you, though. I'm terrible with directions. Oh, and I always have to pee like every half hour."

"Road warrior you are not. I'll keep it in mind."

He kisses me on the cheek, his hands wandering.

"Hold on a second," I say, playfully redirecting his attention but finding it difficult to focus. "When are we going?"

"Let's leave Wednesday night. We're both off work for a few days, and I don't have any editing deadlines coming up."

"Wait, this Wednesday?" I ask, pushing back from him to look at his face.

"Why not?" he inquires.

"It's Thanksgiving this week. And that means we're leaving tomorrow."

"Exactly. Perfect time. It'll be sort of festive. Well, not really. But you know what I mean."

I look away in thought for a second. It's a holiday. A family holiday. This doesn't seem right.

"I don't know. What about family? Turkey? Traditions?"

"Hey," he says, grounding me, calming me. "I know it's kind of spontaneous, but maybe that's what we need. You've been so focused on everyone else lately. Do something for you. Let's do something we'll remember, something we'll be talking about decades from now."

I warm to the idea. "Well, Thanksgiving hasn't really been the same since Mom and Dad died. Mitch and I tried to keep up some of the traditions, but I don't know. So much is changing. He's probably going to want to spend time with Josephine and her family anyway."

"And my mom's not coming home for Thanksgiving, and I wasn't planning on going there."

"So," I say, twirling a piece of hair. "I guess it's settled. Get your witch hat ready."

"I believe I would be a warlock."

"I don't care who you are."

"So you kiss all the guys like this, then?"

I rub my nose against his. "Shut up, writer boy. We've got a trip to plan and packing to do."

"First," he says, his voice coming from a throaty place. He plants a kiss on my neck, right at the spot that sends shivers down my spine. I bite my lip and inhale, my mind still trying to wrap itself around the fact Benson is now mine.

CHAPTER TWENTY-EIGHT

"Okay, so now that we're back on Pennsylvania soil, I'm starting to wonder if this many souvenirs were necessary," I admit, lugging an entire suitcase of faux "witch's potions," black pointy hats, T-shirts, and every other piece of travel hoopla one could buy. Yeah, I think I had the word "tourist" stamped on my head. But really… a cauldron-shaped coffee mug? How could I resist?

"We did go a bit over budget on shopping, but I'm okay with it. Definitely better than watching the parade on television and eating pounds of stuffing, right?"

I pause, mostly as an excuse to wipe the sweat off my head, but also to cherish this moment. "I had the best time ever, Benson. Thank you."

It's true. I'm not just swept up in the romance of the trip—I mean, it was a trip about the Salem Witch Trials, for God's sake. I might be weird, but I'm not a sadist.

The past few days have taught me a lot about witches and Salem's history. They've also taught me that without a doubt, Benson is good for me. He's patient. He's loving. He's devoted.

He's everything I could want in a man. Add in a dash of sexiness, a dash of expertise in the bedroom, and a dash of intellectual conversations, and I might just be set for life.

I smile, probably looking like a fool on the steps of our apartment building. I don't want this moment to end.

"You know, you don't have to go back to reality," Benson offers. "You already have some bags packed. You could always just stow them at my place. The log cabin is pretty lonely at night when you're not there."

I exhale. This subject came up a few times on the trip to Salem. Our trial run of "living together" for a few days in a hotel had gone marvelously. I'm still not sure if I'm ready for the next step, though. The man who shall no longer be named—and no, not Voldemort, although he does share some characteristics—sort of made me a bit gun-shy, I guess.

"I just need some more time. I love you. I do."

"No pressure," Benson says, and I know he means it. "I'll take what I can get."

He follows me down the hall, my suitcase wheel screeching. I get to the familiar door and push it open. I yell very loudly, "I'm home," before really eying up the place. I don't want any repeats from before. I've learned my lesson.

"Hey, welcome back," Mitch says, taking the suitcase from my hand when I come in the door. He proceeds to stow it away before shaking hands with Benson.

"Well, you're being mighty friendly," I comment, eying Mitch suspiciously.

From back of the hallway, a familiar shape comes waltzing into the kitchen. She's wearing a robe and has a hot-pink bath towel wrapped in a turban in her hair.

I bite my lip. The towel is mighty familiar. As in, it's mine.

It's just a towel. *It's not a big deal*, I remind myself.

"Hey, guys! How was your little spooky trip?"

"It was wonderful. How was your tofurkey?" I ask snidely, smiling at my cleverness.

"It was great. Mitch and I have had a wonderful few days," she says.

"I'll bet you have," I say with as much genuineness as I can muster.

I head to the counter to sort through my mail, trying to just settle back in. I notice it's not where it usually is.

Instead, there are some health nut magazines and a few weird recipe cards.

"Mitch, where's my mail?"

"Oh, I just moved it. It's over there." Josephine points to the top of the refrigerator. You know, the area where random dust bunnies and matchsticks find themselves collecting? The place no regular human being ever looks? Or can even reach?

She *would* move my stuff while I was gone. What, does she think she lives here?

I sigh. "Help yourself to a drink or whatever," I say to Benson, motioning toward the fridge. I head down the hallway to freshen up a bit. When I step into the bathroom, though, I notice a few odd things.

There is suddenly a slew of vegan shampoos and hairsprays. There are six different curling irons that aren't mine. It's like a hair salon in here. Which is strange. Why would she need so much stuff for a few days? It's almost as if….

No. It can't be. Mitch and I talked about this.

Obviously, I know I have to figure out the living arrangement by next month. Living with your brother is weird. Living with your newly married brother… over the line. I've been looking into some cheap apartments. I planned to call a few this week to look into it, to make a decision.

Josephine isn't moving in until after the wedding, though. I have a whole month. Mitch wouldn't just move her in….

I saunter back up the hallway and peek in the open door to Mitch's room.

There's a clothing rack with a million yoga pants hanging on hangers. Who hangs up their yoga pants?

Certainly not my brother.

I stomp back out to the kitchen. I notice Benson is drinking alkaline water—definitely not Mitch's.

"So when were you going to tell me Josephine moved in? You wait until I'm in a different state and decide to sneak her in and shove me out?"

"Maylee, it's not like that. You're not being shoved out. I know you need some more time."

"Well, it just would've been nice to have a heads-up."

"Maylee, I'm sorry," Josephine says. "This is my fault. Listen, I just thought with the wedding planning and all, it would be easier if I were here. You are welcome to stay as long as you need. You don't have to rush. Mitch and I would love to have you stay in our place, even if it takes a little longer than January."

My blood bubbles at her insipid calmness. "Your place? You just moved your damn curling irons in what, two days ago? And now it's your place?"

"Can Maylee and I have a minute, Josephine?"

She nods, her picture-perfect grin on her face as always. This just infuriates me more. She leads herself back down the hallway, as if she owns the place. I suppose she now does. Mitch walks closer to me, sighing.

"Mays," Mitch says, squinting. "Honestly. I didn't mean to do this behind your back. It's just been crazy with the wedding planning and all. Josephine ended up coming here so we could get some details ironed out, and it was just easier for her to stay. I wasn't thinking, though, of how it would make you feel. It was a real dick move. Seriously, I should've talked to you about it. It was shitty of me. I'm sorry, I really am. I know this hasn't been easy on you and I've asked a lot of you. I know it's been rough, and this isn't helping. It's my fault, though, not hers. Blame me."

"It *was* pretty shitty of you," I say.

"I know. I really do. I am sorry. I know I haven't been the best brother lately."

"Not really," I say, shrugging a little.

He sighs. "Thanks for making me feel better."

"You shouldn't apologize so I make you feel better, you ass. Oh, and you shouldn't move your sister's archenemy in while she's out of town. Pretty sure that's in the sibling honor code, too."

"You're right. I know. But the wedding's coming soon, and we really need to sort this all out."

I scowl, but I know he's right. I know this isn't really a big deal or a surprise. It's not my place to scrutinize this decision. Things are changing.

"I just hate I had to find out this way. You could've told me, you know." I move the mood back to serious.

"I know. It was just last-minute. It's no excuse, I know. It was a jerk move." Mitch looks sincere, and I can tell he realizes now how much this sucks for me. As much as I want to be mad at him, I can't be completely pissed. I get it. He's busy. Life's changing for him. It's kind of crazy for me to think he's going to keep my feelings his focus all the time. That's pretty shitty, pretty unreasonable of me, too.

Josephine comes back into the room, lurking in the corner like she's been lurking in my life. My almost-ready-to-forgive-Mitch mood fades to black.

The sight of her standing here, the thought that she's taking over everything in my life—it's still not sitting well. I need to get out of here.

"It's fine. I'll grab a bag for tonight. I'll get the rest out tomorrow." The edginess is back in my voice.

"Maylee, be reasonable. You don't have to move out tonight. Stay."

"Look, I know you didn't mean to be a jerk or insensitive, but I'm not living here with her. I'm sorry. Maid of honor is one thing. Living with her? Nope. I'm out."

"Where are you going to go?"

"I don't know."

Benson grabs my suitcases. "Come on, it's all good."

I wheel the screechy suitcase out and don't look back.

In the hallway, I stand in confusion as Benson shuts the door.

"I overreacted. I know. You don't have to say it."

"Hey. I don't think you did. I think this whole situation is messed up, you know? If you ask me, Mitch is being insensitive. I don't think he means to. I think he's just blinded by love. I get it."

I pinch the bridge of my nose. "I didn't want to say anything, but honestly, I don't know where I'm going to go."

Benson comes closer, slowly. He turns me around and puts his arms around my waist. "Really? You don't have any clue of a place you could stay?"

"Ten minutes ago I was telling you why I can't move in with you."

"Things have changed now."

"I know but—"

"But what? What are you so afraid of?"

I sit down now on the edge of the suitcase, head in my hands. "I don't know. I just…. Things are going so well with us, but I thought that with Jeremy. What if we move in and we decide this was all just a whirlwind situation? What if it falls apart? What if in six months or a year or two years you decide this isn't what you want, you decide I'm just the mousey Maylee I was in high school?"

Benson crouches down to eye level with me, taking my hands. "Stop it. You're right. Things are good between us. Moving in is only going to make us closer. We're crazy about each other. Yes, this is moving kind of fast and unexpectedly. But I love you. I don't think you falling head over heels, literally speaking, at the reunion was an accident. I think it was fate."

I look at him, tears in my eyes. "What if it all goes wrong?"

"What if it all goes right, Maylee? You need to stop living your life tiptoeing around. You work at the preschool because you're afraid to put yourself out there and dream bigger. You live in an apartment with your brother because you're afraid of what might happen if you stand on your own two feet. You hold back with me because you're afraid we might not work out."

I never really thought about all of this, but he's right. I've been holding back in every aspect of my life. Where did the eighteen-year-old fearless girl go? Where did the girl with all the dreams go?

"Look, you might be right. It might fail miserably. You might decide you can't stand how I stack the garbage can too high or how I leave the bar of soap on the edge of the tub. You might hate how I roll the toothpaste and how I sing in the shower. You might change your mind about me. But then what? What's the worse that will happen? You'll love and lose? That's not the worst tragedy in life."

"I don't want to get hurt again. I don't want to fall completely in only to have to crawl completely out of this whole thing."

Benson cradles my face in his hands. "Maylee, look at me." I comply. There's a long moment of silence before he says the thing I need to hear.

"I'm not Jeremy. You're not Kate. We're different. We're different than we were in high school. We're different than we were last year. We're different people when we're together, and if you ask me, that's a good thing. It's a good different. So jump in with me. Say yes."

My head tells me no, to play it safe. My head tells me it would be safer and more sure to live in a cardboard box outside the apartment building than to put my heart on the chopping block again.

But my heart, well, it seems to want to take the risk. Because I look at Benson, I see those eyes, and I say, "Yes."

Benson kisses me, and I almost tip off the suitcase. He steadies us and pulls me to my feet.

"Listen, if you want to ease in, I do have a spare bedroom in the basement. You could sort of live there first, almost like a renter."

I shake my head. "No way, buddy. If we're going in, we're going all-in. I don't play half-assed."

His smile grows. "Good. Same here." He kisses the top of my head as I lean in to hug him.

"Oh, and by the way," he adds.

"I love you, too," I reply before running back inside what is now my former apartment. I call for Nelson, ask Benson to grab his supplies, and we head off into the sunset... or the dusky atmosphere of our apartment building hallway.

CHAPTER TWENTY-NINE

"Seriously. This is the only job I can't get fired from even though I'm trying. I could hospitalize Josephine, run her over with my car, and she'd still keep me as maid of honor just to spite me."

"Wait, you're not considering that, are you?" Benson asks over his Frosted Flakes a week later. We've fallen into a simple yet comfortable routine. In some ways, I can't believe I almost didn't move in with him.

"Listen, I draw the line at jail visits," he says through a mouthful of cereal.

"I look ravishing in the color orange," I tease, raising my eyebrows creepily.

I down the final cup of coffee—Benson's a Folgers man, which happens to be my favorite brand, thankfully. Then I give Benson a quick kiss and head out the door to decorate for the event of the century—or at least of the week.

The wedding shower.

So even though I'm maid of honor, my experience with

wedding showers is limited. Extremely limited.

I remember going to one of my mom's friend's wedding showers as a little girl. All I remember were some shrieks over lingerie. Grandma Sally, who was alive at the time, chuckled because she was the one who had bought it.

I remember thinking grandmas shouldn't be buying lingerie, and if this was what wedding showers were all about, I wanted no part of them.

Except now I am a part of it. A big part of it.

For once, though, I'm glad Josephine's mother is as much of a control freak as her daughter. From what I hear, most showers are basically left up to the maid of honor. There's no way Margaret trusts little old me with the event of the century. I really don't know much about what's going down today, other than the fact I had to buy three fifty-dollar door prizes—what happened to winning a car air freshener?—and make some fancy salad with fruit in it.

Who eats fruit on their salad?

Josephine does.

I pull up to Shauni's apartment and honk the horn. I wait a while and honk again.

Finally, she comes dashing out the front door, pulling down the skirt of her black dress. She's smiling ear to ear.

"Getting in a little action before this stiff-collared event?" I ask as she leaps in. I'm so glad she's going to be there to share in incessant eye rolls with me.

"Hey, I've got to get my excitement in early I think." She winks at me.

"You do know the shower isn't black-tie formal, right?"

Shauni is wearing a short yet fancy black dress.

"Hey, I don't want to break any rules. I know I am so lucky to be on the invite list," she says, hand in the air in a mock prim-and-proper gesture.

I shake my head.

It's true. Shauni almost didn't make the cut.

I'd had to fight and beg and argue with Josephine to get her on the list. Mitch had finally stepped in for me.

Then there was hurdle two—getting Shauni to agree to go. The wedding is, of course, going to be a black-tie event. Not really Shauni's thing. It's going to be at the Lakeshore Country Club, complete with caviar, light big band music for dinner, and probably more champagne toasts than I'll be able to handle.

Honestly, it's not really Mitch's style either, but he wants to make his "blushing bride" happy.

"You sure you don't want to skip this thing, head to the casino or something?" Shauni asks, reapplying some hot-pink lipstick.

"I wish."

"Then let's do it. Stop being so passive."

"Trust me, I want nothing more than to screw her over. But I'm really trying here to get along."

"You're a bigger person than me."

"I know," I say, laughing as I turn up Taylor Swift on the radio.

Before we know it, we're at the Northshore Banquet Hall.

Don't get the wrong idea. This is not your typical fire hall, church basement establishment. Of course not. This is an exclusive, members-only sort of place. This is a multiple forks, fountain in the front of the building, gold statues of people I don't recognize kind of place.

This is a Crawford kind of place.

We park my ramshackle car between two cars worth more than my biggest dream home. I grab the gift from the backseat, hand the door prizes to Shauni, and also grab the Tupperware of the salad I made.

"Here we go," I say as we slink toward the front door.

We don't have to struggle to get in, though. The doorman is already in place.

***

"Oh dear, Maylee, we thought you'd never get here!" Josephine says, running toward me.

Actually, it's more like skidding toward me in her ridiculous six-inch heels and her white dress that barely covers anything at all. Perhaps the Bedazzler caught on her dress. She's covered in gemstones. I mean covered. Her dress was probably painful to put on.

"Oh, we're here."

"Shauni, nice to see you. I didn't realize you'd be coming to help with décor," Josephine adds with an air of annoyance.

"Wouldn't miss a chance to help," Shauni says, shoving the door prizes at her.

"Well, listen, Erica and Roslyn have the script, so why don't you go check with them. Mom, do you have the nonalcoholic punch labeled? I don't want a catastrophe if someone accidentally drinks the wrong punch. Oh, and, Carlos, are you sure the vinaigrette is vegan?"

Josephine is running around in circles, barking orders so fast I think she might pass out.

Shauni stands dumbstruck. "You are definitely a bigger person than me," she says, heading straight for the punch.

The alcoholic kind. Thank goodness Margaret is a drinker and demanded alcoholic beverages here.

I sigh, heading to Erica. "So is there a script or something?"

Erica smiles her Stepford smile. "Here you go. Your parts are highlighted!"

I shake my head. "Wait, wait. She was serious? There's a script?"

"Yes. Now, as soon as you review your lines, can you please come help us fluff the poinsettias on the tables?"

"They look quite fluffy to me." I groan. Erica and Roslyn look at me like I've just said I hate stilettos or kittens or weddings.

I exhale. I do this a lot lately. I head over to grab some punch with Shauni before getting to my fluffing duties.

"What is that?" Shauni asks, referring to the stapled packet in my hands.

"A script."

She laughs. I don't.

"Wait, you're serious? A script? Give me it." She starts flipping pages.

"Oh my God. This bitch is crazy."

I chug a glass of punch, leaning over to look over the script with Shauni.

The "script" is a minute-by-minute detailed list of everything we are to say. Every single minute of the shower is scripted, from "hello" to "farewell." And yes, she used the word "farewell."

It's as if I'm rehearsing for a play, not attending a wedding shower.

"Look at this! Look at your lines for 2:36."

I skim them.

Maylee: And I knew from the moment I saw Josephine and Mitch together there was something special. I knew she was the one he'd been waiting for. All those wrong turns, all those women before Josephine were nothing compared to her. I'm so blessed to finally see my brother so in love.

"I'm going to vomit. Seriously. What the hell is this propaganda?" I practically spew my punch across the room.

"Well, I just would put my foot down."

"There are going to be one hundred women here, all of whom love her. I can't just rebel."

"Why the hell not? This is ludicrous."

I shrug. I can't argue with her. I'm seething.

"Why don't you pretend to lose the script?"

"I'm sure she has extra copies."

We both stand, watching Margaret and Josephine flutter about the room, fixing tablecloths, and scattering poinsettia leaves in perfect arrays. I swallow more punch, still pinching myself. This is actually my reality. This is going to be my family.

"You're right. I think you should just ad-lib. Read the script, but maybe add a few extra sentences, you know?"

"I don't know, Shauni. Maybe I should just go with it."

Shauni, at this, gives me a light tap on the chin.

"Hey, bitch, what was that?"

"I'm knocking some sense into you. This woman's going too far."

"You're right. Listen, I'll figure it out."

I'm mulling over it as I "fluff" some poinsettias. Honestly. This is absurd. "If I ever get married and act like this or demand you to fluff poinsettias…." I say to Shauni, who is standing beside me.

"Don't worry. I'll slap you. Hard."

"Deal."

"Oh, no, no, no, Maylee. That's not right," Josephine says, hovering over me. She rushes in, practically shoving me out of the way. She reaches in to fluff the poinsettia properly. "Sorry, this just has to be perfect."

"Oh, of course it does," I murmur. I drink some more punch.

"Oh, and go easy on the punch. We don't want you slurring your words for your lines," she says.

I cough. This woman is, in fact, ludicrous.

***

"Places everyone," Josephine sings at exactly 1:58 p.m. Pretty soon, the shower of the century will be unveiled.

Queasiness takes over my system, and my head pounds. I definitely overdid the punch. Oh well. Maybe it'll help me get through.

I hiccup as the first guests arrive to the chorus of some ritzy classical song. Shauni sits at a table near the front, looking absolutely bored to tears. She gives me a conspiratorial wink.

Women flood in decorated in diamonds and furs, making

me feel like I'm actually on the Titanic or a part of the *Great Gatsby* cast. I stand quietly, still guzzling punch, watching the minute hand tick. I watch Josephine flitter about, still wondering how the hell this woman weaseled her way into the family.

I mercifully greet a few familiar faces—some distant cousins, my aunt, and a few others. Mostly, the ones I recognize are the ones not sporting the elaborate flapper-style garb. They're in the minority, for sure.

After the guests have sauntered to their assigned seats and the boisterous women have been shushed, the script begins. Erica and Roslyn read their lines, welcoming everyone and talking about how lovely Josephine is. I stare at the clock some more.

Someone nudges me in the ribs, a hard nudge. It's Josephine. I've missed my first line.

"Oh. Hi. I am so thrilled you are here today to celebrate this lovely event. I could not be more excited to see my brother marry Josephine." I read my lines in the most obvious way, holding the paper up high for all to see. I read in a robotic monotone voice. Shauni, also a bit drunk on the punch, laughs out loud. Some guests turn to look at her.

Erica tries to smooth it over, quickly jumping to her line about games.

I assist Margaret in delivering door prizes as guests try to guess Josephine's favorite restaurant and other senseless information no one really cares about. I stumble through the crowd, an aimless servant instead of maid of honor.

Only a few more hours, I tell myself. *You've got this.*

Before I know it, it's time for Josephine to give heartfelt thank-yous to the bridal party and talk about how much we each mean to her. She talks about Erica's "crazy times" with her in college. She talks about what a lovely cousin Roslyn has been.

And then she's standing by me. Shauni raises her eyebrows.

"And of course, my maid of honor, Maylee. The sister I never had." She actually wraps an arm around me now. I slink back noticeably.

"Maylee and I go way back. We were dear friends back in high school. Inseparable really. She was just a dear to me."

I shake my head. The punch really must be strong. Because I swear Josephine just said I was dear to her.

Shauni's jaw is open. Nope. I didn't hear wrong.

As the guests are clapping, I put my hands up. "Wait, you mean before or after you single-handedly ruined my high school reputation? Before or after you tortured me with your total witch moves? Before or after your slutty self blackmailed me?"

Josephine's jaw is now the one open. Oops. I think I just said everything out loud.

Shauni actually starts clapping. The crowd of women looks simultaneously horrified and entertained. This is probably the most exciting thing they've ever seen at a stuffy wedding shower.

Margaret is at our table faster than you can imagine. "Get out," she orders. The room is so quiet, so still, we can hear the minute hand ticking on the clock.

"Mother, don't do this. Not here. It's okay," Josephine says in a hushed whisper.

"No. She's not going to embarrass you, not here."

"It's fine, I'm leaving. I'm done." I nod to Shauni, and we head for the door. Josephine rushes toward me as the murmuring of the crowd gets louder.

"Don't do this," Josephine begs at the door.

"I'm done playing your fucking games," I say. And then I'm out. Out of the shower, out of the wedding.

Out of Josephine's life.

"That was awesome," Shauni shrieks when we get to the parking lot.

I don't feel awesome. I feel like everything is just falling apart.

HIGH SCHOOL
SENIOR YEAR

I dash through the crowd, searching for the familiar faces. Mitch is in a huddle with his hockey buddies. They're slapping each other's backs, hooting and hollering. I shake my head, the tassel on my hat naturally hitting me in the eye. I rub it before scanning the crowd of picture-taking parents.

"Maylee!" Mom yells from across the field. She's jumping up and down. I don't know how I missed her in her neon-yellow shirt and bell-bottoms. Dad is right beside her, the trustworthy camera snapping enough pictures to make a flipbook.

Mom wraps me in her arms. "I'm so dang proud of you and your brother. I can't believe my babies are all grown up." Tears are flooding down her face, a head scarf hiding her now-bald head. Still, despite all breast cancer's taken from her, it hasn't taken the signature smile. If anything, she's been more optimistic since her diagnosis, taking every opportunity, breathing in every moment.

I hug her close. I don't say it, don't even really want to admit it to myself, but this moment means so much. Mom's cancer has taught me nothing can be taken for granted. It's made me appreciate every moment with her a little more.

I pull back from my hug. My dad, looking a little less

certain, leans in. "Congratulations, baby," he says. I can read hesitancy on his face. I hope Mom can't. I stiffen but let him hug me.

I'm still pissed at him, still want to rip out his throat. I paint on the smile I've grown accustomed to. I have to act like nothing's happened, at least for Mom's sake.

Mitch comes rushing over, almost bowling me over as he gives high fives to Mom and Dad.

"Get close," my dad orders, and Mom, Mitch, and I smile for another dozen pictures. As my face gets tired from being frozen in a smile, I glance to the right.

That's when I see her.

Prancing around in her cap and gown, a few boys following her like paparazzi, is Josephine. She's smiling like she's just won Miss America. She's parading around like she's the only one who achieved the great honor of graduating, Josiah trailing her like a lost puppy.

I scowl at her, but she just winks and moves on.

"Maylee, smile!" Dad orders, and I snap back to the moment, pretending everything is fine, as I've grown accustomed to doing.

At least you'll never see her again. After today, she's out of your life for good, I promise myself.

Thank goodness, because seeing the witch for the last time cannot come soon enough.

CHAPTER THIRTY

I sit on the park bench, my feet dangling as I watch a pigeon peck at a crumb of bread.

"I hate how we're falling apart," Mitch says, sitting beside me, arms crossed.

"Me too."

"Look. I get it. This is a lot to ask of you. I've been insensitive. And this is moving so fast. I didn't do this to hurt you, Maylee."

"I know. I know that. I know you wouldn't be marrying her if you didn't love her. I don't claim to understand it. I don't claim to see what you see in her. But I know for some godforsaken reason, she's the one."

"I love her, Mays. You just don't see the side of her I see."

"You're right. I don't."

"I understand why you can't be in the wedding. It was dumb of us from the start. I just thought… I don't know. I thought maybe if you saw what I see in her, if you spent time with her, maybe you'd realize she's changed."

"She hasn't."

"I think you're just toxic together. I think maybe it's just never going to be okay with you two."

"I hate this. This isn't how I pictured things."

"I know, Maylee. Let's just go one step at a time. Let's not rush it. I think I just wanted everything to be perfect."

It's been two days since the wedding shower incident. Mitch and I have been through the screaming, fighting stage. We've been through the, "I'm quitting the wedding," and the "You're fired from the wedding," stages.

Now we're just at the calm after the storm. The despondent, everything's-a-mess calm.

"Maylee, I want you to know you'll always be my best friend. This doesn't change anything."

"Of course it does. Don't you see? She's already changed us. She's ripped us apart."

"No, *she* hasn't."

"You think I'm responsible?"

"I think you're letting her get the best of you. You're just so stuck on who she used to be. I understand, I do. After everything, I get why you'd be hesitant. But Maylee, she's changed."

I sigh. "I don't know."

"Look, don't get mad, but did you ever think maybe she's not the one holding on to the past? Maybe you're the one who hasn't changed."

I want to scream and get pissed and punch him.

I don't.

Because maybe he's right. Maybe this isn't about Josephine

and the stupid drama and the picture and the blackmail.

Maybe it's me.

Maybe this is about the fact I'm not where I wanted to be in life. Maybe it's about the fact I've always felt the need to compete with Josephine, and I'm always left feeling like a failure.

"Can I still come to the wedding?"

"Do you want to?"

"Yeah. For you."

"Yeah."

"Shouldn't you check with Josephine first?"

"No. She would want you to come."

I roll my eyes.

"And the gift you gave her was lovely. Seriously. Too bad you couldn't tough it out to stay and give it to her."

I shrug. "I tried, Mitch."

"I know. I really know." He pats my hand, and I lean on his shoulder. Life is such a disaster.

***

Bleary-eyed and morose, I walk through the door at Benson's— my place now, I correct myself. Nelson meows, already settling into the homey cabin in the middle of nowhere. He was thrilled by the prospect of constant bug hunting as soon as we moved in.

I take off my shoes at the door and immediately sink into the recliner in the living room by the fireplace. Benson has a fire roaring, and I tuck my feet underneath myself, Nelson joining me. I pet the cat for I don't even know how long, thinking about how messed up everything is.

"Hey, I didn't hear you come in," Benson says as he walks into the room sometime later. I don't turn my head, the tears cascading into my lap.

He kneels down in front of me, his flannel shirt open to reveal a gray muscle shirt underneath. His gorgeous muscles, his toned stomach visible through his shirt grab my attention. I smile in spite of my current state.

"A girl could get used to this," I say.

"What? The fire? The crying?"

"You." I wink at him in what is assuredly a creepy move. He raises an eyebrow back and takes my hands, Nelson vying for his attention and head butting his arm.

"What's wrong?"

"Everything. Absolutely everything."

Benson exhales loudly through his nose. "It's not so bad, right? I mean, you get to live with a somewhat crazy writer man in the middle of the woods now, huh?"

"This is how horror films start."

"Horror's not my genre, so no need to worry."

He kisses my hand. "Tell me what's up."

"I just feel like shit. My life is nowhere near where I wanted it to be. Don't get me wrong, I'm excited to be living here. I love you. I do. But the whole Josephine thing has me feeling like shit. On one hand, I feel like a crazy bitch who is being super immature and whiny. On the other hand, I want to ram her with my car for everything she did to me, to my family, and what she's still doing. She's going to hurt him, but he's blinded by her. He can't even see all the stunts she's pulling."

Benson pauses, wincing. He seems to be thinking about his words.

"What is it?"

"I don't know. Please don't get mad...."

"Oh no. Please do not tell me you're in camp Josephine now, too. Please don't even. Because if you do, I may stab you with the fire poker."

"Maybe I should be worried about the whole horror film thing," he says, pretending to scooch back.

"See? This is what she does to me. It scares me how angry she makes me."

"Look, it's understandable. Josephine is totally in the wrong with all the crap she's pulling on you. Totally. The thing is, Maylee, why is it getting to you so much? I know you love your brother. I know you're worried about him and don't want him to get hurt. I just don't think it's all that's going on here."

"Oh really, Dr. Phil? What do you think, then?"

"I think you're upset because, like you said, your life isn't where you want it. Josephine is just an in-your-face reminder of the girl you used to be, the girl who dreamt big and had vision for her life, well she's sort of been on hiatus."

"I still have goals," I retort, getting huffy.

"I know. But what are you doing about them?"

"Well, it's not so easy you know. Teaching jobs aren't just out there for the taking, full-time ones."

"So, how many teaching jobs have you applied for in the past year?"

I stare sheepishly into the fire, averting my eyes from him. I've really got no defense to this question.

"That's what I thought. Maylee, life isn't going to hand

you the reality you want. You have to be brave enough to go after it. What are you so afraid of?"

"I'm not."

"I think you're just afraid of failing."

"Well, yeah."

"Who cares? You know how many times I've failed? Do you know how many people look at me and wonder what I'm doing with my life, bartending and then writing romance novels that up until a while ago weren't even under contract? Stop worrying about failure and people judging you. Stop living your life in comparison with others. Do what makes you happy, Maylee. Then this whole Josephine thing and the whole high school thing and the whole almost thirty thing, well, it won't even matter."

I look into those eyes I've come to love and trust. In them, I see the truth I haven't wanted to see. This isn't all about Josephine. It's about me. It's about the fact I'm not who I want to be.

When I was in high school, I pictured my life in ten years. I pictured a life of travel and fun. I pictured me working a full-time job teaching high school English, traveling over the summers, potentially a husband and kids. I pictured me trying new things—taking a dance class, learning to paint, going skydiving.

Am I doing any of these things?

No.

At twenty-eight, up until very recently, I lived in an apartment with my twin brother, watching him live his life while I was a sidekick. I work in a preschool, not because it's what I really want, but because it's the job I could get and my best friend works there.

My biggest excitement? Netflix and Nelson. That's it.

"You know what, Benson Drake. You're right."

"Wait, what?"

I huff. "I said you're right."

"Oh yeah. High-five it, Nelson. The lady admits we're right."

"He's my cat. Don't get any ideas he likes you more. You are right. I need to stop whining, stop letting Josephine make me feel inferior. I need to start worrying about myself and what I want."

"So what's this mean?"

"Well, for starters, I'm going to start looking for a job, a job I want."

"Awesome. What else?"

"Um, I think maybe I'll sign up for a painting class. I've always wanted to do that."

"Good. Anything else?"

"Well, if you're looking for a proposal, I think it's a bit soon." I wink. He laughs.

"I'm flattered, but when we get engaged, I'll be doing the asking. Come on. I write love stories. At least let me handle that part."

I blush, unexpected butterflies fluttering in my stomach at his words.

He didn't say if. He said when.

And the most shocking part? It doesn't scare the hell out of me. Sitting here by the fire, Nelson on my lap, I can see myself here, permanently. I can see myself taking the leap with Benson, chasing this crazy life we're building together. I can see him standing beside me, chasing dreams and making memories.

Because, by this fire—which I'm starting to think has magic powers—I've seen quite a few truths tonight.

I've been making excuses to not live my life. From fear of failure, to my parents' deaths, to Josephine, I've been finding reasons to focus on everything except what I really want to do with my life. It ends tonight.

Second, I've learned that as much as Jeremy burned me, all love isn't like this. Benson isn't Jeremy, not even close.

"Anyway, what I was getting at was, what about Josephine?" He looks at me expectantly, and I smirk.

"So you're asking, yet again, if I'm going to play nice?"

"And?"

"And… I still wish everyone would stop looking at me. She's the one who is being a total—"

"Okay, okay. Enough counseling for tonight, I suppose. Baby steps."

"Baby steps. So, are you done with your editing yet?"

"No. But I mean, if the right offer came along, I could probably be swayed to take a break for the rest of the night.…"

"Hmm, what kind of offer?"

"Use your imagination," he says, leaning in and kissing my neck.

"You're the one with the imagination in this relationship."

"I thought we just talked about expanding your horizons."

He keeps kissing me, and poor Nelson gets the boot. Before

I can come up with a witty comeback, he's picking me up and carrying me up the steps into the loft bedroom.

CHAPTER THIRTY-ONE

There are highs and lows after you are a total bitch who makes a scene at someone's wedding shower.

The lows? Everyone who hears about it looks at you like you're a bitch. It stings, even if you know you deserve it a bit. And of course your brother, who is being brainwashed by said bride you told off, is a bit cold toward you, even if he claims things are okay.

The highs? After being booted from the wedding party, I no longer have to organize the lovely crafting parties or be at Josephine's beck and call to answer questions about tie colors. I don't have to make the twenty-dozen cookies or scrutinize the shade of the bow on party favors. I am, in many ways, off the hook.

Obviously, this is a good thing because I cannot stand Josephine, despite any epiphanies I've had lately.

It's also a good thing because right now, I don't really have time to deal with Pinterest crafts and wedding luncheons.

Because I've started a new job.

Benson's pep talk—and the activity that followed—sank in. So the next day, I combed the classifieds for jobs, applying for three.

Within a week, I'd received a call from an all-girls' private school across town. Their English teacher was having a baby, due any day, and they needed a teacher for the rest of the year.

It was a tough decision. I'd agonized, not sure if I should give up security—and Shauni—at my job for a temporary position.

Benson, of course, helped me see clearly.

"Stop living so safely," he said. "Do what makes you happy. Worry about the rest later."

So I accepted.

And then a few days before Christmas break, the English teacher went into labor. In the classroom. Yikes.

So here I am, painstakingly curling my hair, smoothing my skirt, which I ironed—yeah, it's that serious. I'm making sure my nails aren't chipped and flying around Benson's kitchen—I mean my kitchen—scrambling to make coffee.

Benson wanders in, still in his pajamas. The life of a writer. I'm jealous.

"How do I look? Do I look like a teacher? Do I look authoritative?"

He kisses me on the cheek. "You look gorgeous."

"I don't want to look gorgeous. I want to look smart."

"Hey, breathe. You're going to be fine. They're teenagers, not wolverines. This is what you want. Go get it."

I exhale, nodding, but I'm not feeling brave or fine. I'm feeling like I'm going to vomit.

How am I going to go in there and teach a bunch of teenagers? What if they don't like me? What if they think I'm stupid? What if I *am* stupid? I've been away from my content for so long… what if I screw up?

I glance at the clock. Shit. I was supposed to leave five minutes ago. "I have to go, love you," I shout as I propel myself out the door into the new future.

I know Benson had a point. I need to pursue my dreams.

But sometimes dreams are scary and exhausting.

***

I slump through the door, limping on my broken heel. My makeup is melting off, and I'm pretty sure my clinical deodorant stopped working five hours ago, leaving pit stains the size of saucers. I'm exhausted, I'm worn, and I want to face-plant into the couch.

I stroll to the kitchen, Nelson meowing at my feet.

There's a banner hanging in the kitchen reading, Congratulations! and a homemade cake on the stove. The table is set with candles and a box of pizza.

Benson strolls into the kitchen and wraps his arms around me. "How was it? Did you have fun?"

I just stare at him, and his smile fades. I think the look on my face probably says it all.

"Here, sit," he says, offering me a chair. I slump into it.

"Tell me about it."

I bury my head in my arms on the table, my hair flying onto the pizza box.

"Careful, there's a candle," Benson shouts, and I lift my head just enough to make sure my hair isn't on fire.

"Babe? Come on, it can't be so bad."

I look at him, the tears flowing. "I quit."

"Wait, what?"

"I quit. I'm done. I gave my notice. My life is a mess."

He sits, stunned, not saying a word, Nelson's meows echoing in the kitchen. He blows out the candles, giving me a few moments before he scooches his chair beside me.

"Tell me about it," he says, and the story pours out.

***

The morning started off okay, I suppose, despite the fact I thought I was seriously going to barf up my granola bar. Hands shaking, I'd written my name on the whiteboard and stood behind my empty desk, waiting to face the girls. The classroom was what you'd expect of a private school classroom—clean, utilitarian, full of technology.

To me, it looked totally boring, but I told myself there'd be time to fix it.

I smoothed my skirt as the bell rang, awaiting the students with shaky hands.

"Good morning," I sang, hating the fakeness in my voice. I expected the girls to skip in, smiling, anxious to meet their new teacher.

Instead, I got two glares, one "Who the hell are you?" and ten complete disregards of my welcome.

I exhaled the breath I didn't expect.

"Okay, everyone, good morning, I'm Ms. Keagan," I stated, a huge smile plastered to cover my vomit feeling.

No one made direct eye contact, smirking at me as they gave me the once over.

"So, from what I understand, you just finished reading *Hamlet*, one of my favorite plays. To follow, we're going to read some Sophocles. I thought it would go nicely with the tragedy theme."

I waited for a response or acknowledgement, any sign of life really, that never came.

I started passing out the books, so unsure of myself. I felt like an alien on a different planet, except this planet was way too sparkly and designer necklace-y for my taste.

"I've read this," a girl in the front row said.

I turned to her. "What's your name?"

"Brittany."

"Well, Brittany, it can't hurt to read it again, right? Maybe you'll notice some things you didn't before? I'm sure together we can delve deeper."

"Who are you kidding? You think you, some last-minute substitute, are going to teach me about Sophocles? When was he born?"

"Um, well, see... I'm not just a substitute, I have my credentials and—"

"So tell me, when was Sophocles born? When did he write *Antigone*? Tell me about the Greek questioning of prophecy."

My heart stopped. This was so different than the ABC song I taught in preschool. I knew it. I'm out of my league.

"Well, I haven't had a chance—"

"That's what I thought," she smirked, and the girls around her started to laugh at me, rolling their eyes and looking at each other like they'd won.

I felt a loss of patience happening, worse than when Jack

ate paste every time I turned around. I reminded myself to breathe, to just let it go. This was just some sassy sixteen-year-old needing to assert herself. I didn't need to compete with her.

"Well, Brittany, we will find out all of the answers to your questions on page one of the introduction as we read together." I flip my book to the page and some girls start to do the same.

"Sophocles was born around 496 BCE in Colonus, from what we understand. At the time, the Greeks were starting to question prophecy, so he wrote the Oedipus Cycle to bring the issue to light. *Antigone* was first performed around 442 BCE," Brittany recited from memory, not touching her book. Her arms crossed, she eyed me smugly.

I stared at this human marvel, actually impressed by her abilities.

I was not, however, impressed by the smirk on her face or the crossed arms or the screaming of defiance coming off her entire aura.

"Wow, Brittany. How impressive. Thank you."

And then I just flipped to page one of the Oedipus Cycle, hoping one of her facts would be wrong. They weren't, and she made sure to tell me.

"So, we're not going to learn anything in here, I'm assuming?" Brittany asked as soon as we were done reading the background information.

"You know what we're going to learn? We're going to learn how not to be a condescending jerk of a person. That's what we're going to learn. And some of you have quite a lot of progress to make in that arena," I spouted without thinking.

The girls, jaws open, stared in silence.

Suddenly, I felt like such an idiot. Had I really lost my temper on the first day? With the first class? Had I argued with a girl who clearly was a genius, clearly smarter than me? What the hell was I thinking?

"Um, on that note, please read the first twenty pages of *Oedipus the King* tonight. Thank you." I added a sugary-sweet smile. The girls didn't move. Except Brittany. She just kept staring at me, challenging me to say something else.

I realized it was going to be a tough road, not just because I felt unconfident in front of the class, but because, just like in high school, there would be girls out to make me fail. Oh, and it also didn't help that Brittany, who had quickly become the bane of my teaching existence, had perfect blonde hair.

I regrouped from my first class, though, hoping the morning would get better.

It didn't.

I lost copies of the handouts I'd wanted to give out to third period. I accidentally passed out an Edgar Allan Poe story to my fourth period class, which was British Literature. I couldn't find the bathroom in the school for ten minutes and, when I did, it was the men's room. And I walked in on a colleague. Oops.

My teaching career, the thing I thought I'd wanted all along, was quickly going down the tubes.

And then came eighth period, the period that would completely hammer the final nail into my teaching career coffin, at least at The Mapleson School for Girls.

***

"Oh, look, I'm back in the incompetent teacher's class," Brittany snarled as she walked through the door.

"What are you doing here?" I asked with a little more edge than intended.

"Well, if you'd checked your roster, you'd know I have creative writing this period."

Shit, I thought. One period of this snarky girl was going to be tough. Two periods? Impossible.

"Well, I'm so glad to have you."

"Wish I could say the same."

"Okay, you know what? Your defiance has to stop."

"Or what?"

"Or I'll write you up."

"Too bad my daddy's the top funder of this school. So if you want to keep your paycheck, I probably wouldn't."

A tiny brunette in the back corner of the room, thick glasses and four books on her desk, looked at me empathetically, nodding.

Double shit.

A few stragglers meandered through the aisles to their desks as class began.

"Okay, so this is creative writing. How many of you in here are dreaming of being writers?" I asked, trying to ignore Brittany and focusing on the other girls.

The sweet girl from the back corner raised her hand.

"What's your name?"

"Lisa."

"Lisa, great to meet you. So, why don't you tell me a little about your writing and what you want to do?"

She kept her eyes averted. She wasn't much of a public speaker, I gathered. "Um, I write romance. I have a few books finished I'm hoping to get published," she practically squeaked, and I smiled. See, I could do this. There were plenty of great students. I was just getting ready to continue the conversation when it happened.

The comment that sealed my fate.

"Ha. Romance? What in God's name could you possibly know about romance? What, did you pay a boy to kiss you so you could write about it?"

It was Brittany. She was turning to a few girls around her, girls who clearly worshipped the ground she walked on.

I felt my fists clenching. I peered at Lisa, who now looked teary-eyed. I decided, money or not, contributor to the school or not, I couldn't let this go.

I stomped toward Brittany's desk. I reminded myself to stay calm. It was my first day.

I just couldn't.

"You think you're so amazing and hot and great, huh? You think because you have boyfriends crawling at your feet, because your daddy's rich, you're better than everyone? Sorry, honey. Here's the real world talking. You're a stuck-up little bitch."

As soon as the words, especially the last word, flew out of my mouth, I froze.

I'd been trained for teaching, and trained well. I'd passed student teaching with flying colors. I'd always been rational and calm.

But this girl, this school, it wore on me. The look on Lisa's face wore on me. And I'd snapped.

There was no recovering from calling a student a bitch. There was no recovering from calling the biggest contributor to the school's daughter a bitch.

No one said anything. I stomped back to my phone, called the principal, and said, "Hi. I'm sorry, but I'm quitting. Right now."

Brittany's eyes were wide. I thought I saw a tear on her face. I tried not to dwell on it, though.

As the principal, dumbstruck, walked into my room to take over, I looked back at Lisa.

She was no longer embarrassed or ready to cry. She was smiling.

I might have lost my job, lost all hope of getting another one. I might have made a fool of myself. But the smile on Lisa's face made it all worth it.

***

"I told you. I'm a wreck. You should probably just kick me out. I'll just live in a box on the street and beg for change. It's the only thing I might be capable of."

"Stop. It's going to be okay."

"I don't have a job. I went for my dreams… and now I have nothing."

"Okay, this isn't quite what I thought would happen. I'm still proud of you."

"For being a failure? For screwing up my entire life?"

"No. For being brave enough to go after something. It didn't turn out quite like you expected. So what? It's not the end of the world. I'm proud of you for standing up for that girl. You may have just changed everything for her."

"I called a girl a bitch."

"Sounds like she deserved it, honestly."

"I have no job."

"I'm sure the preschool would take you back. Or, you could try another school. It was one bad experience. One bad fit. It's not the end of the world."

"Feels like it."

"Well, it's not. Come on," he says, pulling my hand.

"What are we doing?"

"You are going to take a long, hot bath with a glass of wine. Then, we're going to eat pizza and watch some stupid movie on Netflix to make us laugh until we're practically unconscious."

"How is that going to help anything?"

"Because. You just need time. Time to figure out what you want. So this maybe wasn't it. One thing crossed off. Tomorrow's another day, Maylee. Tomorrow, you can be whatever you want to be. You can start over. You don't have to lock yourself into this single identity, this single picture you have for your life. Explore a little."

"You make it sound adventurous."

"It is."

"Except for one thing. I need my little adventure to pay the bills."

"Well, you see, you jumped on this golden ticket train right in time. Because, I mean, heck, in a year, I'll probably be rich and famous."

"I'm not a gold digger."

"I'm kidding. Calm down."

"Sorry. I didn't mean to snap."

"It's fine. Cut yourself some slack. You don't have to be perfect all the time, Maylee, not with me."

I looked into the eyes of the man who'd convinced me to quit my job, which turned out to be the worst mistake ever. Instead of anger, I felt gratitude.

He'd saved me from my rut. He was right. I'd done something. Maybe it wasn't the right move, but at least it was a move.

I'm not standing still anymore. I'm not just settling into the mold everyone wants me to. For now, that's good enough.

CHAPTER THIRTY-TWO

Nelson scurries off my lap as I get up to answer the door. I'm a little peeved—it's time for *The Price is Right* to start, the show for the elderly, kids home sick from school, or the unemployed.

Unfortunately, these days, I fall into the latter category.

I brush some cookie crumbs off my shirt, yelling, "I'll get it." Benson's working away on edits; I'm just working away at my pricing skills.

At the door, I freeze in surprise as snow whips in. I wrap my robe tighter around me, shivering.

I was not expecting him, not today.

"Hey, stranger," I say.

Mitch eyes up my outfit. "Wow. This is worse than I thought."

"Shut up, jerk. What are you doing here?"

"Coming to see you. I heard about the job situation."

I usher Mitch in, Nelson meowing at his feet. We stand uncomfortably, the formality between us obvious. Things are still tense, despite our talk, as evidenced by how out of touch we are. Not very long ago, Mitch would've been the first to know about my job disaster. Now he'd heard it through the grapevine.

"I'm a screwup. Tell me something I don't know."

"Stop. I didn't come here to hear you pity yourself."

"Wow. Thanks for the support," I joke, heading to the sofa. "What are you here for then?"

"Two things actually. An offer and a favor."

"Intriguing. Shoot."

"First, I have an offer. I know of a job that might be perfect for you."

"If it involves working with people, I'm pretty sure it's a no go."

"It does. But it's working with little people. There's a nonprofit looking for a coordinator for their after-school program down in the Meadowview Project Area. It's for underprivileged elementary school kids. You'd be coordinating it."

I shrug. It sounds interesting. "How did you find out about it?"

Mitch looks at the floor, and I instantly know.

"No. I will not be Josephine's charity case."

"It's not like that. Listen, her mom is friends with a lady on the board. She just tossed your name out there."

"No way."

"Maylee, don't let your pride get in the way. This could be really good for you."

I sigh. "I'll think about it. What's the favor?"

Mitch takes a seat on the couch now. "I was wondering if you could do something for me at the reception."

"Oh no. Here we go. I thought I was fired."

"You were. You are. But this is something for me, not for Josephine."

I eye him curiously. He reaches into his pocket. "I wanted to know if you could read this."

I glance at the envelope he's holding. It's slightly discolored, but the scrawl on the front is distinct. My eyes well up. I'd know the handwriting anywhere.

It's addressed to Mitch.

"What is it? I don't understand."

Mitch takes an audible breath before speaking. "Look, you're not the only one with secrets. When Mom was sick and thought she wasn't going to make it, she wrote this. She wrote two actually—one for me, and one for you. She gave them to me, made me promise not to open until my wedding day. She asked me to save your letter for your wedding day, too. I think it was just her way of being there for the momentous day she'd miss."

Tears are flowing now. Nelson is head butting me, and I aimlessly pet him. To have this letter, to have a piece of Mom… it's a miracle.

"Why didn't she trust me with it?"

"Come on, Maylee, really? You think you would have been able to leave it unopened?"

I scowl. He's right. But still. To think all this time, there's been a piece of Mom waiting for me.

"I think she also didn't want to worry you. She was worried

you couldn't handle knowing how scared she was that she wasn't going to make it."

"So did you read it?"

Mitch holds up the back of the envelope. It's still sealed.

"I thought it would be special if you could read it at the reception. It would be like a piece of her is there."

"Don't you think that's going to be tough to hear? Are you sure you want to do that in front of all those people?"

Mitch sighs. "Maylee, look. It's going to be tough because Mom's not there. I know our family wasn't perfect. That's become really clear to me in recent months. Still, it's hard to think of parents without thinking of love. I wish they were here for me tomorrow. I wish I didn't have to have Mom there in a letter. But it's the best we've got."

"What if there's something embarrassing in here?"

"Then I'd hope you'd use your judgement. Although that's been questionable."

"Keep it up, and I'll ad-lib something embarrassing."

"No way. We all know what happens when you ad-lib."

Mitch hands me the letter, and my heart flutters at the sensation of it in my hands. Holding that piece of paper between my fingers, it's like Mom's there. It's like despite all the crap that's happened, all the drama and anger and hurt, I feel a tiny bit of clarity.

Mom's not here, and neither is Dad. But Mitch and I are. Despite all the stuff we've been through these past months, despite our disagreements over Josephine and hurt feelings, we're family. We need to hang onto that.

I can't forget what Josephine's done, and I can't let go of

all the old resentments. I can't completely say I agree with Mitch's choice or that I approve of this relationship, at least not right now. But I also can't say I'm willing to let go of Mitch, of my family, over this. I might not be crazy about Josephine, and I might still think this is going to end in disaster... but I also know this is Mitch's choice. I need to be there for my brother in any way I can.

"So you'll do this?" he asks, eying me hopefully.

"Of course, Mitch. I love you. I miss you. I want you to be happy."

"Then be happy for me. Because I'm happy, except I miss my sister."

I lean in for a hug now, my tears wetting his shirt. "I miss you too."

I pull back, our sentimental moment over. Nelson meows loudly. "So, big bachelor party plans tonight?"

"No. We've had enough drama. Josephine and I are just watching a movie at home tonight. No crazy stuff."

I smile. "I guess it makes sense."

"Well, I'm going to get going. A lot to do for tomorrow."

"It was good to see you. I'm excited for you."

"Thanks."

"Oh, wait, while you're here, I have something for you."

I rush back to my bedroom and rustle through the jewelry box. I find what I'm looking for, shove them in a box, and rush back to Mitch.

"What's this?"

"Mom's blue diamond earrings." I hand them to Mitch.

"What are these for?"

I grin. "Something blue, and also something borrowed. As maid of honor, this would have been my job. I know I blew the title, but I thought it would mean a lot for you to have these to give to Josephine."

"Maylee, you don't have to."

"I know," I say stoically. "I want to. Look, I have fought you the whole way to the altar. I was trying to look out for you, but I think in trying to look out for you, I just hurt you even more. I'll never be thrilled about this whole thing, and I can't say with certainty you're not making a mistake. But I also know this is a big moment for you, and I want you to know I love you and support you, even if I can't agree with you."

"Love you, Maylee. You're the best."

"Do you mean that?"

Mitch holds up a hand in a so-so position. I give him a slap. "Get out of here, wedding boy. I'll see you tomorrow."

He gives me a quick peck on the cheek, takes the earrings, and leaves.

I exhale. Tomorrow's the day. There's no turning back.

Josephine Crawford is going to become Josephine Keagan.

The scary part?

I don't think I can stop it.

CHAPTER THIRTY-THREE

"Ouch!"

I jump awake, the scratching on my arm jolting me out of sweet dreams. I cover my eyes with my hand, the sun streaming through the window.

"Dammit, Nelson. What time is it?" I shriek, feeling like hell. I roll toward the alarm clock. It's 7:03 a.m. Ugh.

Benson stirs, too, stretching an arm over me as he pulls me in. Despite my rage at the cat for waking me out of my beauty sleep, my anger disintegrates in Benson's arms.

He squints at me as I nuzzle closer. He doesn't give me any "good morning" cheesy lines. He simply leans in to kiss me. We ignore the morning breath, the messy hair, the grogginess, and we just kiss for a long moment.

I've never been a morning person—but waking up to this sight might make a believer out of me.

When we pull apart, I aimlessly run a hand through my hair, sighing.

Benson smirks. "You're so transparent. Anyone tell you

that you wear your emotions all over your face?"

"It's seven in the morning. The only emotion I have is exhaustion."

"You're dreading today. It's all over your face."

I roll to my back, Benson's arm still around me. "Well, obviously. You don't have to be a psychic to know today is probably not going to be one of my top tens."

Benson reaches for my hand under the covers, pulling it to his lips. "I know, babe. But let's just make the best of it, okay? I mean, free drinks, cake. I'm sure Josephine pulled out all the stops with the catering. Plus, I might not get to shred the bridesmaid dress off you with my teeth, but I think we can still have a pretty amazing night."

I smile, glancing at him. "You're right. I need to just let go."

"Like the song from *Frozen*?"

"Please don't start singing."

"It's too early. Later."

I fiddle with the comforter in front of me. "Today is just not what I pictured, you know? Growing up, I just always had this vision of Mitch's wedding day being such a happy day. I'd be welcoming a new sister into the family. Mom and Dad would be there, and we'd just all be having a great time. I know, it's stupid."

"It's not stupid. You have the right to be upset. I mean, obviously Josephine isn't quite the girl you imagined welcoming to your family. Plus, it has to be tough not having your parents here. It's just hard all around."

"Yeah, and I just took a tough situation and made it worse.

I feel like shit. I feel like I should be there for Mitch, you know? Mom would've wanted that. I'm not even going to be there for him on his wedding day."

"But you will. You'll be sitting there in the crowd. Just because you're not standing beside Josephine doesn't mean you won't be there for him. With the situation, I think Mitch will just be happy you're there."

"I just wonder if maybe I should've tried harder. Which is ridiculous because it's a little late now."

"Hey, stop beating yourself up. Mitch knows you did your best."

"I know. But like it or not, Josephine is a part of our family after today. I need to find a way to accept it."

"Well, today's the first step. We'll go to the wedding and be supportive. We won't cause a scene or call Josephine any names. We won't even move a muscle during the objections part. Right?"

"Hey, really? You think I'd do that?"

Benson wiggles his eyebrows, causing me to laugh.

"Okay, so it may have crossed my mind. And Shauni may have suggested it."

Benson pokes me in the rib. "But we're not going to do it," I say between gasps.

"Are you sure?"

"Pinkie swear." I grab his hand and hook pinkies with him.

"Wow, really? We're at this point in our lives now? Pinkie swearing?"

I giggle. "Oh, I do have some good news for you."

"What's that?"

"You know the shredding the bridesmaid dress with your teeth thing? Well, remember how I had to buy said bridesmaid dress?"

Benson raises an eyebrow. "I'm listening."

"I still have it, you know. I tossed it in the back of the closet."

Benson props himself up. "You know, we don't have to wait until after the reception to shred that sucker, since you're not wearing it or anything."

I smile. "I like what you're thinking, but how about we just skip the whole dress thing and cut right to the post-shredding part? It's pretty ugly anyway."

Benson answers me with a kiss, rolling on top of me in response to my proposal.

We spend the morning in bed. Suddenly, I'm not so depressed about attending this wedding.

***

"You ready?"

"Let's do this," I say, exhaling as we step into the church, my hand clutching Benson's arm. I study him; he looks damn good in a suit.

I pull on the hem of my midthigh-length dress, feeling self-conscious as we walk down the aisle. I'm not crazy—at least ten pairs of eyes are staring at us as we make our entrance, probably whispering about the terrible sister I am. Benson squeezes my fingers with his free hand, and I relax, smiling as we make our way to the second pew on the groom's side.

Soft violin music fills the church, gorgeous red roses and poinsettias dotting almost every inch of the space. I shiver, pulling my wrap tighter around me. Benson puts an arm around me, rubbing me to bring warmth back to my body.

"Remind me again why they picked December. It's freezing," I whisper.

"I could warm you up," he says, creepily winking with extra emphasis, and I laugh. I cover my mouth with my hand, trying to get serious as we settle in.

Before we get too comfortable, though, there's a tap on my shoulder that startles me.

"Maylee?" a female voice whispers, and I turn to see who is behind me. A girl in a familiar, flashy bridesmaid dress is leaning over the pew directly behind us. This must be one of the fill-in bridesmaids courtesy of the maid of honor vacancy I left. I don't recognize her.

"Uh, yeah?" The violin music is still playing. It's about a half hour until the wedding, so I have no idea what she could possibly be doing.

"Josephine asked to see you. She's downstairs. I can show you."

I turn to Benson, confused and unsure of what to do. He shrugs, and I inhale. This seems like an absolutely horrific idea. My gut is telling me not to go. What could she possibly want to see me for? I take a moment to think but decide I don't want to make any more of a scene—I can feel people staring at the encounter.

"Okay," I whisper, standing to follow her. I was right. People are staring and whispering. I try to ignore it, following the substitute bridesmaid toward the back of the church and down the stairs.

My heart is fluttering from nerves as I head down the stairs to where Josephine and the other bridesmaids are. I feel like I'm about to be interrogated, kidnapped, or tortured. Maybe I've been watching too many horror films with Benson.

As we enter the makeshift bridal suite—which is more like a church office—the giddy female voices from the bridal party quiet. Everyone turns to eye me. Josephine turns to face me, a calm look on her face.

The first thing I notice is how she looks drop-dead gorgeous. I'm talking movie star, magazine quality gorgeous. Her sequined, mermaid-style wedding gown looks stunning on her, tight in all the right places. Elegant beading decorates the bodice. On anyone but Josephine, the dress would look like hell.

On her, it looks angelic.

Her makeup is perfect, and her hair floats effortlessly around her face, framing it with soft curls. She wears no veil, but a diamond headband. Her makeup is airbrushed delicately, and she's wearing the perfect amount of jewelry. I notice she's got the blue diamonds in, and my heart flutters a little at the thought that a piece of Mom is here, no matter what the circumstances.

"Can Maylee and I have a moment, girls?" her voice says, breaking me out of my semistalkerish stare.

The women, also looking like they stepped out of magazines, vacate the room. Some go slowly, as if they hope by lingering they can hear some juicy tidbits from our encounter. I'm sure they won't go far, needing to eavesdrop. The way things have been lately, they're probably right to expect drama.

For a long moment, we stand, two women in what feels like a momentous exchange, tension palpable. We stare, two "once" friends turned enemies turned into this odd state we're in now.

"So," Josephine begins. "This is awkward, huh?" She smiles, and I find myself grinning a little, relieved to have the tension eased or at least acknowledged.

"Yeah, you could say that."

She exhales out a breath of what is probably nervous tension. "I know this isn't exactly the best time for this conversation to happen. I know it should've probably happened a long time ago. But the thing is, in a little bit, I'm going to walk down that aisle and marry your brother. I thought this thing between us wouldn't matter. I thought I could just sweep it aside like it didn't affect anything. But it does matter, Maylee. When Mitch gave me those earrings from your mother that you gave to him, it hit me. I'm going to be a part of this family. That's not just Mitch. That's you. That's your parents, even though they're not here to witness it. I should've seen it before today, but those earrings just made it click into place. We need to settle this thing between us because it does matter. It matters so much that I realized I can't walk down that aisle until I said a few things to you."

I inhale now and exhale forcefully. I knew it. This is going to get ugly. I mentally brace myself for the onslaught of words that will come my way—the blame, the anger, the frustration she must certainly be ready to hurdle at me. In truth, I know I'm not blameless. I know I probably deserve some of her anger. I haven't exactly been an angel in all of this.

But what comes out of her mouth next is probably worse than a verbal assault—because it almost knocks me straight to the floor.

"Maylee, I want to say I'm sorry."

I don't respond. I wait for the punchline. I wait for the typical Josephine manipulation, the angle she's playing to reveal itself. But nothing else comes. She doesn't try to justify her words or defend herself. She doesn't lather on sympathy or regret to make me feel bad.

She just bites her lip and nods.

For a moment, I wonder if Mitch put her up to this. I even consider accusing her, but stop myself as she continues.

"I know things between us are never going to be good. Hell, they might never be okay. The damage is done. I think sometimes two people just don't work as friends. I also know the things I've done are unforgivable, unforgettable. But I want you to know, despite what you might think, I do love him, Maylee. I didn't plan on this happening. Hell, I didn't even want it to happen. But Mitch makes me happy. We make each other happy. I don't expect you to understand it or even support it. I don't expect you to ever be okay with me. I realize now what a mistake it was for us to ask you to be in the wedding—not because I don't want you to be a part of this, but because it was just too much pressure. It was wrong of us, wrong of me especially, to expect you to do that. I'm sorry. I do hope, though, at some point, we can come to terms with the fact we're in the same family. I want that for us. I want some kind of mutual peace. I'm vowing today to love your brother forever, but I want you to know I'm also vowing to try harder to make amends, to be a better person. I was never good to you, it's true. I deserved all the things you said at the shower and probably worse. I just—I don't want who we used to be or even who we are now to get in the way of either of our lives. We both love Mitch. Maybe we can find some common ground in that."

For the first time maybe ever, I look at Josephine and don't see my biggest rival, archenemy, or opponent. I don't see the flaunty, manipulative, flashy girl I once knew. I don't see the woman I would do anything to get rid of from our lives.

I just see Josephine, a woman who, like me, is trying to find some kind of happiness in this world.

Looking at the woman my brother's about to marry, I don't see a future best friend or my first pick for a sister-in-law, it's true. I don't see a woman I adore or can really even say a whole heck of a lot of good things about. I don't see mani Mondays in our future anytime soon.

Nonetheless, in her words, I see what I think is a genuine white flag and, with it, a hope that our now intertwined lives will find a way to work out.

"Thank you. I'm sorry, too. I hope you make each other happy," I say, and genuinely mean it this time.

Then, something crazy happens. In fact, I even think I hear a gasp from the eavesdropping posse behind us.

I bridge the gap between Josephine to reach in and give her a quick hug.

I pull back, give her a smile, and turn to leave, passing by the bridesmaids who quickly try to pretend they weren't just eavesdropping.

I head back up the stairs to the wedding, feeling a little bit more confident I will be able to stay quiet during the objections part of the ceremony.

***

"And?" Benson asks expectantly as I return to my seat, his toe tapping nervously. I'm sure he probably expected there to be police sirens.

I turn to him, leaning against his shoulder. "And, I think things are going to be okay," I say.

He raises an eyebrow, as if to ask what my cryptic words mean. I suppose he decides against it, figuring if I came back without a black eye, things are, in fact, pretty okay.

We sit for a few minutes, the music lulling me into a whimsical state. I must admit Josephine's outdone herself—not that I'm really surprised. It looks like a magical holiday wonderland in here. It's gorgeous.

"We're here," a voice whispers from behind us. The whisper is more like a shriek, and wedding guests collectively turn to see where it is coming from.

I don't have to turn to figure out who the voice belongs to.

Shauni slides into the pew beside me, Matt with her. She's wearing a sparkly black dress—and black Ugg boots.

I eye her footwear blatantly, raising an eyebrow.

"What?" she asks. "It's damn cold out, and there's snow. I mean, really, who gets married in December in Pennsylvania?"

I look past Shauni to see a woman in the pew to our left, mouth open, shaking her head. I smirk. So much for not causing a scene.

"It's fine."

"How are you holding up?" Shauni whispers.

"Okay." I grin, thinking about what Shauni would say about my hug with Josephine. I decide to leave it out for now, not wanting to cause a scene with what will surely be squeals from Shauni.

"Any big plans?"

I exhale. "No. We're not going to ruin this, remember? Acceptance is our motto today."

"Darn. I was hoping to have some fun. But okay. Whatever you say."

The music changes, marking the beginning of the ceremony. Mitch enters from the room beside the altar, his groomsmen in tow. They all take their places, the priest also walking out to his spot.

Before the ceremony continues, though, Mitch turns to the priest and holds up a finger. He rushes down from the altar. *What the hell is he doing?*

Everyone is staring, and the groomsmen murmur to each other, wondering what's happening.

Mitch makes a beeline for me.

"What are you doing?" I hiss, but he reaches for my hand. He pulls me up, leans in, and gives me a hug.

"Thank you for being here, sis. I love you. I know this is hard, but I'm glad you're here."

I hug him back, stunned by the simple gesture. After everything I've done, after all the turmoil, he's still the same caring brother he's always been.

The hug means a lot. It's a symbol things haven't changed between us, despite everything.

I let go of him, smile, and take my seat. I have a tear in my eye; I swipe it away.

"I thought he was making a run for it," Benson whispers to me. I squeeze his hand.

Josephine's mom comes down the aisle, followed by the bridesmaids. My stomach knots a bit, thinking it should've been me there. I feel like everyone is looking at me and thinking the same thing.

Then, the music happens. The familiar anthem announces her arrival. I hear three-hundred-plus people stand in unison, the joyous mood noticeable.

She stands, confident and poised, at the end of the aisle. Her oversized bouquet of roses only makes her look tinier.

Seeing her walking down the aisle, I think again how she looks envy-worthy. On any other day, I'd be complaining about how flaunty she looks or how perfect she looks.

Today, I just smile. I can't begrudge her anything today.

Because it's not just her perfect dress I notice. It's not just the fact she makes a perfect bride. It's not the fact she's just sort of tried to make things right between us or the fact I've finally seen a side of her today, the side Mitch maybe fell in love with.

It's the look in her eye—the look she's giving my brother.

It's a look of sheer excitement for what she's about to do. I see in her look a woman who is so crazy about my brother, so in love with him, she'd pledge her life to him. I turn now, eying Mitch at the end of the aisle.

He has the same look.

For the past few months, I've fought this with everything

in me. I let my hatred for Josephine, for who she was in the past, cloud everything. I grasped every harsh word from her, every annoying moment, and let it overshadow what mattered most. I let it turn me into someone I hated just for the sake of winning.

She made a lot of mistakes. She hurt me, hurt my family. She's done some things that are downright wrong. Still, though, I can't help but think it doesn't matter right now. The comments, the stunts, the attitude, it all dissipates as I look at her walking toward my brother. I don't see the snarky, sassy blonde who undermines and manipulates. I don't see the girl who stirred an ugly side in me, who brought out the worst in me. I don't see a woman who will stomp on Mitch's heart, who will tear him to shreds.

As she walks down the aisle past us, I see just one thing.

Love.

Sheer, pure, genuine, life-enduring love between Mitch and Josephine. I don't claim to understand it. I don't claim to have been a proponent for it. I do know, however, that from where I'm standing—my perspective finally unclouded—it looks genuine. Call it wedding magic, call it Christmas magic, call it a miracle, but suddenly, I realize they're going to be okay. Mitch is going to be more than okay.

Our family *is* going to be okay. And after hearing Josephine's words, I think she believes it too.

The preacher begins the ceremony as Shauni turns to me. "Are you feeling okay?"

"Yeah, why?"

"It looks like you're crying. Like happy crying."

"I think I am."

"Okay, are you sure you don't need an ambulance?"

The preacher stops his words, staring into the crowd, apparently looking for the culprit of the too-loud whispers. Shauni mouths "sorry," and I blush, averting my eyes to the ground.

After the opening prayer, I lean in to her. "I just, I think I realized Josephine might actually be good for my brother."

"What?"

"Shh," Matt says, elbowing Shauni.

"I'm serious. I think she might be."

"If you say so." Shauni grins, shaking her head.

I can't blame her. It sounds crazy, after all this time. After all the resentment, the plots, and the burning hatred.

As the ceremony rolls on, I find myself beaming. Through the vows, the exchange of rings, and the first kiss, it all becomes apparent, as if a heavenly light were shining on them.

They really do love each other... and I think they'll be happy.

***

We are the last to pass through the receiving line, thanks to our seats up front. When we get to the bride and groom, I reach for my brother.

"Congratulations!" I exclaim. "I'm so happy for you."

Mitch grins. "You sure?"

"Of course," I say, slapping him on the shoulder. "It was a nice wedding. I made sure I snapped some pics of you tearing up."

"I was not tearing up. There was something in my eye."

"Sure," I say, smirking.

"I'm glad you came, Maylee," Josephine says, smiling. Her words are gracious, sincere. She acts as if our conversation earlier didn't happen, making me believe without a doubt they were her own words. Mitch wasn't behind the impromptu moment. He has no idea.

"I'm glad, too." I'm surprised I actually mean the words.

"Listen, we have a limo out front. We just have to finish a few things here before we head for pictures, so you and Benson can just go hop in with the bridal party."

I feel myself blush. "Oh, it's okay, I didn't plan on—"

"It would mean a lot. You're family. I planned on you being in the pictures. Plus, I have something for you."

I look to Benson for guidance. He just nods.

"Okay."

On our way to the limo, I lean in to Benson. "What the heck? This is so awkward. After being fired from the wedding party, I didn't think I'd be in pics."

"It's a nice gesture. I think she wants you to be included."

"If you say so."

But I can't help but worry what the heck Josephine has up her sleeve now. Just when I was starting to let go, to trust her....

***

"Where are we going for pics?" I ask Mitch as he guzzles a glass of champagne.

"Don't know. Josephine wouldn't tell me."

"That's comforting."

Benson elbows me. I snatch his glass of champagne from

him and down it. I've already finished mine off. I've needed it for the limo full of Josephine's bridal party.

Twenty minutes later, the limo stops on a windy road in the middle of nowhere. Snow coats the ground.

"We're here," Josephine announces.

I glance out the window. It's not the place I'd imagined Josephine choosing for wedding pics.

"Isn't it a little cold for this?"

Benson gives me a look that says he is thinking the same thing, but we both just exhale. It's not our wedding, so I have no room to complain.

I get out, Benson holding my hand, and Josephine and the photographer lead us on what must be a two-mile hike. I grip Benson's arm, traipsing through snow, my feet already feeling frostbitten.

"I think she's trying to give me hypothermia. This was a ploy to kill me," I whisper to Benson.

He shivers, rubbing his hands together. "For once, I think you might be right."

"I should've known Miss Yoga would take us out hiking on her wedding day," I whisper.

The group stops, and I look up to assess the situation.

My heart cracks in half. I know this place after all. I know the cabin that's standing right in front of us—or more like falling in front of us. I know the tree, recognize the way the light is coming through the wilderness.

Tears bubble up again.

"Maylee, Mitch, can you come here a second?" Josephine asks, beaming. I look at Benson, who gives me a gentle shove, telling me to go.

Mitch also knows where we are, his somber look telling it all.

"I know you guys are thinking I'm nuts, that it's too cold for this. But I know this place means a lot to you. I know this is where your parents came for pictures for their wedding. I also know how hard it is for both of you not having them here today. I wanted to commemorate them. From what I hear, your parents weren't the "memorial table" or sappy dove release kind of people. I thought this seemed more appropriate. I thought we'd honor them by coming to the place where they first captured their love on their wedding day, a love that has inspired all of us. I wanted to come here so, in a way, they're a part of today, a part of the pictures too."

Okay, the tears are full-on falling now. I put a hand to my mouth, touched by the sentiment.

It's beautiful, selfless, and thoughtful. It's everything I thought Josephine wasn't.

"And for the first picture, I asked the photographer to do a few of you two alone. Maylee, I know we haven't seen eye to eye on a lot of things, but I want you to know this. You're Mitch's best friend. You're everything to him. No matter what, that's not going to change."

I smile at her, the first genuine smile ever. "Thank you."

"Thank you, honey," Mitch says, leaning in to kiss her.

"Now wipe those tears off. You look a little blotchy. Get it together," she orders, smiling. I think she is a little worried my snot and tears will ruin the photos. I, for once, obey Josephine, falling into place beside Mitch as the photographer snaps our photo.

I'm still reeling from the photos, from the sentiment, when Josephine pulls out the final, tear-inducing stop.

"Before we get to the rest of the photos, I have one more thing."

One of the bridesmaids hands Josephine two gift bags. She hands one to each of us.

"Open them," she orders when we stand eying each other. We obey.

I pull out a tiny, red box. When I pop the box open, there's a locket. I open it.

Inside is a tiny version of the picture of Mom and Dad, the one I love in this very spot. I peer at Josephine through the tears.

"I thought when these are printed, you could put the pic of you and Mitch on the other side."

I am literally speechless. This woman I've hated for over a decade, the woman I've tried to ruin, embarrass, and destroy these past few months, has done this for me.

She's selflessly given something to me that is so unspeakably beautiful, I can't even breathe.

"Thank you" is all I can muster through the emotion. I look over at Mitch, who has unwrapped a watch.

"Turn it over," she says, and he obeys. I lean in closer to see what he's smiling at.

On the inside, the word "Love" is engraved twice.

"Is this…?" Mitch asks.

"I found some cards in your stuff from your parents. I hope you don't mind I borrowed them. Those are written in your mom's and dad's handwriting."

At this point, most of the bridal party is sobbing—at least the women.

Mitch wraps his new bride in his arms. "This is beautiful. Thank you."

"Okay, okay, enough mushy stuff," Josephine says. "Let's get the rest of these pics moving before we all freeze to death. Move it, people."

With that, the bossy Josephine is back, the one we all know—and don't love.

I can't stop smiling, though. No matter what happens, I know the real truth now.

She's not the girl she used to be, not at all. She's not the woman I thought she was.

She's a part of our family now, a permanent fixture in my life.

I'm suddenly more than okay with it, at least for the time being.

CHAPTER THIRTY-FOUR

After we all just about succumb to hypothermia, Josephine is finally satisfied with the pictures we've taken. We head to the reception.

My locket around my neck, I aimlessly run my fingers over the smooth silver back in the limo.

"That was pretty amazing of her," Benson murmurs in my ear, leaning in to kiss my cheek while he's there.

"Yeah, it was."

"Does this mean you two have turned a corner?"

I smirk, glancing at the handsome man beside me. "Maybe."

"Does this also mean you'll be celebrating with some drunken debauchery at the reception?"

"Perhaps. I've heard there are some pretty hunky men up for grabs there."

"Oh yeah? I better keep my eyes open then." He winks at me. He still likes to bring up the fact I thought he was gay, from time to time. I nudge him.

When we pull up to the reception, Benson and I get out and start walking toward the door so the bridal party can line up. A hand grabs my arm.

"Maylee, Benson, walk in with us. We'll announce you as the sister of the groom."

I turn to Josephine, seeing her differently than I have so far. "That's sweet. But this is your moment. Honestly. We're going to head inside."

She nods, a grateful smile on her face, and Benson and I head to claim our seats.

The country club is packed, dinner music softly echoing through the immaculately decorated room. All of the wedding crafts adorn the area. It looks like a chic wedding from one of those shows on TLC. It's gorgeous.

Benson and I find our spot near the front of the room and sit. As the deejay announces the bridal party, I cheer along with them, nothing but honest gratitude and water driving my good mood.

Everyone settles in, and it's time for speeches. The bridesmaid slash backup maid of honor gives some speech that drags on for an eternity. She recounts about all these cutesy stories from her wild days with Josephine. They're supposed to be funny—she laughs really hard, trying to convince the crowd to laugh, too—but they're awful. I fiddle with my glass, giving Benson a look that makes him chuckle.

The best man keeps it short, probably just wanting to get back to his Jack and Coke.

"Now, we'd like Maylee Keagan, sister of the groom, to come up for a special moment."

Benson pats me on the back. I take a deep breath, gingerly pulling the letter from my clutch. I wink at Mitch on the way to the microphone.

I steady myself, reminding myself I can do this.

I haven't read the letter. I wanted it to be a surprise, wanted it to really feel like Mom were here. I just hope this wasn't a mistake—I hope I can hold it together.

I smile at the crowd, open the envelope, and unfold the letter from the past, a connection to the mom we still love and miss so much.

Dear Mitch,

If you're reading this, it means I'm not there to watch you get married. It means I'm not there to drink too many whiskey sours and claim it's okay because I'm just so happy. I'm not there to embarrass you during the chicken dance or to watch the lovely woman you've picked to become a part of our family walk toward you.

It kills me. Okay, so it was a terrible pun. But seriously, my heart is shredded from the thought.

Still, this letter comforts me. Knowing you'll have these words on the day your life forever changes makes me feel like I'll be a part of your wedding, even if it's just through these words.

I want you to know I'm proud of you. I want you to know I am already proud of the man you've become. I can picture you down the road as this loving guy, loyal to his family and going after what he wants.

Mitch, please know this thing called marriage is never easy. There were plenty of times when your father and I wanted to throw in the towel. Mistakes were made. It was hard, even if we didn't show it.

Still, there was one thing that got us through—love. Pure love.

I hope you've found that with the woman sitting beside you now. Hang on to love with all you've got. Hang on to each other.

Most of all, hang on to family.

It's hard not being there with you, but it's easier knowing you've got amazing people surrounding you, loving you, watching out for you. I know you and Maylee will carry my legacy on in the connection you have with each other.

Finally, to the woman my son's chosen. I don't even know you, probably never even met you, but I love you just the same. The thing is, if my son chose you, you must be some kind of woman. I know you're a kindhearted woman who might not be perfect but who loves perfectly. Make him happy. Let him make you happy. Stand proud knowing you are now a part of this family. We're a goofy lot. We're nerdy and quirky, and we don't always get along.

But, to the new Mrs. Keagan, know we have one thing going for us.

Loyalty.

We will have your back no matter what.

So now that I've utterly depressed you guys, I'm signing off. I hope today is the start of a beautiful forever for you. Just know I'm looking down on you in this moment, doing the chicken dance right along with you.

Have a few drinks for me. I love you.

Love,

Mom

Tears are flowing everywhere. Mitch, Josephine, and I sob. I look over at the woman I've hated for so long, at the woman

I tried to stop from sitting here, and I realize something.

Mom's right. The woman Mitch picks isn't what I thought at all. Underneath the troublesome exterior and the sometimes outrageous stunts, there's a good heart. I saw it today with the pictures and the locket. I see it when she looks at Mitch.

I see it now in the tears she cries for a woman she barely knew.

So call it alcohol or call it raw emotions, but I set the letter down in order to do something crazy.

I walk over to Josephine with extended arms.

"Welcome to the family," I say, hugging her.

We stay in the hug for a while, Mitch looking as if he's seen a ghost.

Finally, I let go to point to the deejay, shouting, "Chicken Dance. Stat."

I march to the dance floor hand in hand with my high school rival and start shaking my stuff like no one is watching.

Someone is. Mom. Although she can't be here beside me, she is in so many ways.

She's here in this family we now have, Mitch, Benson, Josephine, and me.

And we will carry her legacy on.

EPILOGUE

"Last time," I mutter to myself in a rage. This has to work.

I will not be nerd girl, glasses glaring on the beach.

"Will you please just put your glasses on?" Benson asks, wrapping his arms around me. I try not to get mad at the fact he almost made me poke my eye out. It isn't hard to overcome my rage when I look at the gorgeous eyes of the perfect man who is wrapped around me.

"I'll get the hang of these things, I know I will."

"If you say so. Hurry up. The weather's perfect." He kisses my neck, and I turn my head, catching his mouth in mine.

"You know, we could just skip this whole thing," he says. "Stay in bed, find other activities to do."

"We need to go," I say, weaseling away from him. "Mitch and Josephine will be waiting."

"Wonder what Rory is going to do, what with four of us no-shows at her magical reunion."

"Oh no, we won't have a shot at the door prize this year." I grin, finally popping my contact in. I do a celebratory dance around the bathroom, and Benson raises an eyebrow.

"You're such a weirdo."

"And you love it."

"Are you ready?"

"I just have to get into my bikini," I say.

He winks at me. "You know, this year, busting out of your outfit is actually applauded, not frowned upon. Bonus of skipping your eleven-year high school reunion."

I smack his arm, laughing. I head to the bedroom as he heads to the kitchen to get together the last-minute snacks for on the sand—some cookies, Cheetos, and cupcakes. No carrot sticks or celery this year. Another perk.

As I slip into my bikini, I eye myself in the mirror. Definitely not perfect. Not even close. I see the wear and tear on my body that reminds me I'm not eighteen anymore.

But it's okay.

I'm different now. We all are. Life doesn't stay the same. It's about growing, adjusting, and finding a new truth for yourself.

I head to the kitchen, sunglasses on, and Benson whistles as I walk in.

I haven't starved myself for fourteen days. I don't have a drop of makeup on this year. Cellulite chunks are probably noticeable on my legs.

I don't care.

Because this year, for our eleven-year high school reunion, we won't be impressing anyone at a restaurant in town. I won't be squeezing into a way too tight dress or trying to one-up people from my past.

This year, I won't be looking for Josephine, hoping she gained weight.

Because this year, things are so much different.

***

"Where were you two? I'm starving. You said you'd be out in a few."

"Your sister couldn't get her contacts in."

"Nice one, man," Mitch says, giving Benson the "dude" look.

"Stop. He's serious."

"Why didn't you just wear the nerd glasses? We all know you have them," Mitch says, and I toss a cookie at him. To my infuriation, he catches it.

"Mitch, leave your sister alone," Josephine says, one hand on her growing stomach.

I smile, mouthing "thank you."

I drop into the lounge chair beside her. We're under an umbrella, a steady breeze blowing. A few kids play in the surf down from us, but for the most part, the sand belongs to us.

"This is so much better than last year," I admit.

"I agree," Josephine says, Mitch leaning in to give her a kiss.

"Newlyweds," I say, making a gagging motion. Benson and Mitch exchange a wink. What the hell was that about?

"Hey, Jo, do you want to take a walk?" Mitch asks.

"I don't know, I'm kind of hot."

"I know you are. So get your hot body up out of the chair and walk with me," he says. I hear some desperation. Josephine sighs.

"All right, if you insist."

She takes Mitch's arm and heads down the beach, the two giggling and making eyes at each other.

"They're so clingy, it's sickening," I say.

"They're happy."

"I know."

And I do.

I didn't think I'd ever get to this place, a place where I could see Josephine and Mitch together and be okay with it. Be more than okay with it. I didn't think last year I'd be here, a year later, on vacation with my brother and his wife, Josephine.

Or with my boyfriend, Benson.

Life can change so fast. Sometimes it changes from seemingly unimportant moments.

Regardless, despite everything, I'm happy we went to the reunion last year.

Benson sits down beside me after pulling something from the pocket of his shorts.

"What's this?" I ask as he hands me some typed pages.

"Well, you see, my agent just secured a contract for a new novel."

"Are you serious? Baby, that's amazing," I say, jumping into his lap, not even looking at the pages.

We kiss, but he pulls back. "This is the beginning of the story. I wanted to see what you think."

I grab the pages and instantly start reading, anxious to see what he's written.

They didn't mean to fall in love, never saw it coming.

They'd known each other back when they were just two quiet kids, too much in love with books to fall in love with each other.

But ten years later, they found each other again. She walked into their high school reunion, and he walked out a changed man.

I look at Benson curiously. "Is this…?"

"Keep reading," he orders. He looks so nervous.

One year later, here they stood, still in awe of a love they never saw coming.

Things were different now, too. Because in the past year, they'd grown to realize how good they were together.

She made him feel like his whole life was waiting for him, like he hadn't really started living until he'd fallen for her. She made him laugh every single day, made him want to go after his dreams and live life. Her crazy stunts, her blunt nature, her compassion—she was everything he never realized he was looking for. Luckily, she was just his type—he wasn't gay, after all.

"Benson, is this really your book?"

"Just keep reading," he says softly. He's twiddling his thumbs.

There was something he'd been wanting to ask her for a while now, but was too scared. You see, he was a writer man. And although he'd changed from high school and come out of his shell, even though she'd helped him with that, he was still the quiet man at heart. He was still the man who was better with written words than conversation.

So he wrote down the question he'd wanted to ask for months now, but was too afraid to.

He wrote down she was everything to him, everything he could ever want. He wrote down he loved the way she was so loyal to her family, the way she would do anything to protect them. He loved the way she looked first thing in the morning, not a swipe of makeup or a brush of her hair. He loved the way she laughed, the way she talked animatedly with her hands. He loved her and would love her for the rest of his life. He wanted nothing more than to spend every single high school reunion with her, whether actually at the reunion or not. He wanted to grow old with her, to one day go to their own children's high school graduations, to live a life of dreams and craziness with her.

So, in the middle of the sand on the eleven-year anniversary of their high school graduation, one year after they surged back into each other's lives, he went after one of his dreams.

He knelt in front of her and he asked the question, finally brave enough to say it out loud.

I silently study him now, shocked. He quietly gets up from his chair to kneel in the sand before me.

"Maylee, I love you. Will you marry me?"

I drop the pages onto my chair, falling to my knees in the sand. I take his face in my hands.

Life has taken so many turns since high school, but this was undoubtedly the best one.

"Benson Drake, I love you too, by the way. Yes."

We fall back onto the sand kissing wildly and passionately. He pulls back. "Don't you want to see the ring?"

"Well, I suppose," I say, tears in my eyes.

He pulls a ring out of his pocket. It's a small, simple pink diamond.

"It's perfect."

"Look at the inside."

I glance on the inside. He's had it engraved.

"Whatever souls are made of," I read. At this, the tears give way. "Oh my God, you remember."

"One of your favorite books from high school, *Wuthering Heights*. We were in Mrs. Jenkins's class when you proclaimed how much you loved the quote."

"You remembered?"

"Yes. Because even then, I had my eye on you."

It took us ten years to find each other even though we'd been right in front of each other all along. Sometimes that's how life works out. Sometimes it takes a decade for you to sort out what you want, who you are, who you've become.

Sometimes it takes getting over your pride, letting go of the past, and realizing things change.

In the past year with Benson, I've come to learn that who we were isn't who we are today. We're different now, life is different. We've changed and grown, passing through this complex thing called adulthood. Still, who we were helped lead us to this point, to this path, to this moment. Tears gushing as I wrap my head around everything that's happened, everything we are together, I smile. I wouldn't change a single moment, a single thing. In the hot sand, Benson in front of me, I realize this is where we were headed all along, even if we didn't know it.

"I have a question," I say, staring at my ring.

"What is it?"

"Are these really pages from your book?"

"What if it was?"

"Just answer me, please."

"No, it's not. The new book is actually a romantic suspense

that starts with a murder scene. I didn't think it was the way to get a 'yes' from you."

I laugh. "Scary. But I'm glad. Because although it's the sweetest proposal ever, not sure it would be a good book."

"I personally think our love story would be the best book."

"Well, you'll have plenty of time to write it," I say, kissing him.

"Newlyweds," Mitch says, mocking us as he and Josephine walk back toward us. They're looking expectantly.

"Not yet we're not," Benson says.

"Soon," I say, flashing my ring.

"It's gorgeous!" Josephine squeals, and she looks truly happy for us.

She hugs me. I don't flinch. "I'm happy for you," she says.

I believe her.

After we share "congratulations" and "thank-yous," Josephine looks at me.

"So," she says. "If you need a maid of honor or anything…."

Mitch chokes on his soda while Benson eyes us, preparing for a catfight.

I just grin. "I don't think so. That's definitely reserved for Shauni."

Tension builds. I know Mitch is thinking we've just had another setback.

"But," I say, "I could use a bridesmaid, if you're up for it?"

Josephine turns to me, wearing a genuine smile. "I would love to."

It's not the picture-perfect moment of a greeting card. We still have a lot of hard feelings to work out. I don't think she'll ever be my best friend.

I finally get where she's coming from, though, where Mitch is coming from.

Sometimes it takes love for you to find where you're going.

For me, it took love to realize things aren't the same anymore.

Josephine is not the girl she used to be.

Neither am I.

As the four of us walk down to the edge of the water to dip our toes in, I realize I'm thankful for that.

ACKNOWLEDGEMENTS

First, I want to thank my amazing publisher, Hot Tree Publishing. Thank you so much for believing in my writing and helping me shape my stories into the best versions they can be. Thank you to Becky for creating such a supportive environment and tirelessly helping all of us chase our dreams. Thank you, Donna, Justine, Olivia, Peggy, and everyone else who works so hard to make Hot Tree an amazing publisher. I love being a part of the Hot Tree family and am truly grateful to be a part of such an awesome team.

I want to thank my parents for always supporting me and helping me achieve my dreams. You are my best friends, and I wouldn't be where I am in life without your amazing guidance.

Thank you to my husband for being an amazing supporter and man. You make me laugh when I feel like crying, and you push me to keep going when I want to give up. You are an amazing husband, friend, and teammate in this crazy thing called life. I am so blessed to have found you at such a young age.

Thank you to everyone who has supported my writing journey. Thank you to the readers who have taken a chance on a small-town girl's words. Thank you to all of the amazing bloggers who help promote authors and reading. A special thank you goes out to all of the supporters in my life, especially: Grandma Bonnie, Christie James, Kristin Books, Kristin Mathias, Alicia Schmouder, Kay Shuma, Lynette Luke, Jennifer Carney, Kelly Rubritz, Maureen Letcher, Jamie Lynch, and Sandra Corey.

I would also like to thank all the teachers who have helped me gain the confidence and writing skills to follow my passion, especially Sue Gunsallus, Diane Vella, Tom Kunkle, and all of the professors at Mount Aloysius College.

For me, this book hit home because I wrote it the year I celebrated my own ten-year high school reunion. Our high school years shape us, for better or worse, into the people we become. I want to give a shout-out to all the members of the HASD class of 2006. So many of you have impacted me in such positive ways. Thank you for all the memories.

Finally, thank you to my best friend in the entire world, my cupcake-loving mastiff, Henry.

ABOUT THE AUTHOR

A high school English teacher, an author, and a fan of anything pink and/or glittery, Lindsay's the English teacher cliché; she loves cats, reading, Shakespeare, and Poe.

She currently lives in her hometown with her husband, Chad (her junior high sweetheart); their cats, Arya, Amelia, Alice, and Bob; and their Mastiff, Henry.

Lindsay's goal with her writing is to show the power of love and the beauty of life while also instilling a true sense of realism in her work. Some reviewers have noted that her books are not the "typical romance." With her novels coming from a place of honesty, Lindsay examines the difficult questions, looks at the tough emotions, and paints the pictures that are sometimes difficult to look at. She wants her fiction to resonate with readers as realistic, poetic, and powerful. Lindsay wants women readers to be able to say, "I see myself in that novel." She wants to speak to the modern woman's experience while also bringing a twist of something new and exciting. Her aim is for readers to say, "That could happen," or "I feel like the characters are real." That's how she knows she's done her job.

Lindsay's hope is that by becoming a published author, she can inspire some of her students and other aspiring writers to pursue their own passions. She wants them to see that any dream can be attained and publishing a novel isn't out of the realm of possibility.

Discover more about Lindsay:

FACEBOOK: FACEBOOK.COM/LINDSAYANNDETWILER

TWITTER: TWITTER.COM/LINDSAYDETWILER

WEBSITE: LINDSAYDETWILER.COM

ABOUT THE PUBLISHER

Hot Tree Publishing opened its doors in 2015 with an aspiration to bring quality fiction to the world of readers. With the initial focus on romance and a wide spread of romance sub-genres, we envision opening up to alternative genres in the near future.

Firmly seated in the industry as a leading editing provider to independent authors and small publishing houses, Hot Tree Publishing is the sister company to Hot Tree Editing, founded in 2012. Having established in-house editing and promotions, plus having a well-respected market presence, Hot Tree Publishing endeavors to be a leader in bringing quality stories to the world of readers.

Interested in discovering more amazing reads brought to you by Hot Tree Publishing or perhaps you're interested in submitting a manuscript and joining the HTPubs family? Either way, head over to the website for information:

HOTTREEPUBLISHING.COM